Shameless

We'd allowed Bernie to see our scenes, providing him with a live peep-show. He had seen me drunk, tied up, tied down, whipped, fucked and buggered. And now I was his plaything, kept captive in his remote hideaway.

'I want you to wear these pretty little dresses,' he said. 'I don't like those things Jim makes you wear. Those prostitute's clothes. Bernie bought these for you 'cos he loves you and he wants to make you happy.'

He was a very strange man. Not the strangest I had ever known, but strange all the same. He had created a prison with incomprehensible pleasures. Nevertheless, it was still a prison, and I had to escape from it.

For Tom Bell

Shameless

STELLA BLACK

BLACK
lace

Black Lace novels contain sexual fantasies.
In real life, make sure you practise safe sex.

First published in 2000 by
Black Lace
Thames Wharf Studios,
Rainville Road, London W6 9HA

Typeset by SetSystems Ltd, Saffron Walden, Essex
Printed and bound by Mackays of Chatham PLC

ISBN 0 352 33467 3

Chapter One

I, Stella, Stella Black, wear leopard skin to the airport because I am Virginia Mayo in *White Heat*. There are stockings, seamed, and five-inch-high spikes that clack percussively along the floor. There is a push-up bra, black, silk, laced, underwired. There is an expensive black lace garter belt that he bought me once when I was good. I know from the back I am 40s starlet, chin out, chest out, black eyelashes, smooth bob, unruffled. Hips undulate, buttocks slowly swing from side to side. I wear Musk and the knowledge that if a star should doubt, it would immediately go out. I have poise. I am a sophisticate. I am wet.

He is at the US Air desk, waiting. Black hair swept over a lupine forehead, six feet tall, the man. And always in black. A long black cashmere overcoat, leather gloves, dark suit, dark shirt, dark tie. His lips are in an amused, sardonic set. His dark-brown eyes glitter with intelligent cruelty, but sometimes, surprisingly, they melt and something like love softens those deep irises. Not now, however. Now he is irritated.

'Jesus, what's all this?'

1

Well, I have make-up bags and shoe boxes and a case full of accoutrements. They all match. The co-ordination has taken weeks. No tone is wrong. No outfit will be repeated. What's a girl to do when she needs things? But I don't say anything. I don't dare.

He takes the luggage from me and hands them over to an air hostess whose tumescent red lips have settled into a professional rictus grin. Then his own leather hold-all. As I lean over the desk to show my passport, he strokes his hand over my buttocks and feels the outline of my panties. Is he threatening or possessive? I don't know. I know I am his.

'Let's go for a drink,' I say.

But he grabs me by the hand and leads me to the disabled toilet.

'Get in there.'

He pushes me into the loo. Then he locks the door and makes me bend over with my palms resting on the toilet seat so that my face is looking down into the water. Other people's water. Water with repellent origins.

He drags the leopard-skin jersey slowly up my legs and over my waist so that my bottom is presented to him. It is covered, at this point, by a pair of black, lace panties worn over the garter belt and stockings.

He slaps me hard on the upper thigh so that noise rings in my ear and I am grateful that the cubicle is closed off. There is some privacy at least.

'Jesus! What are these? I told you not to wear these. Can't you do anything I ask?'

He grabs the waistband of the underwear with two hands and rips them in two. They slide down my arse and on to the unclean floor.

Oh God, I think. Lipstick, hair. Don't push me in that toilet water.

He doesn't push me in. He snaps the seat down, puts

2

one foot on to it and bends me over his leg so that my gartered derriere is facing up to him, provocatively, no doubt, and begging for admonishment.

He places one leather glove over my mouth and, with the other, strokes the white, soft skin of my buttocks. I sense delicious exposure and know that all he can see are my fleshy orbs framed by lace suspenders and stockings. No panties now. Just bare.

He is silent for a minute, staring. Then he brings his hand down on to my arse and spanks me, very hard, and very fast. Slap, slap, slap. He doesn't hold between smacks. He knows how to hurt. He goes on and on and he is very strong. He spanks with the atrocious force of the true sadist and I know that my shaking buttocks are reddening and the heat is reaching under me to my lips and labia and far into my stomach. Now I am shrieking underneath the slaps, squirming and whining and wanting to get away. I hate him. I love him. I hate him. I love him. I wish I was dead.

Finally the tears start to fall down my face, because now his hands are beating on raw flesh and the pain is intense. Then he pushes a leather finger up into me and pulls it out, dark with the stains of my wetness.

'Do you want me to fuck you?' he asks calmly.

'Yes.'

'Tough.'

He stands me up, pulls my dress down over my burning bum, straightens me up and twists me round to face him. I look up at him. His face is still and expressionless but somewhere, flickering deep in the eyes, there is passion.

'Please,' I moan, for now I feel empty with the grievous loss of pure need.

'No. Do your face.'

I snap open a gold compact. Lids are smudged; lips are no longer there. The eyes are bright with desire; the demeanour is contrite. I dab and retouch. He takes my chin and looks down at me. Eyes meet eyes. His knowing control; mine hoping that he is pleased.

'That's better.'

So I clack after him across the airport, past the Body Shop, and the juice bars, through newspaper stands and expensive handbags and Boots. I am all wet and needy and wanting.

He likes me like that.

Once we are in the departure lounge he is kinder. He allows me to rest my head in his lap so that I can feel he is hard. He strokes my hair and hot, tearful face and I am small and will do anything for him. He knows this. But boy, can he wait. He has more control than I. This is unusual in a man. Unusual and disorientating, as I never know where I am or what I should do next.

Jim.

You might wonder where I met this person.

It was in Harrods, actually. I was trying on shoes, as I quite often do, and there was a pyramid of discards on the floor: fancy spikes, patent pumps, heels, toes. I was being laced into a pair of soft, black leather lace-up boots by a young epicene who was assisting with care, labouring in the knowledge that the four-inch-high stiletto heels could have poked out his eyes at any given moment.

'They're very beautiful, Madam,' the effete attendant whispered with worshipful devotion.

'I know.'

I stood and admired myself in the mirror, chest out, arse up, chin out. Faster, Pussycat ... Bitch Vixen in Harrods. The shop assistant was a vision of supplication.

He was walking past and, noticing me, stopped to stare. He stared for so long that, though my back was towards him, I felt his presence, and thought he might be some voyeur creep, looking me up and down. At first I ignored him. God, catch their eye and they're all over you with their lunacy and loneliness. Then, after several intense minutes, I looked round and saw this long, dark face staring at me as if he had known me all his life.

'Take those,' he instructed, pointing to the boots that I had on, and a desperate little pair of mules trimmed with ostrich feathers.

Then he handed the epicene his credit card.

'Keep them on,' he said, indicating the boots.

So I just followed him out of the shop and to his flat, around the corner, in Hans Crescent.

He had paid so I displayed, slipping out of the black silk shift (I think I was Audrey Hepburn that day) and unhooking the bra. As dusk settled outside, the sun flashed sudden and orange through the heavy velvet curtains, and I lay on a *chaise longue*, naked except for panties, a beautiful peach silk, and the boots, skin-tight, laced, with killer points for heels.

He sat in a leather armchair, smoking long cigarettes through long fingers, silvery wisps of smoke hovering in the air in front of him, one lamp on a table by his side and, as the day slowly died outside, so I became immersed in darkness, a faceless silhouette at the window, all curves and spikes.

'Get on all fours,' he said. 'And don't turn around.'

And so I crouched on my hands and knees, everything displayed to the stare of a stranger.

'Take the pants off. I hate them.'

And then I was naked except for the boots. My butt stared at him; my face stared out of the window. The lights of Harrods came up. I could hear the muted sound of 6 p.m. London and see the taxis and swirling Christmas crowds.

'Don't turn around.'

I felt him walk towards me. Then his hands on the bare flesh of my buttocks, stroking, pushing his fingers in. I moaned. I was ready for him. How could I not have been?

'Very nice,' he said. 'Beautiful.'

And without warning, he brought a riding crop hard down on me.

I had not seen this coming and I shrieked with surprise and pain.

He whipped me again and again. About eight times, very hard, so that it was hot and sharp and the weals rose up, swollen and red. Then, without a word, he dropped the crop. It clattered to the floor and, still wearing his clothes, he lifted my behind to his groin and entered me with one hard thrust.

I knew at once that I was lucky. This was very, very fine. The kind of big, beautiful dick that brings gratitude and melting warmth and makes even the worst sluts behave themselves.

It takes some time to appreciate these things; time and the knowledge that a big dick is not the common offering. Furthermore, some of them are attached to individuals who do not deserve such a gift and do not know how to use their advantage.

Occasionally, though, an organ arrives with a certain personality, a man who just knows, and he emanates a personal assurance that can take him anywhere. Women can smell this confidence as surely as they can smell Chanel Number 5 or baked cakes or the stench of rotting garbage.

And so, in those first moments, neither of us looking at each other, no contact except for dick on labia, shaft inside, me open and full, vulnerable and safe, and hot from the lashing. He thrust relentlessly into me, bringing flushed release and unknown personalities and whining animal drama and all those things that serve to make welcome escape.

I knew that I would always want to please this man because I would always want him inside me. I knew that I would do anything for him, though I would not want to know his life, or his background, or his old photographs, or his mother, or his illegitimate children, or how he made his money, or where he was when Sid Vicious died. God knows I didn't care what he ate or where he went or why he disliked films by Hal Hartley. There was only one part of him that I would ever want.

He took my number and we spent our second date in an alley in Camberwell.

He pushed me up against the wet, brick wall, ripped my shirt away from my chest and pulled off the bra. Then he forced his tongue into my mouth and a leather glove between my legs and far into me, angrily fingering my G-spot until I was whining, nearly coming, wanting him, but trying to fight him off.

'No. I don't want to. Get away from me.'

I shoved him in the chest and he staggered back, then recovered and pushed me even harder. I fell and collapsed on to the ground, so there I was, on my back, supermarket trolley, piles of magazines, black gutter water, cold. Him.

He knelt down over my body, ripped my skirt up past my waist, pulled down my baby-blue silk cami-knickers, spread my legs and fucked me as I lay sprawled and helpless on the ground.

It was very dark. I could hardly see his face, only feel him, know that he was excited. And me? I hardly knew. Out of control, overcome, fleeting seconds of wondering what I was doing, but pleasure. Mostly pleasure.

He held me down and drove into me, again and again, hard and fast, and for me, a short disappearance into the pleasure of him, the fantastic violence of him.

In the end, he helped me to my feet, me bruised, hair filthy and wet, street grime on arms and legs, looking like a police photograph. A victim. He held me very tight and kissed me.

'You –' he said '– are a very lucky girl.'

He is a nasty deviant and sometimes I think I love him.

Once he made me wait in his apartment on all fours wearing a black, satin thong and a pair of black, patent-leather pumps with eight-inch-high needle sharp heels. I waited there, on all fours, for about ten minutes, rear in the air, thinking about him, wanting him. Ready. Very ready. At 7.40 p.m. precisely, he walked in that door. I heard him move into the room but knew I must not look around.

He walked up to me, stroked my naked back, my soft hindquarters, presented as an animal ready for mating. He stroked my thighs, my calves, kissed the back of my neck, and still my eyes were down, gazing at the floor. Then, after kneeling behind me so that my backside was about two inches away from his groin, he parted my wet lips with his fingers, gently kneading me until I oozed and squirmed and wanted him to fuck me. And he did. Nothing was said. I did not look at him. I had not even seen his face, merely felt his presence, and he, hard, pumped into me.

I loved the waiting, the wanting, the silence.

On my birthday about a month later I still didn't know his surname and did not care.

He carried me to his bed and said, 'You may be a year older but you are still spoiled.' Then he gave me quite a lot of things: a pair of white leather sling-backs with stripper platforms, a pair of grey gym culottes, a stainless steel bucket, a mop, some pearls and a Victorian ring with amethysts. All wrapped up. And I sat on

8

his big, double bed, tissue paper everywhere, heels, push-up bra with ribbon trim, and satin thong, always a thong so that he could see the criss-cross lash marks, now a permanent tapestry on my backside.

One of the presents was a Mason and Pearson hairbrush with which he immediately spanked me, not because I had done anything wrong, but because he felt like it. It had a flat back and it was painful, more painful than his hand, and he was merciless.

I was bent over his bed for half an hour taking it, slap, smack, slap, until my buttocks were on fire, my face was red, and I was howling for him to stop, shrieking that I would do anything he said, do as I was told. He paused for a minute and I thought the punishment was over, but he had only stopped to take out some leather wrist restraints with which he fastened me to the bedstead so that I could no longer struggle or wriggle away from him.

And he went on spanking me. Smack, smack with that hairbrush, on and on, right buttock, left buttock, until my lower body throbbed with warmth, until, as he well knew, I was dripping for him. Then he stopped and left the room, leaving me well slapped, well punished, and suffering the blissful sensuality of contrition.

He left me there, face pushed into the pillow, arse up and on fire, begging to be fucked, there and then, face down, weeping into the cotton linen.

It was ten minutes or so before he returned, stroked my red buttocks with his hands, feeling the warmth, examining the scarlet blush that now spread over my extremities. He stroked my belly, my tits, then unbuckled the restraints and kissed me on the mouth.

He pushed my hand down on to his groin where his dick swelled.

'You can wait for this,' he said. 'It's time you learned to wait for things.'

Then he drove me to an old woman who lived in Waterloo. She owned a narrow house in Roupelle Street, one of those London streets that has not changed for a hundred years. You can literally feel Jack the Ripper and the back-alley abortionists and this, indeed, would probably have been her profession a hundred years ago. She had huge, old pots boiling on a black Aga and a kitchen table and was one step away from wearing a Dickensian mob cap. *Our Mutal Friend*.

'So, he wants you to have the Brazilian, does he?' she said, her wrinkled, old features contorting into what I could only assume was a smile.

He wanted my cunt to be naked, like the strippers and porn stars, or naked except for one little horizontal strip of hair above my labia.

'I suppose so,' I said sulkily.

He lifted my skirt and slapped me hard on my already red bottom.

'Where are your manners?' he snapped. 'Do you want me to punish you again, here, in front of Mrs Brandesby?'

Mrs Brandesby, ghastly old crone, looked delighted at this prospect.

Yeah, I thought. You'd like to see me over his knee, bare arse being thrashed. Old perve.

He slapped me again on the thigh.

'Are you going to behave yourself?'

'Yes.'

'Are you?'

'Yes!'

Mrs Brandesby leered through an unruly row of broken, brown teeth which stood in her gums like croutons. Her skin was as shiny as waxed fruit and she was apparelled in an appalling symphony of black acrylic which comprised a dirty, shapeless polo-neck and a pair of tracksuit pants which were supposed to be of a generous cut but, on the round shape of Mrs Brandesby, took on an unsightly effect of tightness. A crucifix hung around her neck, although it was difficult to imagine that Mrs Brandesby was imbued with spirituality.

'Better get her ready, sir. You know the position, I believe?'

Mrs Brandesby pottered around her filthy Aga with little, dancing steps and emitting a high-pitched hum that could have either been singing or an electrical fault. A dirty saucepan emitted the acrid smell of the wax that was warming over it.

He laid me out on the kitchen table, face up, and removed the grey culottes that he had bought me for my birthday. Then the black panties and stay-up stockings. Silently, he lifted my legs so that my knees were up and pushed my feet over my head and fixed my ankles on to the two leather straps attached to the surface of the table just above each shoulder.

So there I was, trussed, legs over head, lower regions exposed, a display of lips and clit and hair and anus, a graphic portrait of pornography.

He showed Mrs Brandesby what he wanted, poking his fingers in and about my inner and outer labia, stroking my anus. Meticulous.

'Everything off here, here and here,' he said.

Mrs Brandesby pushed her face very close to my cunt in order to more effectively note what he was saying and because, I suspected, her interest was as lascivious as it was professional. Then she bore down with wax and spatula and proceeded to place hot segments of wax up and down the fleshy folds around my pudenda.

They were hot but bearable, but after they had cooled slightly, she stripped them off, one by one, an inch at a time, and with them came the pubic hair, and a searing

11

force of agony surged through me, burning my sensitive parts.

As the hideous witch snatched each little segment of hair away I screamed, long and loud, as a woman in labour.

'Oh shush,' she said. 'It's not that bad.'

God, I thought, she should try it, starting with her moustache, perhaps.

'Don't be such a baby,' he said. 'Do you want me to put a dummy in your mouth?'

'No,' I whined, tears running down my face.

He put his hand over my mouth and I bit down on it as Brandesby inserted her wax and her fingers into the last hirsute crevice.

She pulled and snatched. I screamed and bit down on his fingers.

'Nearly there, my lovely.'

But she was lying. There were three more strips to go. And then finally, finally, she backed away with her refuse of hairy cold strips of wax, and he undid the buckles and let my legs down. There I was, naked and smooth and raw, my lips pink from these awful attentions, my sex throbbing and exposed, adorned now with only the little strip of black tendrils floating over my slit.

'Where's the cream?' he said.

Mrs Brandesby brought some aloe vera and he proceeded to smooth it over my bald pudenda.

'That will stop rashes and redness,' she said.

He smoothed the cool cream into my hot lips, kissing me as he did so.

'Good girl,' he whispered. 'Brave for Daddy.'

Mrs Brandesby took the cash from his hand and put it in a china biscuit jar like the sit-com cliché that she was.

Then I was as bare as he wanted me to be.

12

'Do you like it?' he asked.

I looked down, parted my lips and saw, for the first time, that I had a little penis, for the clitoris looks like the shaft. It even has a vein running down the middle of it.

I had not noticed before how alike they are, the male sex and the female sex. The female sex is so secret, but shaven, one could see how it was to be a man with their exposed organs, so much more loud and brutish and unprotected. No wonder they were phallocentric. Now I understood, for like this, I could only think of my clitoris.

Would they protect their sexual organs before they protected their brains? If one threw a cricket ball at a man, would he put a defensive arm up to his head or down to his groin? Which would they prefer? Crushed skull or crushed groin?

He stared and stroked, stroked and stared, lightly licking the tip of his finger and playing with this new gyno-show that he had made for himself. Now my cunt was a flower, he said, and it was to stay that way for him, always smooth and bare.

Then he took me back to his house, tied me down spread-eagled on the bed with silk scarves at my wrists and ankles, and performed oral sex on me, tonguing me for hours, while I writhed and jolted and moaned and he pushed me towards orgasm and away again with cruel intention.

'It's much better this way,' he kept saying. 'Much, much better.'

It has been two years now, but we don't do normal things, hand in hand, chatting. We don't go for walks. There is no past. We don't discuss the future. There will be no children. There will be no ring or conventional ties that bind. We both know that only the strange is truly erotic.

Once he held a dinner party at his house. A smart affair. He employed caterers and maids. He liked the maids, with their traditional uniforms, black and white, aprons, starched caps. He took great delight in telling them what to do, and one in particular – a French girl, Maria – looked at him all goo-eyed as she polished the glasses and folded the white, linen napkins.

I saw him stare at her as she bent over the long, polished walnut dining-room table so that her little black maid's skirt rode up, showing a flash of bare thigh and sheer, white panties through which it was possible to see every dark crevice of her maid's butt.

'If there is one stain, you will go across my knee, Maria,' he said jokingly.

As she giggled and flirted and looked as if she would adore it, my face started to cloud over with dark resentment.

He has a big dining room with dark-red walls and gilt mirrors and lugubrious faces staring down from family portraits, and silver, and decanters of port, and all the other old-fashioned grand things.

I was placed at the bottom of the table, the opposite end to him, so I was the hostess/mistress in a beautiful, white, low-cut dress that he had bought me after seeing it on the runway at the Chanel show in Paris. But I was gloomy with jealousy.

He attended to his guests: he did not attend to me. Women, thoroughbred with jewels and couture; men smart, speaking more than one language, talking of Wall Street and yachts and the fact that the Getty Centre was ruining the international art market.

And he spent his time staring at Maria, devoting himself to ordering her around, and she blossomed in

14

front of him, becoming more bosomy and pouting and French.

God, she was like some bad actress.

'How do you know Jim?'

I don't know Jim. I only know what he does to me. I only know his cock and his rectum. And his hands. I only know his voice and his smell. And his mouth. Though I did not say this.

I drank quite a lot of champagne and wished they would all die in a natural disaster.

Maria tottered around, pushing her breasts down on to everybody's ears along with the various vegetables. She lingered at the top of the table where he could fully appreciate her, and they whispered together so, as she came down to my end, I put my foot out and she went flying, silver bowl, leeks, cutlery everywhere.

There was a clatter as a shower of silver rained down on her. Then silence. Everyone stared at the sprawled, dishevelled girl as the atmosphere became torpid with sympathy and horror. She gathered up her limbs and staggered clumsily to her feet before anyone had time to help her. She looked like a ballet dancer who had tripped up in the middle of *Giselle*. It was fantastic.

I knew she wouldn't recover from the embarrassment. I hoped that there was enough pain to send her home. It was an effective strategy. She did not appear again.

As the cheese was being served by a butler, Jim stood up, walked down the table to me, leaned down and whispered in my ear, 'If you don't start to behave yourself, you can go to bed.'

'I don't care,' I said. 'I will go to bed.'

I got up and flounced out of the room without a word.

I went to his bedroom and lay on his double bed, hot with anger, mentally getting ready to pack my over-

15

night case, go out of the door into the night and never come back.

Tears of self-pity started to well up.

Then I heard the door open and I felt his presence in the room. I kept my face turned away from him. I didn't care about him any more.

I heard him open a drawer where I knew he kept a leather tawse. He had never used it on me before. He had caned me and cropped me; he had whipped my back and slapped my thighs, but he had not used that tawse. It was a fierce thing with two strips of tough leather.

He pulled me off the bed and bent me over the big leather armchair that stood in a corner of the room.

He pushed the evening dress far above my neck, ruffling away its beauty, and dismantling all the dignity finery can bestow. I was wearing only a white, lace garter belt and cream, seamed stockings. Silent, he brought the tawse down on my buttocks, again and again. And again. As each lash stung me, I hated him more. I was silent and angry. I pretended these burning stripes were happening to another person. I refused to interact with him, give him the pleasure of my pain. Ah. But he went on and on and eventually the stinging turned into burning and then agony. I started to shriek and now there was noise for it was very painful.

'Please stop, baby, please stop.'

He still did not say anything. He did not need to. I knew why I was getting it.

A shadow appeared at the light shining through the crack in the door.

'Everything all right in here?'

It was a man's voice. Some suit or other. No one I knew. No one I wanted to know. I did not care that he saw my utter shame, for the pain was the only thing now, the pain and the utter submission of being in

Jim's power. I was ego-less. I made no decisions, emotional or practical. I had escaped from my self, for that is what he did for me, led me to a place where I did not have to know who I was. I could forget everything. It was painful, but strangely relaxing. Jim led; I followed. I abdicated.

He stopped whipping me and spoke for the first time.

'I am teaching her some manners.'

'Ah.'

My face was pushed down into the leather armchair; my dress was above my waist; my hind region was burning and exposed.

I heard the other man enter the room.

'Ah. So you reddened her arse for her. Quite right. Though I prefer the cane myself.'

His hand reached out and touched my scarlet cheeks.

'You've beaten her quite hard, Jim. There'll be bruises tomorrow.'

'She deserved it.'

'I'm sure she did.'

I felt my cheeks being split open and a finger inserted hard and fast into my rectum. My back jolted and I screamed as the alien digit pummelled the tight sphincter.

Then another hand – I don't know whose – lubricated me, gently, ready for that painful thrust that takes you back.

A cock pushed into me, past the pain and far into me, so that I was disgusted and a child and, eventually, slowly, I was nothing, a baby, a tiny thing with no voice, and then it withdrew leaving me in a void from which I could not return.

Jim pulled me up, sat himself in that big armchair, and pulled me across his lap so that my arms were now around his neck. My arse was bare. The stranger had left as silently as he had arrived. We were alone, just my lover and I, the man who knew me so well. Too well perhaps. He stroked my face and rocked me until I came back to him.

'Baby . . .'

He gently carried me to the bed, unzipped the crumpled dress and plucked it delicately from my tired body. Then he knelt down and took the evening shoes off my feet, and peeled down the stockings.

'Not another word, please,' he said, and tucked me in.

There was fire on my flesh and shivers still pulsed in my rectum, but I fell asleep.

Maria could go and fuck herself.

It's a long flight to Phoenix. Ten hours or so. He ignored me for much of it and worked on his laptop. Don't ask me what he did for a living: I assume it was something to do with money. I watched various American film stars shoot each other in the stomachs.

He likes air hostesses. Well, of course he does. He likes their tart make-up, red nails, their easi-girly charms. He sees sex in mundane things: a mop, a nail, a barbed-wire fence, a saddle, a shower curtain. He loves the sight of a stockinged leg struggling to climb out of a car, or over a fence, debilitated by tight skirt and high shoe, involuntarily immersed in all the disabilities of femininity. He loves the inherent unmanageability of womanhood, and all its helplessness. His mind is always on it, creating scenarios. Soon I realised that there were no limits to his inner landscape, where everything could be utilised to stimulate and satisfy him. Once I wondered why he was staring at a plain hotel corridor with a look that was not excited – he never got excited – but was certainly engaged with some unseen mystery.

18

Later that night, he made me crawl naked on all fours up and down it, blindfolded, tail wiggling at him as he stood at the entrance to Room 304, enjoying the knowledge that, at any given moment, any person might come out of their room and see me doing that. For him.

He snapped the laptop closed and turned to me.

'Did you go and buy what I told you to buy?'

'Yes.'

'Put them on, then.'

He had sent me to a tiny shop in Hackney, one of the few left where gloves were hand-made to the specific measurements of the palm and fingers.

The old man knew which material and style 'Mr Jim' wanted. They had a relationship, it seemed. He was not inundated with customers. The counters were dusty; there were piles of yellowing boxes, old-fashioned glass cabinets with trimmings, and hand mannequins with sinister, stretched-out fingers pointing at nothing.

They were long, the gloves. They ran past the elbow and were made of black leather so soft it was almost silk. At each wrist, the craftsman had finished off the slits by embroidering fifteen or so tiny bead buttons. I was measured for them; they were made for me and they cost £500. They were put on an account of some kind. It was, as I said, an old relationship. I longed to ask the old man what he knew about this customer and who all the other gloves had been for. Mistresses? Wives? But I did not. For some reason I just did not. I didn't really want to know. I was the current star of the show. That was all that mattered.

He telephoned the old man while I was in the shop to issue last instructions about the gloves. Did the fingers wrinkle? Were they tight enough on the top of the arm? They had to be skin-tight.

On the plane, I lifted them out of their tissue paper

and smoothed them on to my arms. They were beautiful.

'Good,' he said. 'Now be quiet. I've got to finish this.'

So I sat there with my black gloves on, hot and tired, frustrated and sulky, my arse still smarting from the licking he had given me in the toilet.

'I want to talk,' I said.

'If you say another word, I will beat you here and now in front of that air hostess and that old woman and the mother of two,' he said. 'Do you want me to show every single person on this plane that you are a disobedient little girl and what happens to disobedient little girls? Do you?'

I knew that he would do just that. I knew he would do anything. No. I didn't want that.

'No.'

'I don't want to hear another word from you until this plane lands, do you understand?'

I pouted.

He raised his hand, clean palm, tensed, ready to slap me anywhere. It could have been on the face or the thigh. He would have done it. There might have been a scene. The public don't understand these things. They don't understand the true complexity of a sophisticated foreplay that can go on and on, where only the minds touch, but the effect is the same: to arouse, to frenzy, to desire.

The air miles flyer would not understand that a slap is as good as a kiss, and a threat can be as good as cunnilingus. They would not understand the subtext of fantasy played out.

'Are you going to behave?'

'Yes.'

He ignored me for the rest of the flight.

20

Chapter Two

Jim was thinking Jack Kerouac. I was thinking *Thelma and Louise* and rape at gun-point. The inner scenes were different but the reality was the same. We were driving through the Arizona desert in a green Ford Mustang convertible. The Eagles were on the radio. The Eagles were always on the radio. The shades were on; the Cokes were in the console. The ultimate freedom of America stretched ahead, huge, unfathomable and undiscoverable, begging one to be a bandit, or a bail-jumper, or any of the crowd of rolling-eyed outlaws of movieland.

All around, to the left, to the right, in front, behind, the endless space of low skies; dusty plains had been navigated by miners, farmers, gun-slingers, gamblers, big chiefs, little squaws and caballeros. They rode through hostile land for gold. We drove through for fun. The scenery had not changed. This geologic display had remained immutable since some arcane, Mesozoic mayhem had made it. Metamorphic ridges fractured by seismic upheaval; vast plains once covered by Precambrian seas: these had once been the homes of mastodons and crinoids, now they were fissured shelves of granitic magma and sedimentary layers of Peleozoic deposits. Scarps and basins, ranges and ridges, all the rock formations of unseen ancestry spoke of how it had been when time began.

A palette of ochres, yellows and greys shimmered under the white heat of a dangerous sun. All these sandy seas and barren flats were dry and lifeless. Tumbleweed rolled about the place; an occasional cactus protruded proudly into the air, but this land was bereft of evidence of the breath of any other nature, except for the rare sight of an occasional, solitary eagle calmly riding a thermal. There was no one. No sign of life. No human presence at all.

The only vegetation were the saguaro, the Hotel Cactus, of use to woodpeckers, and those other birds who lived in the old boreholes, but of little support to anyone ignorant of its secret, life-giving properties all carefully protected by those discouraging spikes. The saguaro, like the Barrel, the Cholla, the Cat Claw, the Mormon Tea, and all its other unfriendly cousins, seemed destined to keep its nutrients to itself. The ignorant layman's tongue could swell and fur up as the body convulsed into dehydrated death.

'We could die out here,' I said.

'We could,' he said. 'But we won't.'

I clasped the bottle of Evian water close to my chest and wondered if I was going to be happy on 'the trail'. I was not a prospector or a pioneer. A headscarf, kitten heels, capri pants, pearls and lipstick could only go so far, after all. A girl had to eat. A girl needed a chemist. God Almighty. A girl needed shops.

But here we were smoothing our way through the petrified unknown, where the only landmarks described death. Funeral Peak. Black Mountains. Vulture Valley. Skull Canyon. Dead Man's Gulch. Hell's Gate. Burned Indian Canyon.

An hour went by and then another. I thought of home-style apple pie *à la mode* and longed for a friendly, hometown store selling Native American arts 'n' crafts.

Jim switched the button to another radio station. Creedence Clearwater Revival came on. A winnebago sailed by. Hypnosis settled in and calmed the mind.

I could see Jim as a cowboy, riding into town, all leather chaps, dust and frothing stallion. I could see myself as fallen as it was possible to be, a star of the parlour house, the most expensive prostitute in town.

Not a bad life surely, if one lived one hundred years ago at a time when it was a man's world and the few women who ventured into it bathed luxuriously in undivided attention.

I could see myself paid well. Paid to lounge and dance and pose in lace arrangements that fell off the shoulders and looked as if they would fall off completely if anyone so much as smiled in my direction.

I saw gilt mirrors and shimmering chandeliers of outrageous, dangling pendants. I saw brocade curtains of unashamed opulence, silk wallpaper, golden harps, a piano and beautiful girls in soft, white cottons seducing humble admirers by hypnotising them with glossed, red lips and unblinking stares.

These lovely tarts were special, different from others, as they were rarefied by the immaculate knowledge of the things that pleased men the most. They were set apart by their experience and thus clung together in a fleshy, pussy parade as a union of courtesans who would do anything for anyone.

They were shameless in their slutty, paid promiscuity and that is why they were adored. The porno stars of their day, who understood that for all the arts of teasing, there must be filthy foreplay.

They knew how to put their fannies out, vulgar and powerful. They would lick a man's balls and anus and knead the pumping veins of his trembling cock until he exploded all over their throats and breasts.

They would sit on his face as soon as look at him, make him kiss their lower lips, ride him as he tongued their wet pussies, make him get down and dirty before they lowered their longed-for recess down on to his desperate erection and, at last, after all those days on the road, toughing it out with the whiskey and the bandits and the braggadocio, all the juices of those hard men would ejaculate into those impenitent cunts.

That is what set them apart. That is what always sets the good sluts apart. They are sluts. They do everything and anything and they will go all the way and they are both loved and hated for it. Always have been. Always will be. And I, thanks to strange teachings and deviant leaders, was one of them. I knew it all and I knew that, as the successful gangster is the violent gangster, the successful tart is the rudest tart.

I saw champagne on silver trays and scores of grateful men with money and hard-ons. I felt the notes in my palm and saw myself lead them, one after the other, up polished stairs to some soft boudoir where there was an iron bed, the mattress was deep, and the sheets were crisp and fresh and clean.

The light would shine through long windows that were embraced by muslin and silk and the whole scene would smell of floral heaven.

And for the average client, I would slowly divest, teasing the ribbons from the holes in the front of a tight, little broderie anglaise bodice, allowing the fabric to loosen and then fall to reveal full, white breasts and erect nipples, pert and hard, ready to feel the tongues

of those who watched. And then the long, cotton petti-
coat would slide down my thighs to the floor, revealing
all the things that they wanted.

Then I would lie on that bed, and slowly and mean-
ingfully spread my legs, to show them the vulva and
lips, scarlet and fleshy and shiny, all pulsing, all frothing with anticipation and swollen with intent.

The impatient client would leap on top fully clothed,
pump hard, come and go. Some might spread my legs
further apart so that they could inspect the hair and
folds of the orifice that their gold had bought, and then
watch with surgeon's fascination as their shiny, pink
tools were submerged by my wanton labia. They would
smile, excited, as the hot, lower lips grasped on to their
shaft and pulled it in. There would be a brief moment,
fleeting and anxious, when they would fear that they
would never be able to pull themselves out. Then, as it
was warm and tight and their pelvis filled with
thoughtless pleasure, they would not want to leave this
place that filled their thoughts day and night.

Some would fling my ankles over their necks so that
they could surge in deeper and deeper and hear me
moan and want more.

Some, who made their living by roping, would rope
me, tie me up with their lassoes, bind my legs and
arms, so that I could not move as they took me every
way they felt like, pushing their viscous glans into my
mouth, easing themselves in and out of anus or cunt,
having their orgasms when and how they pleased.

Guns would clatter to the floor, trousers would drop,
dicks would quiver and spring from their cotton open-
ings to greet the most expensive, the most beautiful, the
most flexible whore in the whore house. Nimble, plump
in all the right places, curved at the waist, worth every
dollar that was spent on her, and a lot of dollars would
be spent by those brawny argonauts, for what to do

with all your gold dust but spend it on the fancy ladies in gaudy saloons? I would have the grace of a danseuse and the tarnished charisma of a hurdy-gurdy harlot. Satisfaction would be guaranteed.

I saw the sheriff handcuffed to the iron bedstead with his own manacles. Naked. Firm. Scarred. Young. Fearless. A rock hard phallus bolt upright in his groin, still and very, very ready, but able to wait for as long as it took. And me, hair over my face, smudged, truly decadent, sucking him so that he felt like it was the first time, but powerless to move. Then later, coming back for more and more because he liked having the life sucked out of him by the most wanton throat in the county.

Who could resist that?

Not even a tough man of the law.

Jim would pay as well, it would be better that way, though he would probably be my favourite. He would be a rough customer all right, black stetson, black shirt, black horse.

A silent man in a strange town, he would be a good gambler and a sharp shooter. There would be a scar down one cheek, a mouth that could be cruel and eyes that would glitter with old murders and new robberies.

I could see my waist hourglass-shaped in a tightly stitched, black corset that sent my breasts up and flattened my belly and extenuated my buttocks. I could see him holding a revolver out to me, silver barrel pointed at the middle of my chest, forcing me to strip in front of him.

'Is that a gun or are you just pleased to see me?'

'Both.'

I would slowly untie that corset and allow my breasts to spring out at him. He would pinch my nipples between dry roughrider fingers. Then I would be naked except for black silk stockings held up on the top of my thigh with little garters and a pair of laced boots with pointed toes. There for him, naked, breasts, waist, bush, thighs, hair straggled and shambled, and these stockings with boots.

I could see him brushing my hair brutishly off my face with a hard ivory-and-silver hairbrush and then smacking my bottom with it. I could see him lace me with his riding crop, whipping smooth, white buttocks into a tapestry of crimson stripes as I lay in a vicelike grip between leather-covered legs.

And then, with the gun still held at me, he would command me to lie over the iron frame at the end of the bed and he would push me face down, so white orbs poked right up at him and my forehead was down on the bed, and he would stare at the lobes of my upturned cheeks and he would take me from the back, pushing himself into my seeping hole while kneading my clitoris from the front with firm and knowing fingers. He would lean forward and kiss my neck, whisper awful exhortations into my ear, pull my hair and show me who was boss.

'You little whore, you love this.'

Probing harder and harder with his dick. I was the whore and I did love it, and I wanted it harder and harder until my eyes filled with tears and my brain was about ready to burst out of the top of my head, but he would never stop, kneading my clit into climax while pumping and pumping into me, his dick in my belly, everywhere, unrelenting. I would not want it to stop, but it would. He would discharge and I would slump forward, flushed and grateful, and it would all be quiet until the next time.

Imagining Jim as a rough cowboy made me warm and wet. Seeping started to moisten my panties. His voice pulled me back into the present with a jolt.

'Here we are,' he said. 'Squaw Peak.'

27

And there, with no warning, standing surreal in the middle of the desert, were all the signs of civilisation: hotel schmotel Santa Fe grill and cantina, Cowboy Cafe, Manny's Mercado, Ol Jed's Golden Nugget Saloon, Doc Holliday's Drug Store. An historic barber shop. An historic hardware store. An historic old jail. Ribs, shrimp, black-eye pea, buffalo wing, pecan pie. Food! Souvenirs, artefacts, collectables. Shops!

The guidebook told us that Squaw Peak, once the site of a massacre in the Indian wars, had subsequently become a mining community and then dissolved into a ghost town. The arrival of one 'Black' Jack Robinson III, rich from Vegas slot machines (owning them, not playing them) had resulted in the revival of Squaw Peak. 'Black' Jack had seen the gold glittering in the tourist trade and he had reconstructed the ghost town into a theme-attraction. He made a place for wannabe dudes and good ol' boys to relive the past that had killed so many of their ancestors. Visitors travelled for miles to experience the atmosphere of the Wild West.

It sure looked authentic. The main street was bordered on either side by clapperboard façades, all immaculate with spaghetti-western period detail, from the old-fashioned lettering on the swinging signs, to the wooden walkways that clattered as cowboy boots stomped up and down them. There was an old schoolhouse built out of red brick and a saloon with swing doors. A corral held a herd of cows and, near this, two saddled ponies stood tied up outside a livery stable.

'I'm hungry,' I said, as Jim looked for somewhere to park.

'Stella, if you speak like a spoiled child you will be treated like a spoiled child. It would be a good idea to remember that.'

My mouth clamped shut and I slumped back in my chair, sulking. I was hungry and that was all that mattered. My energy levels were dipping into a realm of serious deprivation which would be accompanied by uncontrollable temper. If he did not feed me soon, I would not be able to take responsibility for my actions.

'Don't you dare sulk!' he snapped.

He looked so strict and frightening, I tried to behave myself and saw with relief that he had slowed down the car at a building that described itself as El Sombrero Cafe.

There were gingham curtains at the windows and, outside, a mannequin figure sat in a rocking chair, dusty stetson on top of his head, whiskers glued on to a waxen chin, glass eyes staring into the middle distance. Over his shoulder, there was a belt of bullets and at his feet, a banjo. A blackboard sitting on his lap declared the SPECIALITY OF THE DAY – YANKEE POT ROAST for a bargain price of $4.95.

'Howdy,' said the waitress.

Her micro-uniform, cut low at the front, had puffed sleeves trimmed with lace and was made of the same blue and white check as the curtains. Her rafia, blonde hair was tied into bunches that stuck out and swung as her head moved, as perky as it was possible to be without actually being Anne of Green Gables.

She gave Jim a glimmer of secret inspection, as I would have done if I had been her, for he was tall and dark after all. He attracted scrutiny as honey attracts bees and, behind Ray Bans, his long, thin face burned by the sun on the road, he was a glamorous spectacle of mystery.

He took off his shades and smiled at her. He rarely smiled but when he did the lucky recipient was treated to a concentrated bliss of sincere appreciation that elevated her to a sex goddess, a perfect model of nature whose beauty had been appreciated for the first time.

'Hullo,' he said politely. 'Table for two, please.'

29

'Oh my God, I love your accent!'

She giggled and wiggled on her high, white pumps to a window destination.

Jim pulled the chair out for me and stroked me possessively on the back of the neck.

'Sit here,' he said. 'And behave yourself.'

The waitress produced two menus the size of broadsheet newspapers. I read mine, although there was little point. Jim always ordered for me and, this time, I was particularly grateful to abnegate the responsibility of a decision, as I was tired and dizzy and the endless lists of items jumped up and down in front of me in a confusing jumble of tostada and enchilada, patti melt and butterfly shrimp. I couldn't have decided between a Navajo taco or a green chilli burrito if I tried.

'We will both have chicken fried steak and fries,' he said.

The waitress did not bat an eyelid at this display of control. Perhaps equality had not yet reached the desert and it was taken for granted that men ordered for women; back where I came from, though, it was frowned upon. Ladies were supposed to have their own tastes, only this lady had long ago surrendered to twisted abdication and carelessly thrown away all those things for which women once threw themselves under horses.

'And to drink, sir?'

'A beer and a lemonade with a straw.'

I swung my legs under the table and slumped my chin on my hand and pouted. I would have preferred a burger and a Coca-Cola, but I did not dare make a fuss. The mood he was in, I would have been dragged out of the restaurant, screaming and still hungry. And it wasn't beyond him to push me over his lap and spank me in front of this over-breasted waitress. He had done it in the past, in a bistro in South Kensington to be exact, though it wasn't until later that I discovered that the *maitre d'* was a friend of his with similar proclivities. He had enjoyed every second of the spectacle that Jim had provided for him, pushing me face down over the table cloth, spreading my legs, lifting up my little summer skirt, pulling down the white, cotton panties. I had waited like that, trembling, with my backside bared for all to see, while his friend the head waiter went to the kitchen and brought back a wooden spoon with which to smack my naked, squirming bum. I had burned with pain and embarassment for the rest of the day.

'Stop kicking the chair leg, Stella, and behave yourself.'

'Will you take me shopping?' I said.

'If you are a very, very good girl.'

The chicken was delicious and afterwards I had a huge sundae with chocolate piled on top of it and fruit at the bottom.

'Go and wash your hands, Stella.'

'I don't want to.'

'Do as I say at once.'

I stared at him, energised by the food and defiant.

He slapped his napkin down on top of the table, leaped to his feet, grabbed me by the hand, got up, and half dragged me to the Ladies.

'No,' I moaned. 'Please, no.'

I didn't know what he was going to do but I knew it was going to be difficult to bear and I was already regretting my resistance.

He kicked open the door of the toilet, pulled down my trousers and pants, and plumped me on the loo as if I was a five-year-old. He watched me relieve myself, wiped my fanny for me and dragged me back to my feet, pulling up my clothes and fastening them, and all this was done so quickly, so firmly, and with such adamantine authority, that all I knew was frenzied mortification as he invaded my privacy.

He pushed my hands down into the sink and washed them with soap and hot water, then, without saying anything, he dried them with a hand-towel and, still in silence and without warning, he slapped me twice, very, very hard, on the top of my thigh, so that I shrieked from the pain. He knew how to slap; his palm was hard and outstretched and he used all his strength. It stung and a tear came into my eye, as much from the humiliation as the shock of infliction.

'Do as you're told!'

He pulled me back into the restaurant, his hand tight on my wrist, me stumbling behind him, angry guardian and naughty girl, not two lovers hand-in-hand, romantic and smooching, but two role players accelerating each other into a frenzy with their own secret power dramas.

Now the waitress was staring, for I was red in the face and embarrassed and the subjugation was beginning to make me want him. My pussy was tingling, and there was an ache climbing from my thighs further and further deep inside me as the chastening excitement of shame penetrated my inner core.

We got outside and now I was meek and silent, stripped of will and moving into a place of total submission. He had won. He had won by being more daring and more skilled in the implementation of indignity. I was a shrew to be tamed and it did not matter to him where this happened. I would have preferred to resist in private, play out the misdemeanours and reprisals in the bedroom, but his arena was wider and I never really knew how far he would go. I was forced to resign to his frightening will as one must sit back in a roller-coaster because one cannot get off. He had won.

I wiped my face with my hand and must have looked a sorry sight, tearful and disgraced.

He leaned forward, softening. Looking into my eyes, he kissed me on the mouth, and I think in those five seconds, as his dark eyes melted and his lips touched mine, I think I was seriously truly and purely in love with him.

'Let's look around,' he said.

There are very few things that I enjoy more than shopping with a rich man who is paying. The idea is hot but the act itself is as sexy as any physical act of intimacy because it stimulates on so many different levels. We were far beyond lust-fuck, Jim and I: we wanted hate-fuck, fight-fuck, fist-fuck, and mind-fuck.

Jim was good at this game. He was generous, he was strict, and he enjoyed it. I was his personal tart, his wife, his pet, his moll, his slave, and he had the ultimate control of money, the final authority. He could withhold it or he could lay it out. All decisions were his to make.

I could wheedle and beg and hope, but if he did not want to buy something, he did not. It was a fine dynamic.

We had not played for some time: six months I think, when he had dressed me up in a femme fatale hobble skirt, spikes, seamed stockings, lacy suspender and no panties. A sheer silk shirt showed that my bare nipples had been rouged so that when erect, which of course they were, they poked through the filmy fabric like two hard, red rubies.

The chauffeur had driven us to Bond Street and waited while Jim walked me into Tiffany.

The result had been a very fine diamond necklace, real old-fashioned mistress jewels. He had undressed me in the back of the Bentley, peeling off the clothes and underwear, spread my legs, and fucked me hard while I was naked except for this prostitute payment. Dressed only in diamonds, skin smoothing against the soft leather of the back seat, receiving Jim's excited erection, first in my tart mouth, and then in my seeping sex, sucking and writhing to pay for those gifts, doing as I was told in order to keep them. This, I think, is the only way to shop.

So I was Marilyn with a big baguette and the woman who got a mink the way that minks got minks. Full-on, paid-up, paid-for courtesan, flattered in the heady way that only jewels can flatter, for only jewels can turn a minx into a vamp. They are the best kind of compliment.

Squaw Peak was not a place full of Tiffanies, of course, replicant town that it was. It was a Wild West theme experience for people who had grown up in Disneyland.

There were shops full of 'treasures from Mexico' (Talavera pottery, Oaxacan wood carvings) and 'Native American arts' (peace pipes and Kachina dolls), shops full of custom-made resort clothing and handmade paper items and, next to a store selling home-made fudge, there was a shop named Treasure and Trash, which Jim said just about summed me up.

He bought me a tiny pair of chamois leather shorts that rode up my arse when I walked, and a pair of cowboy boots, and a stetson, and a suede jacket with tassles, so that I looked like a country-and-western singer turned porno star, all flesh and tits and camp ol' girl, but the little shorts felt as close and soft against my skin as if they were my own skin, and they stretched across each lobe, presenting its every curve and crack to anyone who chose to look. It would have been less provocative to go completely naked.

'God, I want to fuck you right now,' he snarled at me.

I smiled that small smile of smug satisfaction that graces the face when promised certain things.

Big Jack's Leatherwear and Saddlery advertised itself with a swinging picture of a cowboy sitting astride a bucking bull and a complicated arrangement of ropes that hung from hooks outside its door.

Jim's eyes gleamed. Leather and rope. This was his kind of shop. He smelled the air as if fresh flowers had just been arranged and strode in.

Big Jack was indeed big, and fat. He stood like a mountain in a plaid shirt behind a glass counter full of snakeskin belts and ornately carved silver buckles.

Big Jack's own silver buckle was the largest in the shop. The size of a portable television screen, it was carved with a complicated miniature fresco of cowboys and coyotes. His stomach emerged over this panorama, the legacy, presumably, of a life spent eating burritos in El Sombrero cafe. His face had been blasted into fuschia by some element, alcoholic or climatic or otherwise.

There were some black-and-white photographs of Big Jack in his younger days, riding wild horses and wrestling with bulls at the various rodeos that he had once attended. A display of silver cups described his various successes in the arts of goat-tying and horse-taming.

'Were you looking for anything in particular, sir?' said Big Jack.

'Well,' said Jim. 'I'm always looking for something to control my fillies.'

'These deliver quite a sting, sir,' said the burly owner, indicating his range of malicious crops.

Somewhat to my relief, a little old lady with pink hair and a battery car whirred in and diverted Big Jack's attention away from us and any deviant pleasures that we chose to enjoy in his innocent store.

Jim could be a liablity in a place like this.

'You folks all make yourself at home,' Big Jack told us. 'Just ask if you need any help.'

Big Jack had a very fine and comprehensive collection of imported Mexican bullwhips, six feet long and made of pliant, black leather. Jim fingered them lovingly and, as my heart began to beat uncomfortably, moved on to a back room where a row of saddles was displayed on stands.

'These are good,' he said. 'Sit on that one, Stella; see how it feels.'

I did as I was told and sat astride the polished leather, the little mound pressed against my barely clad mons venus, and rubbed it gently.

'Mmm, nice,' he said. 'Turn the other way.'

I turned around and lay over the saddle so that my chamois-leather cheeks were poking up at him.

'Even nicer,' he said, stroking my buttocks gently. 'We must find a stable sometime.'

Only Jim would see the potential of an outhouse.

Jim walked towards a range of belts and softly fingered an embossed cowhide strap with a brass plate and enamel buckle, then he wound it around his hand and flicked it so that it snapped spitefully in the air.

Big Jack looked impressed, though slightly confused, for, unlike this customer, he did not see the belt as a tool of sexual control and stimulation. As the proprietor turned back to the old woman, Jim wound the belt around his waist and, of course, now he was the sheriff of my day-dreams.

'I'll take this,' he said.

Jim handed over his platinum American Express card with a masterful flick of the wrist whose action itself was erotic, promising, as it did, of expertise in the flicking of that threatening slip of cruel leather later on, when we were alone. I knew what he wanted that belt for. And it was not to keep his trousers up.

36

'And –' he said '– I'll take five metres of that rope, up there, the thin, white cord.'

'Yes siree,' said Big Jack. 'Finest steer-tying rope there is.'

The Rodeo Queen Motel was at the end of town. The guidebook told us it had once been a hog-ranch, domain of Abilene Purtyman, a lady of negotiable virtue who had run it as a successful brothel until a mad muleskinner had shot her in the head in 1889.

Now it had been modified and made into 'unique lodging for all adult cowboys and girls looking for an alternative western experience'.

Outside, there was a replica stagecoach and real cacti; inside, a courtyard of cubicle rooms were arranged around a swimming pool, as were cheesecake and beefcake in various supine poses of glistening musculature and anointed breast.

Each room was fronted with a double window whose sliding doors led out to the lawns, patio and pool. The idea of these was that those who wished to perform to an audience simply drew back their curtains and allowed any passing observer to watch what was going on in the bedroom. The window-pane became a 'screen' into which the voyeur could observe various performances, all framed and all live.

The facility was being used with various degrees of enthusiasm by the inhabitants of the motel's rooms, and small pockets of spectators had gathered around the windows belonging to those who had decided to put on a lewd 'peep show'.

Couples, trebles, men, women, and vibrating techno-toys were combining to engage in various stages of athletic exhibitionism.

As Jim led me down the patio towards our room, we

were assailed by a live art gallery of pussy eating and clit nibbling, cluster fucking and cowgirl bounce.

In Room Two, a plastic-breasted generic blonde wearing a neon yellow bikini top was easing herself off with a u-shaped, double action self-pleasuriser that stimulated her anus and vagina at the same time.

Next door, two sailors were posing with full erections held straight by pearl-beaded 'prolong' rings, and in Room Ten, a tattooed Asian hussy, naked except for black stilettos and latex evening gloves, was going down on a lithe black girl, whose long limbs were oiled and whose breasts were bouncing out of a silver bra-let. Her feet kicked in silvery peep-toe platforms with perspex heels as her back arched in true bend-back porno horniness while the Asian girl delicately licked her clit with her pierced tongue. As the black girl's red button peeked out of its dark folds, she trembled, and her nipples, big, black, jewelled with gold rings, sprang out of the flimsy cover of the silver lamé and, as the Asian girl twisted them with her thumb and forefinger, her lover juddered and flung back her throat and howled out her orgasms.

In Room Eleven, a bouncy sorority kitten was being body searched by a man dressed in a customs uniform. He bent her over a chair, and pushed the tiny cheer-leader skirt up on to her back so that her white panties were exposed over two perky lobes. Pulling these down with one cruel movement, he spread her cheeks, spat on to her sphincter and dug in two fingers so that her legs trembled.

While she jumped and moaned, he massaged her clit with his other hand and, as she was about to climax with little cheerleading yelps, he reached back into her bung-hole and delicately, very, very slowly, brought out a row of small, back anal balls, all on a thread, like a row of decadent pearls. Working these out of her

38

shivering cheeks, he continued to work on her front, bringing her to a shrieking crescendo that had her falling backwards into his arms.

In Room Twelve there was a subtle tableau with much subtext but no explanation. A beautiful, long-legged brunette with hair cut into a fierce, geometric bob and a tattoo on her shoulder was lying on the bed naked except for a moulded, silver chastity belt. Next to her, a Japanese girl in a school uniform sat on the edge of the bed, spread her legs towards the audience, and slowly, teasingly, rubbed her fingers over the mound under her grey gym-slip.

In Room Fourteen, a big-breasted, big-bottomed red-head was on all fours on the bed being drilled from the back by a tough-looking biker character with beard and belly. His friend, huge in a Harley Davidson T-shirt and leather jerkin, was holding a slip of a Chinese girl upside down by her feet while licking her out, his mouth deep in between her legs as she writhed and moaned.

And finally, in Room Fifteen, two tiny, muscular yogi were indulging in naked asanas, twisting their flexible rubbery limbs around themselves, exposing their undu-lating perineums, muscular buttocks and hirsute back passages with equal verve as a series of exercises dis-played their suppleness and dexterity.

These culminated in a bizarre finale of twisting and folding, where both proved that they could go down on themselves. The woman, in a variation of the lotus position, sat cross-legged on the floor, and leaned for-ward to drop her mouth into her crotch. The man achieved his feat by lying on the floor, swinging his legs above his head and adapting the plough to drop his erection towards his tongue, a manoeuvre which ignited a spontaneous round of applause from the group of admirers watching them.

'Not many people can do that,' said Jim, and put the key into the lock of Room Sixteen.

Room Sixteen, like the rest of the Rodeo Queen Motel, had succumbed to the theme of the 'old west' and, to this end, was decked with Navajo Indian bedspreads, pictures of Calamity Jane, and frescoes of cacti. This was enhanced by an old-fashioned iron bed as I had imagined in my bordello fantasy, so similar it was almost uncanny. There was also a sunken bath, pink, with four-speed jacuzzi, and baskets of complimentary Day-Glo condoms and edible underwear.

The Room Service Menu (delivered by 'your friendly stud from our very own gourmet Swingers' Bar') continued the adult-orientated theme, offering the usual sandwiches, soups and french fries, along with yohimbe ('potent prosexual stimulant') ginseng, Astroglide, and lickable penis massage creams in four different 'natural' flavours.

The back pages bore photographs of 'exclusive' merchandise that could also be delivered straight to the room along with the chilli fries and butterscotch sundaes. A wide variety of neon-coloured vibrators included one in the shape of Orca, the killer whale ('let him nudge his nose against your coral reef!').

The television was pumping the authorised version of Pamela Anderson and her husband entwined in the intimate relations of happier times.

I lay on the bed and looked at Jim and wondered what scenes of orgiastic depravity were playing through his sick head.

I wondered if he had an erection.

He opened the curtains of the window to provide the obliging vista then, without saying anything, opened my suitcase and found a pair of four-inch-high slut shoes in red plastic and put them on my feet.

The room was dark except for one scented candle and a display light at the window which shone down, making the area into a tiny stage.

'Go over to the window, Stella, and take your clothes off.'

He put a tape into the cassette player and I moved my body slowly to Jim Morrison's shamanic exhortation. 'Come on baby, light my fire . . .'

Gyrating my shoulders and massaging my breasts, excited now, with hard nipples, I swung my legs over the chair and fucked it with my pelvis.

Turning around to face the growing audience of faces pressed to the window, I removed the tassled cowgirl jacket and threw it off, then slowly removed my little vest until I was just bra and shorts and shoes.

I undid the clasp in front of the bra, which was a pink, lurex number with a tiny G-string to match, and I threw it behind my head and thrust my breasts forward to the growing crowd of male faces now breathing on the glass in front of me.

Twisting down, I licked my own nipples and jiggled them, teasing the gawping expressions of excitement. Then, very slowly, I pushed my hands down into those tiny, tight little shorts – which were hardly more than pants anyway – turned around, and bent over so that they could see my fabulous buttocks and excited pudenda, although all the porno-gyno trimmings were to come. They knew it. I knew it. I was going to give it all up.

Facing away from them and towards Jim, I shimmied slowly and seductively out of the shorts so that I was naked now except for the G-string and shoes.

I placed one shoe on the chair, one hand up the crack of my arse, and swung my hair around in the frenzy of some dance orgasm, then pushed my bunghole towards them, my clit towards Jim, removed the G-string so now they had it all, hair, buttocks, breasts, all resplendently thrust out and up by the shoes.

Slowly, deliberately, I turned around to face the rows of faces now pressed against the window, naked now except for the shoes. Staring at them as if I wanted to fuck them all, I sat down in the chair, lifted my legs up and out into the splits, popped a finger in my mouth and pressed it down into my gaping hole, grinding my hips and moaning, as if to bring myself into orgasm, which I would have done if Jim hadn't strode up and slapped my hand away.

'Not now,' he said. 'Get up, stand up, turn around, bend over and touch your toes.'

I did as I was bade, and touched my toes, so that my arse cheeks pointed towards the window.

Jim stood behind me and pushed his fingers into me to make sure that I was wet. I was.

So there I was, moons out, showing everything to an audience of perverts and swingers and casual passers-by like some Amsterdam hooker offering it up in a window in the red-light district.

Jim waited patiently, watching the watchers. My face was turned away from them so I could not see them, but he could, and after ten minutes or so, I heard the door open.

'This gentleman would like to fuck you, Stella. Are you agreeable?'

'Yes.'

I turned around to see one of the most attractive men I have ever seen.

What was this film star doing in an adult motel? I don't know. What were we doing in an adult motel? He was blonde, not as in Aryan youth, to which I have never been drawn. Staring blue eyes and straw fringe are not *pour moi*, but this charming individual did not have the Hitler youth thing going on; he was lean and

42

gaunt and muscular, a Kurt Cobain type, and he smelled of some delicious old musk and had a smile that lit up his eyes and invited you to partake in mischief. Amusement is an aphrodisiac and this guy was amused.

He sat on the edge of the bed and took off his T-shirt to show a small tattoo of an eagle and a hairless chest. He had beautiful long legs, and a long, lean body. There was something female and graceful about him and I realised that he had all the customary ambience of a bisexual man.

My favourite. I love a bi-guy.

'What's your name?' he said.

'Stella.'

'I'm Nick.'

'Suck Nick, Stella,' said Jim. 'Make him feel at home.'

'God,' said Nick. 'You English. You'll do anything.'

Nick had a great cock. Big, clean, circumcised, rock hard. And I did suck it for him. I wanted to please this beauty, keep him excited and sit on that dick as soon as possible. I hoped that I was going to be allowed to.

Jim liked to watch me fuck and so I guessed I was going to get this pleasing member inside me.

'Doggy for Nick, I think,' said Jim.

Nick's eyes were closing and he was about to come. I pushed my hand down on the base of his shaft to prolong him, keep him connected. I didn't want him to go. Control was the thing. Control was everything.

'Not yet, sweetie,' I said. 'Not yet . . .'

'You'll want what I say you want,' said Jim. 'Get up on all fours.'

I did as I was told and assumed the dog position on the bed. The golden boy knelt behind me and caressed my nipples and then, lower down, started to play with my clitoris.

'You want his cock, don't you?' said Jim.

It was a rhetorical question.

'Yes,' I moaned.

'Do you?'

'Yes! Yes! I want his cock.'

'Tell him you want it, you little whore.'

'I want your cock, I want your cock,' I moaned. 'Get that big dick into me. Please fuck me.'

The boy's hard member did not falter; it drove into me, pumping me hard as some instinct told him that I wanted.

'She likes it hard,' said Jim. 'Very hard. Pump her good. Pump her so she can feel you all the way.'

He did as he was told, driving into me harder and harder, until I gasped and pushed my weeping hole up to him, and he went on and on, until I reached the inexplicable anguish of sensation and exploded inside. But Lord knows, one is never enough, and why have one when you can have six? I reached down with my finger and massaged my clitoris and brought myself to another and another as he released himself into me, yelling and still smiling as he did so.

And, as he pulled out of me, there was that terrible nano-second of grief when the world is no longer full of unifying love and I had to address the desperate fact that I would never see this smiling lover again. Our souls had met for ten or twenty minutes, they had melded as closely as it was possible to unite, but now he was pulling on his jeans and his boots and he was moving away from me, and he would go out of the room and stride into some distant horizon and I would never, ever see him again.

Something deep in my womb moved, revolted even, against this hard severance, and I wanted to weep.

I turned my face and looked out at the window. Twenty faces, whiskered and otherwise, were staring at

44

me lying on the bed. Some of the shorter men were pushing and shoving and jumping, trying to get a better view.

'Next,' said Jim.

So I yielded to the erotomania of unknown opportunists and submitted to assault and flattery, naked, legs spread, as permissive as it was possible to be. They filed in, rednecks and ranch-hands, tough guys and old guys, all smelling the musky scent of a free whore and hardening at the promise of all the possibilities.

What was I? A lost soul, wild and unblushing? A servant of Jim's amused expectation? Acting out. Acting up. Endorsing the final taboo, that slippery gang-bang slicked with the superfice of passive assent but, in fact, exposing the true nature so long smothered by untrue expectation.

True nature is polygamous and promiscuous when unbound by the bondage of society and politics and religion. A female monkey will fuck any monkey. She doesn't care. And neither did I. We were all primates copulating in the lens of the anthropologist's binoculars. The freedom invigorated me; extremism propelled me.

I was an anonymous aperture. They were incubi, whispering dirty words into my ear and possessing me with their evil lusts so that I twitched and writhed as madly as the nuns at Loudun, possessed by the Devil, and adulterated by the exciting stigmata of true hysteria.

But I was also sacred, a priestess in charge of my own temple and a mistress to myself. I did not surrender my basic divine right. This was not rape. I could have stood up and stopped them all. Jim would have deflected them: he was the protector, watching how far we should go, ensuring that no nasty miscreants polluted the pleasure dome with their beastly misunderstandings. It was a friable protocol, retaining the semblances of subtle dignities, but necessary to safety and pleasure, after all. Who wants to be carelessly wounded or thoughtlessly contaminated? Not I. There is common sense even in the exploitation of unorthodox decadence.

To some of them, I was merely a receptacle; to others an x-rated glory-hole, a free sex show as good as any Bangkok babe firing darts from acrobatic cunt muscles.

'You are getting the fucking that you deserve,' said Jim, as they arrived, one by one.

They slid in and pumped, drilling and thrusting with their tools, all so different. Some were fabulous, though to know the dick was not to know the man; some you wondered whether they were in or out. I did not kiss them. There was no lip-homage. This was not a romance after all: this was the mystery of genetic imprint, a shifting miasma of archetypal forces where all explanations are inept. No. This was not romance. This was a ceremony of clitoral and vaginal excitation, an inundation of phallic force where I was testing my limits and they, delighted, surprised, sometimes unnerved, were getting it for free.

By the fourth or fifth father, brother, son, husband, dick, I had entered a stage of multiple orgasm. All my nerves were on fire.

A sixteen-year-old with a glossy forehead and thin hair and a wide, satisfying shaft said that this was his first time. An older geezer, crimson from unfamiliar exertion, thrust with the last vestiges of his life force, pushing my ankles above my head, coming with the growl of an old dog.

Sometimes I closed my eyes and merely sensated the simple friction of pulsing erections slamming into my stickiness, coming and coming as they heaved their hopes of manhood into me, some caring, some wanting the accolade of causing enjoyment, most not. Some adored me momentarily, a sex goddess providing precious minutes of bliss for no reason other than that I wanted to.

These, the good lovers, saw my beauty and appreciated it and understood the dimensionality of liaison. They gave to please me, because to please me was to please themselves. They were generous. They wanted me to enjoy myself and they made sure that I was. They asked me where I wanted it and took me doggie with good, hard care. To most, though, I was a service as inhuman as a waitress or a maid, a neutral vessel for the expulsion of their fluid. It was 'blow me, bitch' and 'show us your arse, whore' and 'swallow or spit'.

They studied me as they proudly presented the throbbing totems of personal prestige. They wanted to inspect the crude gyno-detail, the engorged flaps of my slutty ruin. My vulva, tumescent, became exaggerated, like some fertility statuette where the genitals are huge and exposed because they were created when birth was all that mattered.

They pushed themselves into the dripping lubrication of evanescent excitation, shining shafts dipping through the swollen labia and deep into my fleshy recess. They cajoled and shot their load, possessed me without the duty of civilised expectation. This, surely, was the truest and purest obedience. Rough hand on smooth throat, hair pulled, pressed down, flipped over, caressed, groped, slapped, fucked.

'You gonna take it up the arse, baby.'

A statement, not a question, from a broad-shouldered roughneck in a denim vest.

Jellied fingers slithered like eels into my back passage, massaging and stimulating.

'Relax, baby.'

'Relax, Stella,' said Jim.

'Relax, baby.'

I did as I was told and he squeezed in, slowly and carefully at first; I wouldn't say gently, but with some consideration, at least. Then through the sphincter, the pierce of pain, and full in, probing deep.

'I can't take it,' I moaned, tears finally welling underneath the lids of my closed eyes.

'Relax, baby.'

He slapped me twice on the buttocks: the snap of hand on flesh echoed in the room, and my flesh burned.

'Relax.'

This, then, was a liberation from all the lies and commerce of merchandised expectation. To know neutral sex with strangers is to gain the necessary wisdom of the cynic and become a wild woman, witch and princess, too knowing for everybody's comfort, for this sex makes things known, and those things are not sold in card shops or Persil advertisements or magazines. Nor does it suffice to say all men are bastards: this is unsophisticated. It suffices to say that some of us become wild when we shrug off the trappings of society's endless demands; to know fleeting intimacy with many callers is to know the true nature of man and your own true nature. Scary boundaries broken by temporary nymphomania leave one with truth, and that truth gave me transcendental knowing. I knew what lurked, dark and dangerous, in the depths of my id, and I knew what men were really like underneath the suits and shirts and hats and howdies.

They were not all rapists, but they were all surprisingly simple and they were all the victims of the cardiovascular vagaries where manhood was by no means guaranteed.

Twenty was enough. I had come and come; I had been fucked for hours; I had seen alien glans wave in my face, and been offered dicks to suck, one after

48

another. There had been an orgy of wet and flesh and tease and fuck. I was satisifed and so were they. They all filed out, obediently, one by one, though the sixteen-year-old said, 'Ma'am, I will never forget you as long as I live.'

Jim lifted me from the bed and lowered me gently into a warm, bubbling jacuzzi and I felt the jets massage my muscles and wash out the slimes of gang-bang sex. He kissed me gently on the mouth, towelled my body with a soft, white towel, and carried me to bed, where I fell asleep immediately.

Chapter Three

*T*he 'Laughing Apache' trail leads deep into the Arizona desert to an oasis. It is a day's trip on horseback, winding through the wilderness of the Painted Desert, a scorching, dusty wasteland of some 43,000 acres.

Jim and I hired two horses from the 'Lucky Cowpoke' Dude Ranch; a mare for me and a chestnut gelding for him. Both animals were accustomed to making this trip, according to 'Whistling' Jeff Bonanzo, the jovial owner of the Dude Ranch.

'You go careful, now,' he said. 'Take plenny a water and watch out for rattlers. It's a funny place, that there desert. It will kill ya as soon as look at ya. The mare will follow the chestnut, wherever he goes, so make sure he knows where he's goin' . . .'

Jim helped me mount the mare, caressing my thighs as I struggled up on to the saddle. I wondered, not for the first time, if this expedition was merely an excuse to see me in jodhpurs and riding boots, an ensemble for which he had a particular and peculiar predilection.

I had chosen an old-fashioned beige pair that fitted

like a second skin and extenuated the curves of my buttocks and thighs. I had teamed this with a white shirt, knotted at the waist, and a wide-brimmed picture hat, under which I had tied a headscarf.

Jim was wearing a black stetson, shades, a white T-shirt, black Levis and a pair of scuffed, black cowboy boots.

There was a spotted handkerchief around his neck to prevent the dust blowing into his face. Ropes and a whip hung from his saddle, as well as water and the camping equipment. He looked as if he was about to rob a stagecoach. He looked like the real thing.

I sat on the mare, who was old and slightly dopey, opened a neat gold compact, and applied a generous application of Paloma Picasso lipstick.

'Stella! For God's sake, concentrate,' said Jim, pulling at the neck of his horse who was friskier, livelier and a great deal younger than my mount. 'I'm going to have enough to do reading the map without looking out for you as well.'

I looked over the lip of the compact and glared at him through my cat's eye shades.

'I didn't want to come on this hot trip,' I said. 'Why would I want to be bitten to death by scorpions and then eaten by vultures when I could be lying by a swimming pool with a Bacardi and coke? It's going to be dusty and boring and very, very uncivilised. I hate camping!'

'You'll know the meaning of the word uncivilised if you don't shut your mouth,' he snorted. 'If I had wanted to date a princess I would have hung out in a disco in Monaco. You're a spoiled little bitch and it's about time you learned to rough it. It will do you good.'

'I'm roughing it going out with you, you fucking creep,' I snapped, realising that we were having a fight

51

and it was beginning to turn me on. I shifted myself in the saddle so that the leather pressed against the ache that was beginning to grow between my legs.

Jim slowly walked his horse so that it was next to mine.

I continued applying lipstick as if I hadn't seen him.

'I'd be careful,' he said, his voice low and cold with menace. 'We're riding into the desert, miles from anywhere. There won't be anyone around to hear you scream. There won't be anyone to save you. I will be able to do what I choose with you and, if you carry on like this, I can assure you it won't be pleasant . . .'

'Do what you want, motherfucker.' I snapped the compact shut. 'I'm not scared of you.'

I kicked the mare in the flanks and trotted away from him, aware that my jodhpured arse was rising up and down in the saddle, providing him with a delightful view of my bouncing buttocks and thighs.

We rode slowly through the arid badlands. Surrounded by sandstone buttes and harsh scrub, hills striped red from iron oxide were the only landmarks.

As we rode further and further away from civilisation and all was dust and heat, my mind began to fixate more and more on the delights of a swimming pool and how much happier I would have been lying comfortably on a lounger in an over-priced Calvin bikini, mules accentuating painted toe-nails, settled beautifully with *Vogue* and vodka and studying the other shiny, bronzed bodies around the pool. This was my idea of a holiday, not all this traipsing around as if one was a bit part in the *Big Seven*, overheated, with muscles aching, hungry, with the dry desert drafts blasting on to the face and wreaking havoc with the skin.

I did not mind studying lizards in their natural habitat, but I did not want to become one. It would be Jim's fault if I came back looking like one of the prehistoric fossils that lurked deep in the fissures of these geological formations.

I sucked disconsolately on the Evian water, and thought of age and death.

'Stella,' he said. 'Come here.'

I kicked the mare and rode up to him.

'Dismount and get up here.'

He indicated the front of his saddle.

'What about the mare?'

'Whistling Jeff said she would follow.'

'Well, let's hope so . . .'

'Just get up here, Stella. Now.'

He reached down and swung me up in front of him, like some Turkish soldier taking a village woman to ravage. I sat in front of him, facing him, my legs on either side.

He kicked the horse into a gallop, kissing me as he did so. Then, as the horse slowed down to a canter, I sat on top of his thighs, feeling his erection press into me.

Still silent, he took a knife out of his belt. Slowly, with a surgeon's skill, he cut the seam of the jodhpurs with the knife and made a slit in the middle of my legs through which he pressed two fingers.

'Sit on me,' he ordered.

He wedged his dick in between the cut seam of the jodhpurs and pushed it up into me, synchronising himself with the rhythm of the rocking horse.

I, feeling him deep inside me, allowed myself to go with him, riding up and down on top of him, controlling my muscles and pushing my hips down until he jolted and ejaculated into me. Moaning, he kissed me.

The sun began to sink, a flaring, orange ball low in the sky, and I remounted the mare that had, as he had said it would, followed patiently behind.

We came to the oasis which rose as an underwater spring into a small lake surrounded by palm trees. I dismounted, tired and thirsty and aching and wanting to be served dinner rather than cooking it from scratch.

But the duties had only just begun. Jim set up the tent and watered the horses while I made a fire, except that I don't know how to make fires. Who does? *Pas moi*. Never had to, don't want to. I am not Pocahontas.

I struck matches, fiddled about with twigs and paper, struck more matches and blew. Nothing. I crouched further down so that my face was nearer and blew again. Dust went into my eyes.

'Oh for God's sake, Stella,' he said, snatching the matches away from me. 'Can't you do anything?'

Furious, I kicked the fire. 'I've had enough of you,' I shouted. 'I hate this bloody trip!'

He grabbed me by the hand and dragged me over to the mare's saddle which he had placed on a boulder. Then he pushed me down, face down on it, so that my arse was pointing towards him, and tied my hands with a rope over my head.

He pulled down the tight jodhpurs and, as I wasn't wearing any panties, I was immediately naked.

'You can scream, Stella, but no one will hear, and you deserve this; you've been a bitch all day.'

He went over to the other saddle where the crop was and I saw him untie it from his hook. It was 26 inches long with a yellow, braided nylon cover over a fibre-glass centre. The thing had an unbearable sting. He slipped his hand through the wrist-loop to maximise the strength of his grip. Then, without saying anything, he stood behind me. I could feel the warmth of his body and his strength and he brought that crop down on my buttocks with a merciless, searing pain.

I twitched and screeched.

'Please. No! No!'

He merely slashed it down again. The pain started to seep into me and, with the third slash, I started to go into another place, a place of sheer, wet excitement where pain mingled exactly with pleasure and both were the same.

I could smell the sweat on my arms. I could yell and struggle but I could not move, except to jiggle my flaming behind and provide him with a more enticing target.

He beat me again and again, the hardest he had ever beaten me. My buttocks were hot and seared and, when he came to untie me, I had difficulty pulling up the jodhpurs over my throbbing lobes.

I had left resistance behind and now I was his. I would do anything for him.

He knew he had pushed through this barrier: he knew how to break it down. And now I was his good little wifelet, with a hot ache between my legs, and a burning pain over my lower body, and it all melding into one another.

Meek now, I made corned-beef hash in a frying pan.

I served them up to him and poured him a beer and we sat on the rug by the flickering fire. It was dark and the stars were sparkly like diamonds. We were the only people in the world, and it was incredible. He was silent, the flames flickering in his eyes. It seemed that he was miles away, in a world of his own that did not include me and featured memories and characters and old pains of which I would never know and, suddenly and unexpectedly, I felt terribly alone. Then he seemed to shift, remember me, see that I was there, and he pushed me on the shoulder with his hands so that I was lying on the rug with my legs towards him.

His fingers pushed throught the frayed hole in the jodhpurs, straight into my wet pussy, which he jabbed and fondled with skilled ease until my pelvis was gyrating.

I spread my legs and offered myself up to him with arched back, my glistening pussy poking through the slit in the jodhpurs.

He dragged my ankles up to his shoulders and shoved his lips between my legs, teasing my already throbbing clit with his cruel tongue, knowing exactly what he was doing, making me wait, because all I ever wanted, really, was him, the full length and shaft of it, the width of it. Him.

'Please fuck me,' I begged, knowing that he liked me to beg.

'I don't know that you deserve it, Stella.'

'I do, I do, I do. Please!'

'Are you sorry?'

'Yes!'

'Ah, you say that now, but tomorrow you'll be the same rude, spoiled princess.'

'I won't!'

He smiled sardonically and separated my legs so that the cut seam split some more, making a ripping noise. Then he pulled out his cock and entered me and fucked me, hard, on and on, until I was screaming into the desert night. And he was right. No one could hear.

We fell asleep fully clothed in each other's arms by the dying fire.

The next morning we bathed in the lake and ate fried eggs and bread out of the frying pan and I was secretly glad that we were going back. My hair was dirty. I was dirty. I longed for an orange. And a loo. But I didn't say anything and I did not dare to complain. The whip and the dick had won. I was silent and polite all the way home.

That night, we stayed in the Lucky Cowpoke Dude

Ranch. The next morning, we dropped the car back at the rental agency and went to the airport to meet my friend Mel, with whom we were going to spend the rest of the holiday.

Chapter Four

Mel met us at Phoenix airport. Towering in heels, she was wearing a pair of skintight, black leather trousers, a studded belt, a leather jacket and a black T-shirt saying, 'Jesus is Lord'. Black haired, black lipped, black nailed, black humoured, she wafted the scent of cigarettes, Opium and engine oil.

We had been best friends at a convent in Highgate, where we had both managed to wreak an unsettling influence due to our predilection for being punished by the nuns. Powerless over us in all but incitement to onanism, the sisters had seen us as the offerings of Satan, incomprehensible, twisted and dangerous. And we had luxuriated in our insouciant nubility: Mel, tall, big breasted, arrogant; I, tiny, silent and without qualm.

They had strapped our bare bottoms with their tawses, caned us, tried to bring us down with their blows, but we had pulled up our knickers, grown warm with the heat, laughed and wanked, wanked and smoked.

I remember Sister Ignatia, in particular. She taught geography, which was not a subject that interested anybody, including Sister Ignatia, who delivered monotonous lectures about land formations in an accent resonating her Scarborough birthplace, an accent that was imitated loudly by both Mel and myself at any given opportunity and always within the nun's earshot. We were terrible. We deserved everything we got.

Sister Ignatia spent her increments of forty minutes allowing herself to be sent wild with fury by either myself, or Mel, or both. Mel, though, was the ringleader: always ruder, more daring and louder. I was drawn into delinquency by a need to prove audacity, to show her that she was not the only defiant one, nor the only clever one.

We competed in transgression and vied for punishment. Sister Ignatia's pleasure was our pleasure.

Ah, those dark corridors, those leaded, Victorian windows, those prison beds. The smell of toast and beans and girls. The basic boredom. And everywhere you looked, there was Christ, weeping, lacerated and bleeding, and smiling images of Satan, drinking and exuberant. And everywhere you looked there were nuns, whispering words of prayerful piety.

It was lucky that neither Mel nor I ever became infected by the God they tried to sell us. We were guilt free and detached with amorality. Our eyes were lowered in prayer, but inside we were children of the streets.

Mel and I were atheists. He did not exist for us, so we were borne by careless existentialism, and this grew into a more sophisticated sensuality when Mel stole a copy of *Juliette* from a book shop. Reading it secretly by torchlight, our unformed and impressionable minds were quickly stimulated by de Sade's idea of erotic diversion.

Possessed by spirits that drove us to voluptuous experiment, we were twisted carnal symbols of traditional penance, as bloodied as medieval masochists, as exuberant as original sinners desperate to be purged. We went down on each other in the confession box, fingered each other in the cold night of the chapel, opened up our labia and pointed our clitorises at each other amongst the reliquary and statuary. And no thunderbolt carried us away.

Sister Ignatia would tell us to stay behind after the bell had rung for the end of her class. As everyone filed away for break, we were instructed to bend over the desks in the front row of the classroom.

They were small, these desks, and our bodies would touch. We could feel each other move, hear each other breathe, although our faces were pushed down on to the carved wood so that the unyielding surface pressed against our foreheads and we could see nothing. It was as if we were blindfolded. We knew only sound and sensation and the delicious foreknowledge of abandonment.

She would then instruct us to lift our navy-blue pinafores so that our official white knickers were exposed to her view.

We were told to pull down our pants ourselves. We took great pleasure in performing this very slowly, not because we dreaded the whipping that Sister Ignatia was going to deliver, but because we knew that our slow strip teased her and ignited passions that could never be consummated.

Sister Ignatia had never known sex and this was the nearest thing she was going to get to it. Mel and I both enjoyed this and we used it to our benefit, to our advantage and to our mutual satisfaction.

And so our young cheeks, smooth, unblemished, would offer themselves to the sister and the sister would be silent for some minutes, making out that she was allowing us to dwell on our iniquity, to know the fear of the fires of Hell, and that she, Sister Ignatia, was going to do her best for us, purge us of our sins by beating them out of us.

But we knew that her old eyes glinted behind her thick spectacles, that somewhere underneath that habit a woman was growing wet, while a mind cowed by Old Testament threat saw rivers of blood as the body rebelled against Him.

She did hurt us. There is no denying that. She did not smack our bottoms with her bare hand; she used a wooden paddle that hung on the door and must have been designed for this purpose as there seemed to be no other.

She would spank us both red so that it was difficult to sit down for the rest of the day. Mel tended to get it first, for no reason really, except that she was bigger, naughtier and a more obvious presence. I would be bent over next to her, my arse waiting for what she was getting, my body feeling the tremors of her body as every jolt went through her. I felt her every deep breath of excitement, heard every slap as the leather hit her upturned buttocks. And I longed for the same.

Then it would be me. My bare bottom, smaller than Mel's, would take the frenzy of Sister Ignatia's passion, my white flesh growing warm and scarlet as the paddle slapped down on it again and again.

Once, I remember, as we waited face down, side by side, Mel managed to push her hand underneath my chest and gently stroke my breasts as I was being beaten. She caressed me and felt the fierce beat of my heart as Sister Ignatia tormented me with that paddle, ignited my hindquarters, and pleasured me with the fantastic bliss of reprisal.

When she had finished, we could almost smell the disappointment on her. She dared not spank us for too long, although we knew she would have gone on all

61

morning if there had been no God or Mother Superior or laws or timetables. As it was, she tended to bring that slapper down for the full half hour of break-time, so that anyone passing down the catacomb corridors would hear the recognisable thwack of two young bottoms being reddened, and more than one interested observer would poke their head around the door to watch the punishment.

'Pull up your pants and leave this room without speaking,' she would say. 'And pray to the Good Lord our Father that he shall deliver you from evil and grant you forgiveness for your sins.'

'As far as I know, my father is playing golf in Palm Springs,' I once told Mel.

And so we would draw our cotton panties up from our ankles, pull down our navy-blue skirts, and leave the room with faces flushed and pussies moist.

Whipped and excited, we would immediately run to our dormitory and fall on each other's fannies, rubbing and kneading, knowing that we had to bring each other to the orgasm that Sister Ignatia had so kindly started to stimulate.

I would kiss Mel on the mouth with abandoned passion as she pushed her fingers up into me, bringing me to orgasm after orgasm.

We were seventeen. Too old to be locked up.

It was some years before I realised that men could also bring these pleasures, for here, in this Gothic place of repression and fun, I was educated to believe that women and women alone are the harbingers of delight.

As the term drew on, Sister Ignatia would become more frenzied and, by the last three weeks, she was almost mad with hysteria. This motivated us to mock her more. We would stand outside her bedroom door and tell each other in loud voices that Sister Ignatia was possessed and that she should be exorcised.

As Sister Ignatia began to appreciate the full extent of her powerlessness, her eyes would glitter with sadism. She became transported by frustration. The spankings, more impassioned, were delivered more frequently. Sister Ignatia's brow and body would soak in the sweat of her illegal ardour. She was insatiable.

Mel and I continued to do as we pleased because she pleased us. She never scared us. Bonded by mutual deviance and sensual empathy, we rolled our eyes, mocked her, imitated her in grotesque, needling voices, met her glare with provocative sneers, and stared out of the window as if she did not exist. It was a fervent *ménage* and a strange love.

Finally she resorted to the cane. She had to receive permission to carry out this punishment from the Mother Superior, for it was considered to be a harsh measure, reserved for only the most extreme misbehaviour.

We had to receive it in Mother Superior's office, for the principal had to be an official witness and sign a book to confirm the number of strokes that had been administered.

It was a delightful afternoon of waiting until, at 4 p.m., with little panties moist, and agitated libidos, we sat on a polished bench outside this sanctum.

We had often challenged each other to incite the Mother Superior but, unfortunately for us, she was cool and wise and swept about the corridors wedded to God, never noticing two A level students who devoted their energies to attracting her attention so that they could feel the hot, sexy heat of her anger.

We had often longed to be pushed into Mother Superior's study, to see her sanctum, feel her hard, flat palm smack down on our wiggling posteriors. Now we had succeeded. Now that cool eye would stare at our nudity.

On instruction, we entered. Mother Superior, pious and sad, stood with her back to the window, her two hands folded over the crucifix that hung down to her waist. She, unlike the rest of the sisterhood, wore a long, grey habit.

Sister Ignatia, in black, wearing an expression of triumph and ill-concealed enthusiasm, held the cane in her hand. It was long and white, with a crooked handle.

A decipherable patch of pink graced the cheeks of each sister's face. They were tangibly flushed and their breasts heaved with the breath of their deviant euphony.

Sister Ignatia could hardly speak.

'Our Mother Superior, in all her blessed wisdom, has permitted me to cane you,' she said. 'We have prayed for guidance, and the Lord has answered our prayers with instructions to favour you with penance. Thus, by purging your bodies with austere discipline, you will be released to the Kingdom of Heaven.'

Mother Superior opened a little white Bible and read an edifying passage while we stared out of the window.

'Walk over to Mother Superior's desk and bend over it.'

We did as we were told.

There was silence. We looked down on to the desk. It smelled of leather and polished wood and it had been cleared of books and papers in readiness to receive us.

This time there was no titillating undressing to excite Sister Ignatia. Mother Superior walked to the desk, stood behind us and, without saying a word, lifted up our skirts and pulled down our pants so that they lay in pools at our ankles.

'Proceed with the punishment, Sister Ignatia,' she said.

At this point, my stomach dropped with excitement

and my pussy oozed so that I was frightened my secret would glisten on the edge of my lips or run down my leg, telling the mistresses that all was pleasure.

Sister Ignatia meant business with that cane. It was made of bamboo and it was thin and hard, with little give.

She started with Mel, as she always started with Mel. She walked behind her then, to both our surprise, took a little run at her, using the steps to increase the power in her right arm, and brought down the thin rod as hard as her strength allowed, across Mel's round buttocks.

And Mel, even strong Mel, who loved punishment, and who was inured to it, bent double and let out an involuntary shriek of genuine agony.

Sister Ignatia swiped Mel's arse six times until she was shrieking, sobbing and crying, something I had never seen before.

After the sixth stroke, Mel reached down to her ankles in order to pull her cotton knickers back over her bottom, but Sister Ignatia pushed her back down over the desk.

'I have not finished with you yet, miss.'

While Mel lay on the desk sobbing, the nun came over to my side and – the same thing – ran up to my fleshy target and swiped my buttocks with all her might. A surge of sheer fire swept through my lower body. A sting, a burn, a never-ending sear of pain. Whack, whack, whack. Fast, strong, merciless.

I thought six would be our punishment, but it was not. To my horror, having caned me six times, she returned to Mel and caned her again, fresh, harsh strokes over the livid, red lines that were sprouting up and smudging Mel's naked buttocks, swiping her again on top of the burning weals. Now that behind was a criss-cross of crimson and Mel was writhing and weeping with terrible abandon.

And the same for me, six more, so I could bear it no longer. The tears flowed, followed by cathartic sobs.

And then the grovelling apology and begging for mercy and promises that we would never, ever again disobey.

The pain was such that we were immersed in genuine contrition and we believed our words of abject purity.

Sister Ignatia listened in silence, watching our heaving bodies and seeing the tears run down our flushed faces.

'Pull up your pants, girls,' she said. 'And pay your respects.'

We both curtsied to the Mother Superior and kissed her crucifix.

She patted our sweating heads with a benign smile.

'Go now, girls,' she said. 'Pray for forgiveness and I will pray for your salvation. I do not want to see you again in this study. Do you understand me? If you are brought to me again by good Sister Ignatia, I will be forced to observe the record. You have both received twelve strokes this afternoon. If you are permitted to receive the cane again, there will be eighteen and, after eighteen, twenty-four.'

'Yes, Mother Superior.'

We could not see Sister Ignatia's face as she was standing behind us and our vision was, anyway, blurred by our tears, and our senses were deranged by the stripes on our glowing behinds.

We walked stiffly from that study, the blood throbbing underneath our skirts.

'That was painful,' Mel admitted as she lay on my bed, stuck her finger firmly into my hot gash, and brought me to a warm, wet, shuddering orgasm.

'Yes,' I agreed, returning the compliment by stroking her swollen labia and gently licking the clitoris that stood erect from it, visible and scarlet amongst its fleshy leaves; the little clitoris, excited by its hard beating, now ready to be comforted, and taken to the place where pain blazed the way.

And so, well caned, with pulsing flesh, and minds released by contrition, we sprawled over the iron dorm bed, a flushfaced disarray of hair and panty and long legs, moaning and ecstatic, as Christ looked down from his crucifix, an expression of agonised disappointment that seemed to be reserved for us and for us alone.

Hah. But we did not care. We did not care about anything.

Later, some time after the final A level exams, we were caught drinking wine from the communion decanter and we were finally banished for ever from the circles of Holiness.

We went to London, I sustained by inheritance, Mel by a job as a topless waitress in a club in Soho, a job for which only her breasts qualified her. Her attitude certainly did not. Her attitude, belligerent at the best of times, escalated to outright pugilism in this environment. Strangely, this worked to her advantage the night that a man named Leon walked in. Mel told him that they were closing so he had better order within five minutes or fuck off. He immediately offered her a job.

'I am looking for a mistress,' he said.

'I've never met a man who wasn't,' Mel replied cheekily.

'No, a mistress. A top. A top to be my star.'

Mel did not know what he was talking about, but the money was good and the hours were shorter. She undid her lacy pinny and walked out in the x-rated, neon-specked Soho night with Leon Labrisky, director

67

of such acclaimed adult entertainment hits as *Welcome to Pantyworld*.

Mel became a star in a world full of she-male cowgirls, one-legged Oriental housewives and tattooed dwarves. Leon's company, Rolling Cheeks Productions, had launched itself with a high-concept feature comprising a rollercoaster ride, four South American women and a shaving scene. This was followed by *Enemas of Promise*, which starred a naked cheerleader, several rubber tubes and a hot-water bottle.

Leon longed for arthouse credibility, but all he achieved was some respect amongst his peers for a technical breakthrough in *Depraved Anal Virgins*, in which a camera, attached to a procterscope, recorded the most graphic rectal shots ever to be featured in a porn movie, or anywhere else. Leon was approached by more than one major London hospital to give teaching seminars in these photographic techniques.

Leon dreamed about the Palme d'Or, but all he received was the Big Butt Award for Best Anal Scene. Oppressed by his crew – fast-buck hustlers who terrified him with images of desolate poverty – Leon had to satisfy himself with intellectual discussions about the camera angles deployed by Anatole Litvak and gaze moodily into his beer in the crimson booths of gentlemen's clubs where the girls were paid to make you drink cheap champagne.

Mel starred in *Nasty Nazi Nurse 1* which, unexpectedly, was seen as a ground-breaking drama by those who reviewed such things. It enjoyed enormous sales after word about the controversial 'triple entrance' scene got out. Leon went on to direct *Nasty Nazi Nurse 2, 3, 4,* and *5*. There were also *Nasty Nazi Nurses 7, 8,* and *9*, but Mel became bored with the role and dropped out. By that time she had won the Reel Sex Awards for

Best Tease Performance, Best Group Scene and Best Actress. She was a star.

Leon renegotiated her contract, pushed her to the top of his roster of 'celebrities', and created a new character for her. She became Mistress Electra, grand dominatrix of the House of Lubricity. She was the Queen of Pain at the apex of a miscellany of storylines all dealing with slavery, punishment and merciless mania.

My particular favourite was *The Torture Chamber*, in which Mel – wearing a purple wig, long, purple nails, a silver breast plate, thigh-high PVC stiletto boots and a leather mini-skirt – abducted men from car parks, raped them with a strap-on dildo, and beat them ferociously with a series of whips. All this was accomplished with the help of her nubile 'attendant', Demonica, and a soundtrack by Rossini.

Mel met Pete, a prosperous businessman, when she was signing autographs at a trade convention in Vegas. She had moved to Arizona where they were now renting a ranch. Pete was attending a conference in Tokyo and Mel was on her own.

I was not sure how our *ménage* was to work, or confident of its success.

Mel had dominated me for years. She was a top and, like most tops, she liked the show to be her own. Plus men had to earn her respect: she had been a porn star for too long, seen too many whining gawkers with camcorders, heard too many requests for spit and waterworks. She knew what it was to be worshipped, flattered and obeyed without question. She had seen men in all their snivelling, masochian abnegation.

A newcomer had to prove himself worthy of her attention, let alone her affection. Her manner, honed on the success of the bitch goddess, was cold and indifferent, patronising even, before the individual displayed enough worthy qualities to earn her respect. Until this point, communication was a cold, middle-distance stare and a clipped vocabulary.

Jim was as arrogant. He, too, was accustomed to being number one. He had a will and he was as intelligent. I knew that this relationship could go either way. They could hate each other and I, physically smaller than both of them, and seen as the submissive, could end up in the middle, mediating pathetically, or being punished by both.

Mel inserted her tongue into my mouth and kissed me. Then, dispassionately, she nodded at Jim.

'She's behaving herself,' she said.

'In a manner of speaking.'

Mel took my suitcase. This is the benefit of a dominant. Sometimes they open doors and lift suitcases. She could have made me carry everything, slavish, but though she loved her role of cruelty, she also loved me, and she sensed that I was tired after the trip to the desert. She was bigger and stronger but she did not need to bully me when I was already weak. Furthermore, I knew this gesture was one of possession, a small sally against Jim to undermine any authority that he may think was his.

I knew Mel. Jim could have chosen to carry my suitcase, or to order me to carry his, but this decision, as my master, should have been his. He would have to fight hard if he was to stay ahead of Mel. She had played with sexual power for many years, she knew its subtle vagaries, and she thought of me as hers and hers alone.

I wondered if I was going to enjoy being dominated by two tops in a deserted land from which there was no return.

She was driving a 1965 Buick Skylark. Built like a tank, it purred like a mechanical cat. There was a fur-covered bench seat in the front.

'Nice car,' I said.

'Yes. Not great for the terrain. We've got a jeep, though, as well. It's better in the desert. I use this for shopping, mostly.'

We all sat in a row in the front. I, in the middle, sandwiched between Mel and Jim so that I could feel both their bodies against me.

We travelled into the dark plains of Arizona, where there were no lights except for the occasional glinting speck of a homestead in the distance. We shuttled through tiny towns, banged up and down dirt roads, past Hookers Hot Springs and Safford, through the Dos Cabezas mountains to the New Mexico border.

Rabbits and deer occasionally sprinted across the road, caught in the headlights, a blur of fur and ears and red-eye.

Passing through a crossroads, Mel cut off a man in a huge pick-up truck.

'You're so macho, Mel,' I said.

'Yes,' she agreed. 'And getting more so all the time.'

She pushed my hand down on to the fly of her leather jeans and I felt a hard phallus.

'Unzip it,' she barked, screeching around a hairpin bend.

I did as I was told and eased the strap-on dildo out of her zipper. It stood erect, springing from her dark loin, stiff and pink, looking, for all intents and purposes, like the real thing.

Suddenly Mel was a chick with a dick. I rubbed the weird probe, felts its moulded veins and ribbed head. It was smooth and made from some geloid substance, and it was warm from the heat of Mel's thighs.

So here was Mel with her firm jaw and voluptuous breasts, equipped with a dick that would never go down, a ballsy member that would never wimp out or go soggy.

71

I climbed on to her lap so that I was sitting astride her, my face towards her, my back towards the windscreen.

She continued to look over my shoulder out of the window and steer while I sat against her breasts, looking out of the back window at the empty, black road disappearing into the distance.

Mel put her foot down on the accelerator and pushed the car up to seventy miles an hour.

'Sit on it, you little bitch. Sit on it and fuck me.'

I hoiked my dress above my waist and eased my wet pussy down on to the dildo, feeling its hardness insert itself into me, comforting and gratifying.

I pushed myself up and down slowly and then, as pleasure oozed through me, quick and dirty, tremors turned to surges, faster and faster, until I was riding up and down on her like a frantic piston, whimpering, thinking only of my own pleasure. Mel, driving, occasionally accepted my perfunctory kisses aimed at her breasts and face as I moaned, up and down, up and down.

My leopard-skin dress rose above my thighs and then to my waist, leaving me bare-arsed, with stockings. My lubricated slit took it all in. It was a good feeling, a hard feeling, a sensation that would only stop when I wanted it to. So I pumped up and down on the eternally stiff rod, moulded for excitement, feeling her breasts on mine, feeling her female softness meld with the masculine phallus, up and down, bringing myself to the edge of orgasm, letting myself back again, bringing myself up again, and finally, shivering, letting go with a little whine, shivering again. One is never enough. And so, again and again, because I am greedy and, with the man-made, well, you do because you can.

She could do nothing. She was just the chick with the dick. She had the dick, but the chick had to drive.

It was dark and it was difficult to sensate Jim's reaction. He said nothing, but I could feel his eyes on us, glittering in the black.

When I had finished, I slowly removed my spent puss, easing it up and off the toy.

'Enjoy yourself?' she asked.

'Yes, thank you.'

'Well, if you're a good girl, you might get some more.'

I pulled my skirt down, eased myself carefully out of her lap and over the gear stick, and merged back into my place next to Jim. I could feel his legs against mine, but he remained silent. He did not touch me, on purpose, at least.

Mel had made a claim with her infallible penis. I felt that he did not like it, but he said nothing.

I had immediately gone over to Mel's side. I had sought no advice from him, no permission, but simply slid on to her and pleased myself.

I had not thought about any implication, but now there was his froideur and I wondered if he saw this disloyal hedonism as a slight, a subtle move away from him and towards another party which would exclude him, undermine him, and make him a stranger in this unfamiliar place. I could not imagine that he was intimidated, but I knew enough to imagine that he would be irritated. Jim did not like to be without power, and, if he was forced to be the outsider of this trio, the odd one out, he would lose some of his power.

His mood seemed to worsen as we drove nearer the ranch. It was very cold now. The desert was a huge, clear sweep of black night and stars.

We moved through a porch cluttered with dry skulls and rifles. Mel showed us our room. There was a double bed and cupboards, but I registered very little. I could do nothing except step out of my clothes and in

73

to bed. Jim did not speak to me. He did not touch me. His silence was as cold as the night. I would have been unnerved and apprehensive if I had not been exhausted, but I was too tired to wonder or to worry. I just fell asleep.

We both bolted upright, wide awake, at 4 a.m.

The silver-grey light of early morning shone through a French window.

'Get out of bed and stand by the window,' he said.

It was cold and I was naked, but I did as I was told.

'Put on your black shoes and show me your arse.'

And so, as the silvery dawn flickered through the glass, I looked out on to a terrain with swirling mists. There were outbuildings, tractors, a corral.

'Bend over.'

I bent over, the high heels pushing my cheeks up.

He watched me saw slowly for some minutes and I knew that my body was lean and white in the semi-light. I knew that the skin was luminiscent and flawless. Outside, the moon had disappeared: the room was grey, misty and mysterious. Soon the sun would rise and a surprising yellow orb would bathe this scene in colour.

I pressed my forehead against the cool glass and thrust my buttocks up at him.

There was silence. Then I heard the rustle of cotton covers as he pushed them aside and got out of bed.

I felt his body, naked, ease up behind me. I felt his breath on the back of my neck, his hand on my breast. He squeezed my nipple and then pulled my hair so that my head tilted back and he kissed me on the lips. Then, still without saying anything, he pushed me towards the bed and face down over the edge of it.

He stroked my buttocks with one hand and brought the crop down with the other. I jolted back.

74

'Get that butt up and shut up.'

He heaved my pelvis towards him and let me rest there for a moment, cheeks quivering.

Then I heard the swipe in the air again and the crop slashed down on my behind. Hard. He knew how to use it. It was his favourite weapon, that and a nasty little hacking cane. He swiped again and again, gently at first, then harder and harder until I was kicking and writhing.

'You –' he said '– have an apology to make.'

'I didn't do anything '

He swiped my bottom again, harder this time.

'You will never do anything, and I mean anything, without asking my permission first. Do you understand?'

I was silent. I understood but I did not agree.

He brought the crop down hard on top of my thighs; the most sensitive place and he knew it. He swiped again and again and, eventually, I was no longer defiant. I could not take the stinging, the burning, the sheer agony any more. I had reached my limit. I wanted to stop. I would have done anything for him to stop.

Again he had broken down my defence and routed defiance. The pain shot through my hindquarters in spasms. I could not take any more.

He swiped again, the cool whistle through the air, the heat of the stripe flaring on hot flesh. I doubled up, back arched, sobs gagging my throat. I was a naughty, punished child. Defenceless, vulnerable, exposed, I entered the place of perfect submission.

'I'm sorry,' I sobbed. 'I'm sorry.'

He threw the crop down and it clattered on the wooden floorboards. Then he helped me back into bed, laid me on my front with my poor, laced behind exposed to the cool air. He stroked my hair.

'You remember this,' he whispered. 'You will always do as I say.'

And I knew he was the one with the strongest arm, that I must obey and, tears still running down my cheeks, I whispered, 'I will. I will do as you say.'

I felt his calm fingers push into my wetness, for, as usual, the pain was bringing sexy need. He pushed again and again until, dizzy and aroused, I begged him to fuck me. And he did. My lover fucked me as he always fucked me, his big, beautiful cock thrusting in and out, taking me, penetrating me, making me know who was in charge.

He was strong and diabolic and he never stopped. As the tears of pain turned into the laughter of release, I knew that this was better than any plastic dildo. Yes. Much better.

Chapter Five

The next day, while Jim was asleep, I walked around the ranch. It was noon and the desert sun beat a heat that was friendly to organpipe cacti and gila lizards and men who made spaghetti Westerns.

The house was dark and cool. A sprawling bunga-low, resonant with the echoes of past lives, it was dominated by a huge sitting room where several sofas were scattered around a cavernous fireplace. Above this there was an oil painting of an old man wearing a stetson and the expression of a person who knows he is right Underneath, on the mantlepiece, lay the dried-out, white skulls of old animal heads, large and small, long-nosed and broad-skulled. Reduced to the mysteri-ous phrenology of the cadaver, they were devoid of individual characteristics and it was difficult to tell cat from coon or sheep from bear, but I guessed that they had all been murdered by the man in the stetson and those he called his good old boys.

A glass-eyed moose head stared out from a brown shield, its date of death proudly inscribed on a brass plaque. On either side of this, two glass cabinets contained various hunting rifles and, around the edge of the room, untidy bookcases offered titles about hunting and skinning.

The kitchen, a set from the Waltons, had a stone-flagged floor, a 50s cooker, gingham curtains and a long, wooden table flanked by benches.

The windows looked over to the Indian mountains rambling in the distance, while outside, a dust-covered yard had once been a children's play area. A swing hung from a tree and there was an old pedal car.

I knocked on the door to Mel's bedroom and found it empty. A huge double bed with a brass bedhead had not been made; the polished, wooden floor was an assemblage of shoes and magazines. A French window led to a path through a garden that was not so much a garden as a disarray of dust and unkempt shrubs. Knotted foliage dropped out of flowerpots and entanglements of dry greenery were splashed with exotic flower-heads.

At the end, there was an iron gate which led to a dark-green swimming pool whose paving was cracked with age and bleached by the sun.

There was a small, wooden pool house and, around the edge, several faded loungers. Mel was sprawled face down on one of these. She was naked except for her black fingernails. A tan spread all over her body except for two small, white slits, both v-shaped, one at the top of her buttocks, one over her pussy, both left by the thong that she had obviously worn while sunbathing, a habit she had picked up from her days as a porn star.

She was not fat. Nothing wobbled. But she was big. Her breasts were large and full, decorated with nipples that stood up on them like the teats of a baby bottle begging to be sucked. Both were pierced and adorned with gold rings. Mel had tough tits. Once, when she was a professional top, I had seen a man whip them with a flogger and I had seen another thread a chain through the rings and lead her into a room full of impressed leather dykes.

Her thighs and calves were big, her wrists and shoulders wide. She looked strong, and she was. The sun brought out the auburn flecks in her dark hair. She looked strange and witchy. I wanted her again. I always wanted Mel. Perhaps it was because we did not see each other so often now, but this relationship had lasted ten years, a long time, and longer than any other blow-in boy-toy with whom I had entertained myself. Romances tended to last as long as the strawberry season, but that was the nature of romance.

Staring appreciatively at the round orbs of her tanned buttocks, I slipped out of my cotton shift and lay naked on a lounger beside her.

She raised herself lazily, sipped from a glass of lemon juice through a straw, and squinted at the thick, purple weals that criss-crossed my white arse.

'Mmm,' she said. 'Hard man.'

'Yes.'

'What did you get those for?'

'Fucking you,' I replied.

'Really? Interesting.'

I could see her mind plotting the implications and potentials of this news. Mel enjoyed explosions. She was an emotional pyromaniac. She had had so much sex that it was not exciting to her unless fraught with danger and crackling with the electricity of tension. She was amoral, but so inherently exciting. I sighed and tried to put the precognition of trouble out of my head.

'How's Pete?' I asked.

I had only met her husband once.

'Boring,' she said. 'I'm glad he's away. Anyway, I'm in love with Rick.'

'Rick?'

'The cowboy who owns this ranch. Wait till you see him!'

'How come he's so rich then, having all this?'

I waved my hand to indicate that Rick's land spread as far as the eye could see.

'I don't know. It's mysterious. He didn't inherit it and I don't know how he could afford to buy it. He got drunk one night and said he had seen a man shot in the face, but then he kind of clammed up.'

'Well, we are in the Wild West, I suppose.'

'Yeah. And let's hope it gets wilder.'

'Have you, er, made any progress with Rick?'

'Not exactly. He's married. But he's been around a lot more since Pete has been away, sniffing about.'

She turned over on her back, reached her hand over and gently stroked the livid weals on my buttocks. I was about to climb up on to her lounger and kiss her when he appeared, white trousers, white shirt, shades, black hair glossy in the sun.

He did not acknowledge Mel but addressed me in the firm voice of authority that I knew so well, and whose tone had the same effect as the tip of a finger winding up into me and tickling my G-spot.

'Come into the house, Stella.'

I felt Mel tense up, muscles flexing in that state of stiff, competitive tension before the starter's pistol when everyone will kill to win, when everyone knows that they are going to win, when everyone is pumped up with adrenalin and oxygen and ego. Here he was then. The adversary.

She looked at me, daring me to stay, but not offering any protection if I did. I knew she would not take responsibility for tempting me: she would merely lure me and then watch while I suffered any consequences.

Mel was mercurial. You could only trust her so far.

80

This I knew from years of experience. She was stimulating, but she was dangerous and one played with her very carefully.

And, anyway, it was the first day. To stay with Mel and annoy Jim would be to alienate him. What would be the point?

'You had better go to daddy,' she said.

'Yes,' I agreed.

Naked, I followed Jim into the house.

'I've run you a bath,' he said.

I loved having baths with Jim. We had turned them into our own private scenarios. He had imagination and understood all the elements of fun that could be obtained. So baths were never just baths for us; they were always a drama of foreplay and stimulation and sex. They were head games and cunt games. Sometimes I was his slave and administered to his needs; sometimes I was firmly scrubbed like a child.

It was a good bathroom, old-fashioned, with a free-standing deep tub and big, old taps. The floor was tiled but there was a wide, furry rug. He had put bubbles in the water because he was a nice daddy.

He pushed my hair above my head in a yellow butterfly clip and I sunk into the warm foam while he knelt beside the tub and slowly soaped my body, pushing his fingers under my arms, between my legs, and massaging my neck. I nearly went crazy.

'Get on all fours.'

I did as I was told, allowing my glistening buttocks to poke out of the bubbles as if they floated separately from my body, two white orbs lined with a dark crack. I pushed them up further so that he could see the brown opening that I knew he loved.

He washed me gently and then pulled his finger up and down that dark crack before inserting it gently into my anus.

81

'You know that I am going to fuck you up the arse, don't you?' he said, pushing two fingers into me.

'Yes.'

He raised me out of the bath, dried me with a voluminous cotton towel, then made me lie face up on the fur rug with my knees up and my legs splayed.

He sprinkled talcum powder on to my gash and, taking a razor, gently pulled it over the soft lips of my labia, trimming me into a soft, hairless mound. He wanted me to be baby-soft. So there I was, as exposed as it was possible to be. My clitoris poked out from the powder, scarlet and moist, like a tongue poking through icing sugar.

He put the razor down and lowered his face between my legs, and licked the presented clitoris, making me writhe and groan. As I was coming to the point of orgasm, he inserted his finger into my anus so that now I was only aware of grateful repletion.

'Please fuck me,' I whined. 'Please. I want you to fuck me.'

He stood up and looked down on me, a pathetic wanton mess on the bathroom floor, legs everywhere, pussy glistening, wanting him, knowing that I would do anything for that dick.

He took off his belt and at first I thought he was going to lash me with it, but, in fact, he removed his trousers and at last, at last, I knew I was going to get it.

He kneeled over me and pushed his cock into my mouth. I sucked with the selfish abandon of one who will do anything to get fucked.

'I'm going to take you up the back, you little slut.'

Slowly he moulded a condom over his erection and massaged some KY Jelly over the top of it. Slowly and smoothly he pushed his head, then his shaft, through my sphincter and up my back passage which was relaxed and ready for him. And, as his head worked its way further and further into me, he pushed his fingers deep into my cunt.

As I came again, he eased his dick all the way, so that as I escaped to the moment of pure pleasure, there he was, in me, taking me to that instant, embarrassing primal regression that is anal sex.

Now he was part of me, in a place where he was not supposed to be, but a place full of very old pleasure, the pleasure of pre-conscious shit-obsessed id-crazed sensuality and, as always with him, I went to that place. Jim. He always took me there. He had taken me to so many new places. Even in the hysteria of inarticulate sex, with the tremors cascading through my cervix and womb, I knew I must be careful not to lose this big man who allowed me to have total freedom, let me abdicate adulthood, who knew what to do when he found the child, or the young girl, or the teenager, or the witch, or any of the other personalities that emerge with animal carnality.

Now I knew that I loved him and would do anything for him. I was his. After that I was always his. Long may it last.

I lay on my back on the bathroom floor, arms over my face, exhausted.

'Put these on,' he said.

He handed me a pair of frilly French panties. They were white and tight and, as they moulded into my buttocks, the lace frills stood up, provocative and saucy. Then he tied a tiny, white apron around my waist and made me put on a pair of high white slut-pumps.

'Now you will cook me breakfast.'

'I've got no top on,' I pouted. 'What if Mel's friends come?'

'Well, I expect they will see you as the slut that you are,' he said implacably. 'Do as I say.'

I was nervous, but I was not scared. Jim was not like

83

Mel. He would protect me in the event of an unexpected incident. I knew that he would do as he wished, and delight in demonstrating his control to an audience, but that nobody would harm me. I had faith in Jim. He would not let anyone wound me. This turned me on and I loved him for it.

Empowered by sex and tingling with sensual self-confidence, I enjoyed serving him his bacon and eggs, for I was meek and fucked and we were close with the intimacy of our private world.

I did not need anything else, or anyone. He was my man. My master. Big dad. He made me respect him by bothering to find me out, bothering to discover the things that I liked, and then enjoying it when inhibitions ebbed away and there was only primal savagery and the hollering of the cheerful anthropoid. He was not frightened and he did not judge. He understood brain sex. He was very unusual.

It was one of those pure moments in the sunny kitchen that smelled of coffee and bacon.

The sun shone through the window on to my bare breasts, making them feel warm.

I am small, about five foot five, and I am quite thin, with a small waist and flat stomach. But my arse is round and my breasts are full and firm, slightly larger than they should be in proportion to the rest of me. Nobody has ever complained. They gush out of bras, make a nice cleavage, press themselves out of tight jerseys when I am Hedy Lamarr for the day. The nipples are brown, like coffee beans, sometimes, when they are erect. They were erect now. I watched his dark head and beautiful mouth as he read a newspaper. I knew I had to be silent.

I was making an egg for myself when the door banged open and swung back off its hinges like the bar in the saloon of a B-movie Western.

'Howdy.'

A young man in a black stetson was followed by a shorter, blond youth with wild, blue eyes that darted around in their sockets and looked as if they were about to spring out on stalks.

'Y'all must be Mel's friends from Englan'. I'm Rick and this here is Bernie.'

Bernie emitted a yelp of wild screams as if he was attending a rodeo. A gaping maw revealed a mouth full of horrifying teeth.

'Y'all dress well in Englan',' Rick commented, licking his lips as he stared at my bare breasts.

I stared back. His denim shirt was undone because there were no buttons on it. His chest was brown, his biceps strong. He was lean and muscular, in jeans and cowboy boots.

Bernie also stared. He was short and stocky; his hair stood up vertically on top of his head, thanks to madness, gel or his haircut. I could not tell. I wondered if he was receiving adequate medical help.

'Pleased to meet you,' said Jim calmly.

He got up and shook their hands.

'This is Stella,' he said.

I did not step forward but stared back, silently, protecting myself with distance and detachment. Jim had often told me off for my inadequate social manner; he had spanked me for it in the past. But I felt that this situation was fraught with vagary. I did not want to flirt with these men. I did not know them. I did not know anything about the passions that lurked within their situations. To speak, to converse, was to play, and I did not want to play.

Jim had dressed me up like a little dolly, arse up, frilly knickers, pastiche pinny, high shoes. I was semi-naked. As far as I was concerned, he was in charge of

85

this particular situation. I did not have to interact with it if I did not want to. And I did not want to.

I had to agree with Mel that there was something about Rick, something in the cold, blue eyes. I felt the flicker of tiny fear that often precedes sexual attraction.

Rick drank me in for a couple of slow seconds and then pulled Bernie away.

'I think Mel is by the swimming pool,' said Jim.

'OK. We'll go 'n find her.'

They left. Jim looked at me, smiling at my gauche embarrassment.

'Come and sit here, baby,' he said.

I curled up on that big lap. He gently sucked my hard nipples. My pussy, as always when I was around him, grew wetter, and I wanted to fuck him again. I wondered if he would push me back over that long kitchen table, that wooden platform which had so much potential for activities that were unrelated to eating. I hoped he would tie me down on it. I hoped that he would push me down, spread my legs and drill me with that big cock of his. But he continued teasing me, whispering in my ear.

'You're safe with daddy,' he said. 'Nothing can happen to you when you're with me. You know that, don't you, baby?'

I curled up on him, hugged his big shoulders, and sucked on his fingers.

Nothing could happen to me.

Jim wanted to drive into Complicity but Mel owned the only two cars and I realised that we were trapped. We could not leave this hot, desert place without bending to her will in some way. It was a kind of house arrest, if one should look at it like that. Jim agreed. He liked this idea even less than I and said that he was going to enquire about finding a hire car.

I changed into a tight little top, a pair of 50s-style shorts, a pair of pointed stilettoes and, thinking of the dust and sun, knotted a yellow silk headscarf around my chin and added a pair of black praying-mantis shades.

'You're in the desert,' Jim commented. 'Not *Butterfield 8.*'

'So?'

He looked up at me, his eyes cold and his mouth tight.

'Any more cheek from you, miss, and those shorts will be down to your ankles. Go and get the key from Mel.'

I blushed. I didn't want Jim to whip my backside before a long journey in a bumpy jeep.

I left the bedroom before he told me to change and there was an argument about sensible shoes, which I did not own anyway, and he knew it.

It was his fault. I wore what he liked, and he only liked high heels. Hiking boots were for people who hiked and I did not hike. I lay around. I was very good at lounging. It was my *métier*. And it did not demand a sensible shoe.

I clacked down the lane to the pool. Mel was lying as before, on her lounger, only this time she was wearing a black underwired bikini top, Jayne Mansfield style, with padding.

I guessed she thought that voluptuous reclination rather than forthright nudity would be more effective in the seduction of married cowboy Rick.

Rick was lying on the lounger beside her and Bernie, wearing swimming shorts, was in the pool doing 'bombs' and wrestling with an inflatable turtle. He was obviously a very disturbed young man and I tried not to catch his eye for fear of being swept up in some unwelcome agitation.

'The keys are hanging in the kitchen,' Mel said. 'Get some salad if you can. And beer. We'll have a barbecue tonight.'

Bernie whooped at this news, and splashed water into the air, so I assumed he was under the impression that he was invited.

As I walked back down the lane I heard them all laughing.

Complicity was a small town, one of many small towns, whose only role was to be on the way from somewhere to somewhere, in this case Tucson and New Mexico. That was about all that could be said for it. We were in a land that had seen Indian wars, gold diggers and murder, but Complicity had seen no interesting event. No Indian chief had hidden himself in the woods; no famous on-the-run outlaws had shot each other in the street.

Some towns like Complicity make themselves attractive. They build themselves the biggest thermometer in the world, or they grow a record-breaking rose-bush, or initiate a competition to eat pies made out of locusts, or they launch pow-wows or jazz festivals or trade fairs. But Complicity did not benefit from any of these things. It just lay low, cowed by the brooding, purple mountains, roasted by the blasting, white heat, dusty and quiet except for the occasional bark of a half-breed dog or the whispering rush of a winnebago passing through.

It comprised of one mobile home park, one Jed's Drugs and Hardware, one bar that actually called itself The Saloon, one Good Guys Diner, one Smart Mart, one Canny Critter Trading Post (with provisions and equipment for livestock) one Econo-Lodge, and one Chevron gas station.

Jim and I finished our errands and repaired to The Saloon, a small bar where heads of dead animals stared from the wall, and there were dark polished wood furnishings and a television set showing a programme about cannibalism.

The barlady's stetson balanced precariously on top of a nylon wig whose orange hue was not a colour seen in nature.

She was called 'Jerry Lee' according to a badge on her shirt. She was very small, about five foot three. This would have rendered it difficult for her to see over the bar, had it not been for a pair of white platform boots which she had teamed with a grey, suede mini-skirt.

This choice of footwear enabled her to see over her domain and to present her enormous breasts which floated above the surface of the bar and, presumably, presented the town's only form of live entertainment.

Jerry Lee immediately informed us that she was called Jerry Lee after Jerry Lee Lewis because, 'accordin' to my mama my poppa had great balls of fire'.

She was surrounded by a clientele with whom she was on terms as intimate as if they were members of her family and, in some cases, more so.

The local population obviously treated the bar as an extension of their homes, another living room. The atmosphere was created by people who had known each other for so long that everyone knew everything and there was very little left to say, though to admit to being bored would have been to break the last taboo.

The conversation, then, was general, for the group interacted as one. There were no huddles around tables or couples whispering in corners. The individuals formed one social unit, and behaved as if they were in their own homes.

Jim bought me a Coca-Cola with ice and lemon. He did not ask what I wanted, because that is what I had. He never asked what I wanted when we were out, but made the decision for me. I liked this. It made me hot.

We had had some of our best scenes in restaurants. We had had some of our best rapes in alleys outside restaurants.

Restaurants were nearly as good as baths, except they were public. There was always a waiter who could wonder what we were up to or a barman who might see me outside, skirt up, cunt bare to the night air, being beaten with Jim's hard hand or fucked with his hard cock, taken perfunctorily, as he wished, or slowly, because I was his, all his, to be of service to him when he wished. I liked being his tart. How I liked being his tart. And he knew I always wanted it; to be with him was to want it.

Once I had complained about the meal that he had bought me. It had been our first dinner out, so I did not know what to expect from this dark man.

'I don't like veal,' I had said. 'And I don't want sauces. I hate sauces.'

'One day,' he had replied with genuine anger, 'you will learn to say "please", and "thank you".'

He had pulled me on to the pavement and slapped me quite hard in the face with his hand. As my head rang and tears sprang into my eyes, he had grabbed the back of my neck and forced me over so that I was bent face down over the bonnet of his car. Then he had roughly pulled up my skirt, ripped down my panties, and beaten me with his belt without caring if anyone came or saw or anything.

I had whined and cringed, hardly knowing where I was, not caring, just knowing the lashes and the impetus of retribution, the stinging flesh and the exciting hopelessness of abdication.

Then he had shoved me into the passenger seat so there I was, red faced, lipstick smudged, no panties, punished, aroused. Fifteen minutes later he unlocked the door to his apartment, pushed me down on the hall floor, spread my legs and fucked me.

When I thought about it later, I was confused. I did not know if I was being punished or rewarded. It was all pleasure. I didn't know whether to be bad or try to be good, to do as he said, or disobey. The subtext was too subtle, too diverse, too deviant to understand.

There were rules made to be broken, and rules that were rules. One could only surmise that it was all the same in the end. We would both do as we wished, find out what pleased each other, and please ourselves.

Car parks, alleys, driveways, gutters. You wouldn't think it to look at him. Or perhaps you would.

In The Saloon, we were immediately brought into the conversation. Everyone in the bar wanted to know everything.

'You from Australia?' asked a cattle farmer in a stetson, fat stomach bubbling over a silver buckle.

'No, London.'

'Oh, London, England. We got the London Bridge here, you know. Over there in Lake Havasu. Where y'all staying?'

'Up at the Jackson Ranch.'

The farmer looked silently at his friend, a tall man with long, grey hair, long, grey moustache, green dust-jacket and two guns in holsters at his waist.

Two Native Americans stared silently into space and drank whiskey.

An old man threw back his beer and banged the glass on the table. His torn plaid shirt and whiskers made him an 'old timer' from central casting. I felt that I had seen him in a hundred movies telling Lee Van Cleef, 'They went thataway.' He was a genuine relic.

'The Jackson Ranch, huh? Now I knew the old man Jackson –'

The cattle farmer interrupted him.

'Now you hush up, Vermin.'

'Vernon. The name is Vernon, as you well know, Mr Chuck holier-than-thou Saint-Marie.'

What Chuck was doing with a surname like Saint-Marie I did not know, could not guess and never found out.

'They're staying at the Jackson Ranch, Lee,' Chuck said, as if telling the barwoman gave the fact authenticity.

'The Jackson Ranch, huh?'

There was a silence. They were waiting for Jerry Lee to pass a comment, or judgement, that would give them a lead. She was obviously the law in these parts.

'And how is it up there?' she said in a tone that provided no clue as to the reason for the drama of the silences that mention of the Jackson Ranch had initiated.

'Very nice, thank you,' I said in the English accent that I had inherited from the Lord my father, Sir Henry Wakefield, who spent most of his time in a casino in Monte Carlo.

'No, er, troubles?'

'There been troubles in the past up there!' the old timer shrieked. 'There been troubles sure enough, troubles aplenty.'

'Oh dear,' I said. 'What kind of troubles?'

'Well, listen here, that Rick du Cane, he's had his troubles, and I'll tell you, ma'am, no one knows where his money came from, tha's for sure. One minute the old Jacksons were farming that ranch and the next, there was Mr Rick Sir dudaddy du Cane, all riding it up there with horses and women and the Good Lord knows what . . .'

'Yes, he's had his troubles.'

'And now Bernie is out of prison.'

92

'He's been very kind to that Bernie, gettin' him to help around the place.'

'Yes. But y'all know why?'

'What was Bernie in prison for?' I asked, in an effort to nail down the most important point.

'Well here, ma'am, that's a story.'

The old timer licked his cracked lips, preparing them to describe this story and quite a few others besides. I would not have minded hearing his tales. He was a bizarre person. His revelations could have been unimaginable. Or he could have been a barroom bore, on and on about nothing. Just a drunk. I wondered what Jim would have done if I had prized that old timer's withered pecker out of his dirty trousers, pulled out that aged winkle, cranked it up and into the present. How deviant was Jim? How far would he go to explore oddity?

On the TV screen behind him several naked tribes people started to eat one of their relations.

'The truth is,' said the man in the dust-coat, 'we don't rightly know why. He's not from round here, you see; he comes from the other side of Phoenix, I believe. But Rick told his wife Albertine and Albertine told my sister Lily-Anne that Bernie had some drug problem and he held a store up with a knife, but it wasn't such a success, see, because the man in the store had a gun . . .'

'Aw,' said Jerry Lee, 'Lily-Anne told me that Bernie had raped a girl.'

'If he had raped a girl, he would still be in prison, wouldn't he?'

'Not necessarily. Not in these parts. Nosiree. There's some that think raping is allowed in these parts.'

Jerry Lee had obviously formed her own opinion of the law based on various unpleasant experiences, but she did not reveal any more details.

'Anyway, he's been in prison and paid his debt to society, and he has found God, I believe,' said the farmer.

'Yeah, yeah, yeah,' said Jerry Lee. 'And I once found a good pair of shoes in a thrift store, but I'm telling you this, you can't tame a coyote . . .'

'Now Jerry Lee, is that a Christian attitude?'

'Christian schmistian. My daddy was Jewish. And whatever that Bernie did or did not do, he is not safe. Rick is his cousin or some such, and there's very bad blood in that family. There was problems down in Tucson and I heard Rick shot a man. He's a sly fella, I know that much. Wouldna trust him as far as I could spit.'

I looked at Jim, wondering if he was as unnerved as I was by the fact that we were strangers in a land without law and that Mel's best friends seems to be a gang of psychos and murderers. But his face was calm.

'Well,' he said. 'Nice meeting you all.'

He smiled charmingly at the barmaid, paid her, gave her a generous tip, and helped me down from my bar stool.

'I'm scared,' I said, as the four-wheel drive bumped up and down the dirt track, dust billowing behind us, tumbleweed rolling about in the white sand. 'There's no police here and even if there were, it would take them an hour or more to get to the ranch and that's if they didn't get lost . . .'

'Oh, baby. Don't worry. Sure, they're a bit rough, but they seemed OK to me. You can't believe everything you hear in bars. Darling one. Come here and give daddy a blow job.'

He pulled his hard cock out of his trousers.

I leaned over from the passenger seat, lowered my face into his lap and sucked on his gleaming tip as he drove. His shaft twitched, swelled and stood up, the glans ready to be licked. I brought my lips slowly down and tickled his tip gently with my tongue then, massaging shaft and balls with my hand, pumped up and down on top of his stiff, red cock, sucking it deep down into my throat, and fucking him with my mouth.

I was sure he was wrong.

Chapter Six

I had known Mel for ten years or more. I had watched her star in an ever-playing sequence of surreal scenes in subterranean domains where everyone sweated with sexual contortion and psychodrama. As butterflies must draw to flora, so a cast of exotics clustered around Mel. They were whimsical and bizarre. Some were dandies, some were lug-heads, many were maniacs, but she moved fearlessly amongst them. Implacable and calm, she wore sang-froid as some people wear Diorissima.

I had never seen her anxious and I had never seen her lose her dignity.

Even that first time, the afternoon (a free period) when he fell on top of her, the man retained by the nuns to skulk about on some scarecrow pretext. He was a primitive with a Kawasaki, a chainsaw and stamina.

There was no flirtation, simply a whispered request, nodded agreement and a mutually convenient assignation. The nuns had told us to pray to the Lord for what we wanted, but it seemed simpler to merely ask. His name was Gareth.

'Both of you?' he had inquired, sucking on a roll-up and staring down at us.

'Yes.'

'You sure you're eighteen?'

'Yes.'

The under-used neurotransmitters began to forge links across the primate lobes. Assimilation flickered across his low forehead, followed by shards of enlightenment. Finally, cunning arrived, as he began to understand the full potential of the suggestion.

'There must be others,' he said smugly.

'No,' said Mel. 'Just us.'

We went to the lawnmower shed at about 3 p.m. and he pushed Mel down in a pile of dead leaves. She lay on her back, head inches away from paint tins and logs and parts of machinery. He kneeled down at her feet and gently lifted up her short, grey skirt so that he could see her white schoolpants. He slowly pulled the cotton briefs over her long legs and threw them to the side. So there she was, skirt above her waist, all schoolgirl slit and downward nubility.

He unzipped the buttons on his jeans and pulled out his cock, proudly and with some ceremony, as if it had just won a prize for 'best in show'.

I had never seen one 'live', as it were, and I stared at it as one stares at strange creatures in zoos.

This new specimen was white and fat and hard. The male member is rarely seen erect in pictures. I was accustomed to seeing pendulous organs hidden behind bunches of grapes or hanging limply and bereft of life. I had never seen any evidence that validated their reputation as tools to drive women wild. They had all seemed to be innocent, meek things, unaffected, as they were, by the vigour of tumescence.

Familiar only with the limp representations displayed in biology books, I was, at first, taken aback and slightly intimidated by this imposing erection. Then I wondered how one was supposed to touch it, and where. I was glad Mel was first.

He did not kiss her but simply thrust himself into her and fucked her quite hard, groaning and jolting into her with careless force. There was no pause, or speech. He did not ask if there was any pain. It was as if he did not know that she was a virgin. Later we thought, well, he must fuck like that all the time; same thing, all the time. He had probably never done anything different because he didn't know how.

The first time is never the best time, but it is, unfortunately, the time that is remembered. All the others fade away into distant annals with their pants and chests and attempts. No matter how strong or handsome or skilled they are, some of their names will slip away. But the first, the first is always there, despite the fact that he is usually only a technicality.

I watched carefully, for I was next. This was the agreement.

He pinned her arms down, and she stared up at him while he looked ahead at the wall. Then he shuddered, came, and went, as they do.

'There you are then,' he said, slipping the condom off with perfunctory skill. 'That's it.'

Mel rose gracefully from the mulch, pulled down the navy-blue school pullover, picked some leaves from her skirt, and walked grandly out of the shed as if she had been invested with some ornament of monarchy rather than divested of her virginity.

I presented myself for his second erection and he entered in the same position. He was not an imaginative person nor a sensual one. He performed this service much as he performed any other, the window-cleaning, or drain-clearing, or weeding. They were all part of the working day to be completed by five o'clock so that he could be down The Frog and Firkin by 5.30.

I removed my own pants and laid them carefully on top of an oil can. Then I spread my legs, far apart, for I liked to feel my puss poking up at him, raised and waiting, the air on my clit. I parted my lips with my fingers and stretched my hole for him so that he could come in.

I was smaller than Mel, and the hard shaft, the strength of it, the girth of it, took me by surprise. I should have waited, perhaps, saved my little pussy for a more worthwhile event, but where Mel went, I tended to follow.

He surged in, hard and fast.

'For Christ's sake,' I snapped, pulling my face away from his unshaven mouth. 'You're hurting me.'

'Sorry, love.'

Then it didn't hurt. It intimated warmth and power and waves of sensation, but only intimated. Sex with the gardener was a promise; his contribution was a hint of the fun that we were to have. Only a hint. A small, interesting operation, informative, and useful, but only a start.

There, in this speedily performed scene, my face and ears and hair lay amongst dust and lawn cuttings. As I smelled the motorbike on his clothes, and the unwashed skin, and allowed him to come closer to me than any man had ever been before, I saw Mel's face framed by a mildewed window pane as she stood outside, looking in at us. I thought I saw a tear roll down her cheek, but I was not sure. I did not ask and, over the years, I never saw her cry again.

We were pert pioneers, the first in our class. Boasting to the other girls, we embellished this 'act of love', described his magnificent organ with complimentary adjectives and told of climaxes that were hallucinogenic in their quality. Soon, they all wanted to make out with the gardener. Lucky Gareth.

On stage Mel could smoke a menthylated Dunhill from her pussy and I swear she could blow rings. Later, a little Thai girl who could pick up a razor with her cunt taught Mel how to ejaculate with a yogic contraction of the pelvic muscles. Mel learned that, with concentration, she could 'squirt' as well as any man. She made sure that she was paid for this party trick that mystified or horrified, depending on the inclination of the individual voyeur staring into the scarlet recesses of her pudendum.

I often visited her backstage with the tits and tassles and endless talk of tips. This was in a bad phase when the work places were velour, the waitresses were topless and the sleaze-merchants took 25%. Later, she was discovered by Leon and became his sensational star of adult motion pictures. Then life became easier.

Mel had seen and done many, many things and, though the wild tales were described with unruffled detachment, I noticed that, sometimes, she made love to me in an angry way.

She was always the man, in general, always the man. She overcame me, but sometimes I could not tell if the passion was anger or the anger, passion.

The evening that we returned from our shopping trip to Complicity I found her outside by the pool. Her face was crimson and she seemed very agitated. On some this would have been mortification or fury, but Mel was never complicated by these unhelpful stirrings. Nevertheless her cheeks were flushed and her eyes glittered with unfathomable intent.

I assumed that these signs denoted that she had had sex with Rick.

'Did you have sex with Rick?' I asked.

'No, I did not,' she snapped. 'I'm hot from the bloody barbecue.'

She had bellowed the flames into an intense conflagration that would have mercilessly immolated any steak unlucky enough to be placed anywhere near it.

So there she was, buttocks in tight, spandex pedal-pushers, breasts framed by black scoopneck T-shirt, kitten heels, all curves and fury. I caressed her arse gently, pushing my fingers between her legs as she bent over the fire, but she pushed my hand away from her. She wanted Rick.

This heaving edginess was uncharacteristic. She had better get it soon, I thought. And it had better be the real thing, the pulse that goes all the way into the womb, that ignites and satisfies all at once. It had better be the real thing, I thought, or there is going to be trouble.

I went into the house to change. It was growing cold. The desert chill stabbed the skin and I was beginning to shiver.

I eased myself into a skintight black jersey dress whose folds hung silkily over my knees and which somehow managed to be Bette Davis, dangerous and femme. I enhanced these aspects with a pair of black, calfskin, knee-length boots with four-and-a-half-inch stiletto heels. They were laced up through rows of gold eyelets and clung to my calves as if they had been made for me.

Jim was opening some bottles of wine in the kitchen and it was as if the Devil had decided to update himself with a Brooks Brother shirt. The white cotton made him appear even darker than usual. The raven-black fringe flopped over his face. His thin but sensual lips rested in an expression that, at its least kind, was an amused sneer, but in normal repose showed calm authority.

Sometimes I would just stare at him, quietly subsumed

by wordless amazement and fascinated by the distance that had to exist between us.

He had found places on and in my body I had not even discovered for myself. He could easily bring me to orgasm with his fingers deep inside me and I still did not know how he did it.

He had known from the beginning how to play with me, how to grope and feel and pinch and twist the nerve-endings until I did not know where I was and did not care. He had taught me that, as all dicks are different, so too are all pussies. He knew I liked it hard and deep, that I wanted to feel, but needed to be made to feel. A good belting, a good fingering, a good fucking and then, only then, could I move into the world and make connections. He managed to maintain an endless erotic distance at the same time as pulling me close with his mind.

There was something strangely courtly in his love for he spent a lot of time thinking about me, plotting plans that he knew would entice and excite me. This was the best kind of romantic attention.

The straights might see a bad man teasing a weird woman, but anyone with the smallest understanding of sexual passion would know that by taking time to understand the erotic core of my sexual being, to know and fuck the oddball slave slut, by taking this time, he was the ultimate gentleman and perfect lover.

He was very unusual. Most men cannot be there or are too scared or too tired or too selfish or neurotic. Jim was generous and careful and he had a very high sex-drive. And, of course, he was rich and single, so he was tired by neither labour nor family duties. He could spend as much time as he wished pursuing pleasure and learning what pleased him. He was a sybarite whose understanding had been developed by the long-term and obsessive observation of women.

He was very, very interested in sex and, for the time being, he was interested in me. I had caught his attention, possibly because he sensed that I would meet any challenge that he chose to set and follow him wherever he chose to lead me. He could do anything with me and I would encourage him. He was forty. His only enemy was boredom. I, with all my pure forms of provocation, made him feel alive.

There was love. Not love as it is usually sold, all those amazing sagas of unlikely happiness, not love as presented for entertainment, but the love that springs from surrender, courage and trust.

He had tied me up, hung me up, lashed me, raped me, whipped me, shaved me, slapped me, bent me over a public park bench and buggered me. He had gagged me and threatened me and allowed his friends to bang me.

I had been compelled to trust him with my life.

He had not hurt me yet but I felt that here, in the desert, for the first time, allowing him the freedom to do and be as he chose had the potential to cut my soul to ribbons.

He looked at me, studying my tits that were pushed towards him by the high heels. Then, without saying anything, he pushed his hand between my legs.

'You're wearing panties.'

'Yes. It's cold.'

He sighed.

'Mel's not in a good mood,' I told him.

He didn't answer but his eyes registered amused expectation as the possibilities ran through his imagination.

Jim never took moods seriously. Emotions were toys to be played with and teased until they performed some decadent show-down.

I regretted saying anything. I didn't want Jim to have

any power over Mel, even though she was well able to look after herself. I didn't want him to see her need and direct it, and I didn't particularly want him to find a way to force her to submit. I did not want to see Mel assent. And anyway, I was his girl. One slave should be enough.

Mel and I had always borrowed each other's men as we borrowed each other's money, car-keys and clothes. Anything could be lent for the night, for we had long agreed never to be suffocated by the ludicrous constrictions of monogamy.

It had always worked, but that was then. I was older now, less casual, more aware of and grateful for a skilled lover. I was very close to Jim. There was a unique intimacy and an unusual level of sexual understanding and I did not know how fragile this was, nor how easily it could be broken by Mel who, in the end, had a big ego. She would let the world and his wife lick her pussy just because she liked the proof that they wanted to.

Three is fun but its dynamics are arcane and the choreography complex. Three is an interesting number for sex, but it is not always a successful one. It's risky. Relationships can be broken with a slip of the tongue; enjoyment can dissolve into unexpected jealousies and misread body language. Everyone needs to be attended to and no one can predict the emotional outcome. There are perils in these pleasures.

I wanted Rick to handle Mel; straight Rick should give her what she wanted. But Jim moved in, slow and as sure as a jungle predator. He crept towards her, sniffing the perfume of her and sensing her vulnerabilities.

When I walked back to the barbecue, he was pouring her a glass of wine, charming her, offering to make the potato salad, and worse, worst of all, making her laugh.

I sat at the table and stared at them, smelling the mesquite, gulping white wine.

He fired up a cigarette for her as she performed to the awe of his gaze. She was an antelope in the Serengeti and she didn't stand a chance. He was more powerful, more lethal, and he was ready to spring.

The moon was a mean silver sliver; the sky black. We, the characters, moved in the shadows that lurched between the orange glow of the barbecue and the twitching candlelight.

Then the silence was shattered by rodeo whooping and unnatural shrieking as Rick and Bernie walked down the garden path, playing with their flashlights and pushing each other.

They had dressed up for the evening. Rick was in a suede jacket with tassels and there were new spurs on his black cowboy boots. Bernie wore a plaid arrangement over a T-shirt whose front bore the words GUN-OWNERS OF AMERICA.

They slumped themselves down on the wooden bench so that they were on either side of me, sandwiching me with their bodies. Their Wild West banter came through in stereo as they devoted themselves to warming me with their attention, flattering me as surely as Jim was flattering Mel.

This was not as it should be.

Rick's hand was on my leg.

This was not as it should be.

Why was Rick ignoring Mel?

Why was Jim ignoring me?

Was Bernie on medication?

Perhaps I should become a conventional person. Get married. Settle down. Give up sex.

'You sure are pretty,' Bernie said, staring at me with two blue eyes swivelling in opposite directions. This must have given him the peripheral vision of a hammerhead shark rather than allowed any detailed description of my face.

'There more like you in London?'

'They're all like that in London,' said Rick, stroking my cheeks with one rough digit. 'Trus' me. I'm an authority on English roses.'

He caressed my thigh and eased his mouth so close to my face that I could see where the skin had been chafed in a close shave.

His lips continued to move in homage.

'Are you a supermodel?' he said.

I could have laughed out loud, or I could have chosen to enjoy this fulsome adulation, but instead, I said loudly, so that Jim and Mel would hear:

'And how is your wife, Rick? I'm looking forward to meeting her.'

Rick's face pulled away from mine as if it had been jerked by an invisible string. He paused, as if not knowing whether to shift down to third or go up to fifth.

Jim's head whipped round and he looked at me for the first time in an hour.

It had been a long hour.

'Er . . .' Rick edged his way down the bench away from me. 'She's gone to Phoenix to see Michael Bolton.'

As Jim's attention diverted to this tiny scenario, so Mel, antenna twitching, resumed control.

'It's ready!' she shouted, more loudly than was necessary since no one was sitting in the next state.

Steaks the size of the Isle of Man were thrown on to plates; potatoes were lobbed into dishes; condiments and cutlery were circulated.

Everyone sat at the table, concentrating on knives and napkins and passing the butter.

The conversation focused on the food, and the wine, the food again, the state of the meat, the quality, where it came from and all the steak anecdotes that alfresco eating inevitably initiates.

Mel preened as congratulations were heaped on her and everyone paid tribute to her culinary skills.

Bernie drank alternately from glasses of beer and wine and rolled a joint while performing an extraordinary kinesis of cutlery whereby potatoes leaped up and down on the plate, as if they were possessed, then chunks of meat flew into his mouth via his ears.

As he spoke, he jabbed the knife into the air in a stabbing motion that would have killed anyone who came too near. Stab. Chew, stab, chew. That was Bernie. And then blandishment. A eulogy to my breasts, an endorsement of my legs, all praise and over-promotion.

And, of course, I encouraged him.

Jim's eyes were black, staring from dark eyelashes with the expression that he knew I understood. No one would know what this long gaze meant unless they had been in his scenes. He could do anything with me. Even his silence turned me on with the threat that was always a promise.

I looked at him and looked down, instantly yielding to him, submitting before he had even said anything. Did he scare me? Yes. Always. And I loved this. I loved being scared in the full knowledge that he would never, ever harm me. He would play with me, maul me, humiliate me, hurt me, subordinate me; he would lead me to new places, but he would not leave me there alone and he would never actually scar or maim. Maybe he was the cat, playing with the mouse; perhaps he actually loved me and was devoted to my pleasure. I did not know.

Bernie began to juggle oranges but Jim's gaze held me. It was like a hot kiss after a long, cold swim.

I was in trouble. Delicious trouble. I did not know why, exactly, since he could not have believed that I was actually interested in either Rick or Bernie, but sexual jealousy is an unpredictable thing. Jim played with it, switched it on and off as he felt like it. He was even in control of this emotion.

He could have chosen to give me to Rick or Bernie if he felt like it.

Bernie began to expand on his two favourite subjects: God and the importance of home protection. He carried on and on, and on and on, talking about muzzle loaders and ballistic efficiency, about bullet weights, grain jackets and the importance of loading a Makarov with XTP hollowpoint.

He boasted that he owned a 'loada' police surplus double-action revolvers, a pump-action Remington, a Mossberg, and several hand-grenades.

I looked at him. It was freezing but he did not notice the cold.

He was patently mad.

Then he took my hand and kissed it ostentatiously, as if he was some amateur ham doing Shakespeare in Surrey.

'I want this 'lil lady to marry me,' he said.

I laughed happily and said yes.

'Clear the plates, Stella.'

Jim's voice was quiet and matter-of-fact. The tone expected automatic obedience without the effort of intonation. He knew that I would do as I was told and he knew the power of quiet command.

I pouted.

'Now.'

Mel perked up; her back straightened. She liked this. She was drunk. She was loose. She could go anywhere.

Rick and Bernie were way, way out of their league. They were reprobates moving in a far-flung land full of lost souls. Their lives were probably full of unlawful doings, committed, I suspected, with varying degrees of incompetence. Bernie might have killed a man; perhaps Rick dealt in stolen fire-arms, but we, the sensual outsiders, we were the ones who were truly ungovernable. We annuled all their little psychic rules of decorum. We suspended conformity and pushed them towards a dissolute adventure. They may have broken this law or that law, they might rule the local low-life with their pirate tales and prison stories, but now they were forced to face their own mortification. Would they follow us? Or would they stay scared, swig beer, look askance, prefer straight sex in straight places because to follow us was to surrender control and experiment with forces that were beyond their experience?

These forces, as we know, sometimes serve to intimidate and to repress. The fantasy that stays in the head is the fantasy that festers and often becomes diseased with unnecessary shame. Fantasies should be allowed to break out and feel the fresh air of welcoming reality. Rick and Bernie. They would be better off joining in.

'Now, Stella, or I'll punish you.'

Invisible fingers pinched my labia, there was a warm dribble and a butterfly in the belly. Excitement. Fear. The fabulous unknown.

Rick and Bernie reeled back as if they had both been punched in the face.

'I'm sure Rick and Bernie would be delighted to see . . .' Mel paused mid-sentence. What were they going to see exactly? She did not know herself. The scene had not been planned.

Rick flushed and drank a glass of red wine in one gulp.

'Sure would,' he claimed with magnificent machismo.

'Sure would,' Bernie echoed, confusion driving him to follow Rick's lead.

'Why don't we all go into the sitting room and Stella can serve coffee?' said Mel.

She blew out the candles and led the way.

I cleared the plates. Jim watched me silently for several minutes. He was not touching me, he was ten yards away from me, yet this basilisk stare made me feel as if his body was on top of me and pushing me down.

Then, suddenly, as I leaned over to pick up a final fork, he was behind me. He pulled my body towards him, kissed me on the back of the neck, rubbed his hand over my buttocks and pushed his finger into me.

'You're wet,' he whispered. 'I knew you'd be wet: you're a sick little girl . . .'

'Fuck me now,' I whispered.

He slapped my hand away from his groin and held it behind my back.

'Please, baby . . .'

'You –' he said '– have got to learn to wait . . .'

They all sat in the sitting room, lounging on sofas and smoking joints.

Jim came into the kitchen. I was grinding coffee beans so I did not hear him or sense him until his hand clamped the back of my neck with a grip against which there was no defence.

He pushed my face down so that my cheek was lying on the counter, and lifted up the soft dress so that the fabric was above my waist. Smoothly and still without saying anything, still with one hand pressing down on my neck so that I could not move, he used his right hand to pull down the black lace panties. Easing them slowly down my thighs and past the boots so that they fell as a little pool at my feet.

'Step,' he said.

I lifted one knee like a neat dressage pony, then the

other, and the lace slipped down the shiny boot and over the pointed stiletto heel. Bette. Oh, Bette. You were never as good as this.

He stooped down, rolled the knickers up with one hand and, still with the other hand pressing down on my neck, pushed them into my mouth.

Now I was gagged with my own panties, unable to speak, unable to protest or complain or yell or anything.

Then, still holding me down, he reached to the cupboard above the counter and pulled out a bottle of Crock olive oil.

'Extra virgin,' he said. 'Hardly appropriate for a nasty slut like you.'

So there I was, bent over the counter, neck in his grip, gagged with my own panties, dress up above my waist, bare arse presented to him, shaved arsehole pointing at him. All orifices were his, just as he liked it; they were his and I was helpless. Helpless and shameless.

The kettle started to boil but he kept his hand on the back of my neck.

'Spread your legs,' he ordered.

I did as I was told. The movement, balanced by the high heels of the boots, pushed my buttocks further out to him, and presented the puckered orifice in which he was so endlessly and relentlessy interested.

'More, come on, you know what I want . . .'

I spread my legs further and now my cunt was open and my arse was his and I was exposed, again, exposed to Jim, his to take. God. Would I do anything for this spectator?

Dipping his free hand into the olive oil, he slipped the tips of two fingers on to the edge of my arsehole and slowly insinuated them into my back passage. Warm and oiled, they slipped in, pushing further and further, feeling their way with artless ease to a place that he knew well, a place that he could manipulate with expert knowledge. And so I was forced again to allow him this forced intimacy, so again I submitted to the tingling of the thrill which he directed so well. Need, fear, panic. His fingers were in the soft tunnel that he had discovered and that was his and only his to see. As he pushed that warm, wet digit further and further into me, exploring and groping, I wished that I could see the expression on his face.

What was he looking at? My rump? My legs? The black down of my presented pudenda? Or the glistening opening of my cunt which, seen from the rear, must have been a flower of moist folds, as yet untouched by him, but, nevertheless, swollen and wet.

He pushed further and further into me, three slow fingers now and, though I loved this and loved him and wanted him to have it all, I hoped that my trust was not misplaced. I hoped that he would not present this inner secret to the world, display it to everybody, to inane strangers who I did not know.

I did not know if I wanted to please this audience. But the show was up and running. There was, after all, very little I could do about it. I was gagged and he was holding me down. I was his.

He removed his hand and the jersey folds of my dress fell back to my knees. He pulled me up, turned me round and looked down at my mouth still full of my own panties. He was stern. I wanted him to smile at me, show me he loved me, but he was stern.

'Bring in the coffee now,' he said, reaching into my mouth and pulling out the gag.

Then he left the room.

I clattered around with the little cups and jugs of cream and spoons. I was hot with excitement, in a world of my own now, where I had abnegated most vestiges of true reality and entered a realm where I would do anything and where, as a result, anything could happen.

The humiliation of being forced to serve was nothing, for it was subsumed by anticipation of greater and more interesting excitements. This submission was foreplay.

I walked in, knelt down, and put the tray on a low coffee-table made out of walnut. The ends of the short legs had been carved into bears' feet whose claws, I noticed, had been finished (somewhat eccentrically) in turquoise paint.

Meekly, I asked everybody what they would like and served it to them with my eyes lowered.

I knew that the silky black jersey clung to my every curve, that they could all see the creases between my buttocks and between my erect nipples. This dress was a classical drape. I knew I was the most provocative of all sexy mysteries: the clothed body that revealed everything, while showing nothing

I was the headline act and they were all looking at me, even Mel, who had seen it all before. She was gazing with an interest that she had not shown for some time, as if I was the promise of something new. She knew my body but she did not know Jim. She did not know where he could take us or how far he would go and this is what interested her. He was ready to expose parts of me that she had not seen before and so, in some ways, I was a new plaything.

'Rick wants to see your arse, Stella. Show it to him, please,' said Jim. 'Lift up your skirt. Now.'

'I'm not wearing any underwear,' I said, as if he did not know this.

Bernie, startled by this truth, dropped his full coffee cup on to the carpet.

'Oh, Bernie!' said Mel. 'Stella, get a cloth.'

113

I paused.

'Do as you're told, Stella,' said Jim.

'I don't want to.'

Jim slowly rose from his armchair and, without saying anything at all, picked me up from the floor where I was kneeling next to the coffee-table, twisted me round, bent me over, lifted up my dress and bared my buttocks to the two men sitting on the sofa.

They craned forward, studying my cheeks, and observing the light blemishes left by the various whippings that they had received over the last days.

'Gee,' said Bernie. 'You wop her good then . . .'

'She needs to be taught a lesson,' said Jim, pulling me up so that I was now facing them.

Rick stared at me in silence with his cold, blue eyes. His thin lips were set in a sneer, the *vaquero macho* of one who resented losing the control. He should have been top dog in this particular saloon. But he was aroused, and Mel, I knew, would thank me for this.

'Go and get the crop, Stella,' said Jim.

I flushed. He had never punished me in front of strangers before. Did they deserve the special spectacle of my humiliation? Did I really want to perform for them? What had they ever done for me?

Then a kind of love ran over me. It arrived in the form of sexual generosity: a desire to please Jim, to aid Mel, to arouse Rick, and to further confuse Bernie whose childlike admiration I so flagrantly enjoyed.

This was accompanied by a need to keep my place with Jim. He was fearless and he was easily bored. I wanted to be the only person with whom he could be sure of always finding new excitement, the partner who would always join him in any scenario that he wanted to enact.

I went and fetched the crop from the suitcase. It was made of leather-bound bamboo and had a plaid handle, the end of which was carved silver. Jim owned hacking canes, hunting crops, and miniature stock whips, but this was his favourite. It was old-fashioned, Victorian probably, and he liked the thought of its history, wielded in the hands of some master of hounds, slashing down on the bums of maids or wenches or any other wanton minx who got in the way of it. He had a traditional sadist side to him, did Jim.

'Thank you, Stella. Now go and bend over that chair.'

He had repositioned an armchair so that my bottom would face the audience and my face would be buried in the recesses of the upholstery. At least I could hide my pain and humiliation in the dark.

He tied my hands behind me with some soft, white rope. He was firm, but the rope was too soft to cut my wrists. I knew he had chosen this carefully, as he chose all his accessories carefully. And I knew he would tie me in a way from which it would be impossible to struggle or to escape until he had decided that I should be set free.

I bent over the leg of the armchair so that now all they could see were my buttocks, my shaven arsehole, the back of my puss, my thighs and my beautiful, black, laced boots. A sight, no doubt, that Rick and Bernie had only ever been able to imagine in their heads was now presented in their reality. I wondered how they were coping. I wondered if they wanted to fuck me, or Mel, or each other.

Jim brought the crop down on my buttocks. My body jolted and I screamed loudly, though my voice was muffled by the cushions into which my mouth was pushed. Then the familiar scorching seared over my nether regions. He whipped me again and again, each stroke burning like a row of fire, and soon, as he beat me more and there was only pain, I disappeared out of my body, a sort of shock, but oddly enjoyable. I was no longer aware of the humiliation of public punishment but only the pain and him.

He whipped me for ten minutes. This is a long time to be whipped, and the deviant trauma of this merciless subjection must have drawn the cowboys into a space that they had never entered before. Privilege can be intense.

When he had finished, he lifted me gently out of that makeshift pillory and kissed me hard on the mouth. Sweat glistened on my forehead and tears shone in my eyes. My mouth trembled. I had become vulnerable for him and this, I suppose, was the point: to allow the defences to be destroyed and let him in, let him see me, a person who genuinely believed that it was best to remain a stranger to the world and, if possible, a stranger to oneself.

I could not party with the modern celebrants of vulnerability. This was an impractical concept formulated by psychiatrists, that most self-serving group of medics.

He led me from the room, gently lowered me on to the soft, fur cover of the bed, spread my legs with his hands, and pushed his fingers into the warm lubrication that was my frenzied supplication.

'Now,' he said. 'Do you really want me?'

'Yes. Please, daddy. Yes.'

'Am I going to come all over those tits, those beautiful tits?'

'Yes. Come anywhere. In my mouth, in my hair, in my face . . . Just fuck me. Please fuck me.'

He looked down at me as if wondering how he wanted me. It could be any way he wished. My legs, still in the lace-up boots, were sprawled; my skirt was ruffled above my waist. I was passive, but I was also wanton, for my pelvis, possessed with desire, was grinding and squirming.

At last he brought that cock out; big, beautiful, hard. The veins stood out proudly; the tip, circumcised, was a polished ball. Always so hard. And I knew it would remain like that for as long as I needed it and wished it. He would never fall and fail me. There would never be that sense of deprivation as the dick lost interest, went elsewhere, or actually didn't care that you had been roused and then left there, unfinished, frustrated and ready to kill. This cock did not stop.

He flipped me over, pulled me up on all fours, shot in from the back, big and powerful and, though I had been longing for this all evening, his size still took me by surprise.

I groaned and then screamed with pleasure.

The door of the bedroom was open so, as Jim played me to multiple orgasms, dicking my cunt, hands all over my breasts, in full control as he played me with that relentless organ, I screamed out my needs in an animal drama that we both knew was being heard by everyone in that sitting room a hundred yards away.

They could hear, but they could not see.

Chapter Seven

*T*he next morning I found Mel sitting at the kitchen table. Her black hair fell in deranged tentacles over her face and she was wearing a major negligée.

This frothy spume of chiffon and ruffles was transparent, and her body undulated beneath it. I had forgotten how big she was, this Amazon bitch-goddess, five feet nine without the spikes. There was something magnificent about her this morning, all huge nudity and pie-crust frill. She still fascinated me. I looked at her and a flashback triggered an unexpected shiver of elation as I remembered the month that she had had a leather and spandex panty girdle made for her. It was cut to a 50s design that clipped her waist and flattened her stomach, but its prettiest addition was a thin zip that started at the back and ran to the front. She could be fucked or buggered while wearing that girdle. And she was.

Her arse had looked wonderful encased in that tight, black body-shaper. I had always enjoyed undoing the zip so that her cheeks, loosened from their elastane restraint, suddenly sprang out and offered themselves up to anyone who wanted them. I always did want them.

We really knew how to have fun, Mel and I. I quickly learned how to bring her to orgasm while she was wearing that odd-mother lingerie. She would writhe under the presence of my fingers as they wormed through the open zip and pushed deep inside her to the oily wetness that I knew so well.

She would scream out as the mind abandoned the body but the pelvis would struggle, frustrated, but deliciously imprisoned.

She would moan and complain but I would keep my fingers firmly in her pussy until I felt the muscles of her pelvic wall contract and waves of tiny, electric vibrations kissed my fingers.

'I can't believe you've got lipstick on already,' she commented grumpily.

'It's 11 a.m.,' I said smugly. 'I'm taking advantage of a flat-stomach day.'

I was also taking advantage of a very wonderful new satin-and-lace bra whose whalebone infrastructure pushed my breasts into areas they had never travelled before and gave my baby-pink cashmere jersey an appearance that, in some states, would have carried a prison sentence.

This was teamed with a little, grey, silk skirt. Jim had told me not to wear panties, so I was bare beneath the fabric. He had told me that when he saw me, he wanted to know that my bare flesh was sitting on the bench. I was to lift up the back of my skirt so that I could feel my bruised cheeks rub against the wood.

I obeyed these instructions, noting that my arse hurt from the whippings it had received over the last couple of days, and enjoying the wantonness that an exposed pussy must always precipitate. The surface was cold on my hot flesh. My cunt, though, unrestrained by underwear, was free and available and growing more and more excited all the time.

Jim could fuck my lights out but I always wanted him. I had woken up wanting him, feeling his back and his arms, smelling his musk, sex smells, waking up wet and ready for him. I had climbed all over him, moaning, begging and hoping. I had sucked that morning dick but he was not ready for me. He had slapped me very hard on the thigh and then pushed me away. He (sleepily) told me to get up and get the breakfast. He'd fuck me later, if I was a good girl and did what I was told, but not now: he was tired.

I had sulked but he did not notice. He knew I could never get enough attention but he did not know that I was only interested in dancing to the light from his beam. No matter how much I might twist with the others, lead them on, dip and dart, I was only really interested in one person.

I resolved not to allow Jim to know this because I sensed that it would deflect any affection he had for me, and even repel him. The most determined of free spirits, he would not be constrained by someone else's emotions, and he would feel trapped and nervous if he sensed evidence of any intensity that was likely to suffocate him.

I smoked a cigarette and poured a cup of tea.

Outside plains of dust dotted with sage-brush stretched to the forests and grey mountains that rambled across the horizon. The sky was clear blue and the air hung with the subtle, smoky smell of the now-dead barbecue. The desert was already growing hot, too hot for cashmere.

'So,' I said to Mel. 'Did you have your way with Rick?'

'Finally.' She shrugged. She was nonchalant now the

chase was over. 'Though he was more interested in your arse, kept going on about you.'

'And?'

'Not bad. Big cock. Likes anal.'

'Doesn't everybody?'

'I suppose so.'

'Do you think he'll play?'

'Yeah. He's pretty well up for anything, I think. Well, anything that turns him into a slave. Some cowboy. Just wants me to take him off to the stables and whip his arse. He might be lucky. If I'm bored enough, I might well do that for Rick . . .'

She sighed, uncharacteristically gloomy.

'Sometimes I miss Darlene,' she said.

'I wonder what happened to her.'

We had met Darlene in a fur-lined ladies' room in a nightclub in Soho during an era when you could meet interesting people in designed conveniences and the ladies' were not always full of ladies. She was wearing a skintight, white leather catsuit and carrying a Chanel handbag full of Percodan.

Her long, black hair was cut into a fringe that sat in a fierce, straight line just below her eyebrows and allowed her intelligent, brown eyes to flash from underneath it. Darlene used that fringe like a curtain, darting behind it when she was bored or stoned, reappearing when she was ready to parry. Her mouth sat in a pout of permanent provocation; to see her was to want to kiss her.

She was beautiful. Her mother was Hawaiian; her father a Fiat salesman in South London. I wondered from whom she had inherited her grace, for Darlene moved from her hips, as if on a catwalk, but not so exaggerated. Darlene had studied ballet and she had picked up a lot from watching old Jane Russell movies. She would walk loose but tall, head erect, eyes forward, permanently showing off her clothes and herself and permanently moving in the knowledge that the entire room was staring at her. She assumed the world thought she was ravishing, so the world did think she was ravishing.

I learned a lot about nerve from Darlene. She could get away with anything. I, too, perked up my posture, thrust out my tits, stared into the middle distance and developed an attitude.

We had a limousine that night: I can't remember why, something to do with Grant Plaza, a permanently-waved friend of Mel's who had a song in the charts at the time. It was the eighties. Everyone had a limousine. Leon actually lived in one when the bank repossessed his house. Anyway, we had a limousine and Mel and I lured Darlene into it with promises of champagne.

Mel had employed one of her slaves to act as chauffeur for the night so it did not matter what we did in the back of that vehicle. The slave lurked in front of his window and did as he was told.

Together we peeled Darlene's catsuit away from her body. She shed it and smoothed away from it, as slow and easy and slinky as a snake leaving its old skin.

She had round, firm breasts, a tiny waist, tiny ankles and firm cheeks. She was also the owner of a very fine, fully operational penis.

Mel and I could not believe our luck. We had been looking for a chick with a dick for months.

Darlene fucked us both in the back of the limo that night and the following morning we invited her to move in.

She became the link between Mel and myself and we formed a perfect circle, perhaps because she reflected aspects of our physicality back to us, perhaps because she was a switch bitch. She could be top, mistress,

122

slave. She was all things to both of us and there was nothing she would not do. She/he, I mean,

She was a man and a woman so no one was ever bored. Sex with Darlene provided all the gentle comforts and familiarity of femininity with all the advantages of a good-sized dick. She was more female than male in her sensibilities but, in the end, she could provide an erection and, when she offered us her phallus, she became more aggressive, more like a man, as if the dick somehow took over her brain. She would strut about with her glistening extension, knowing that we wanted it, and her.

Darlene was never ashamed of her manhood. She had learned to live with her cock, use it for her own pleasure and for that of others. She recognised some aspects of her own power, but I think Mel and I encouraged her to see more. Our appreciation cultivated her core as she began to realise, as we knew, that she was lucky. She had been born with more.

I think she was the only person with whom Mel had been in love. She would have done anything for Darlene.

I often wondered why this was and I worked out that Mel felt protective towards her, as one must always feel protective towards those who are freaks in the eyes of the world. These emotions were powerful for Mel, possibly because she had never felt them before, perhaps because they struck at the centre of the womb where the mother was supposed to be.

Mel and I knew the male and the female in ourselves. We had fucked as men and women; we had been fucked by men and women; we were careless in our gender definitions and suffered from no traditional agenda.

Mel tended to prefer to be a man; I tended to like life as a femme. But we could do and be anything. Darlene fell in easily with us because no expectations were made of her. She could play any role she chose. And did.

Darlene always knew what we wanted. I loved having sex with a woman who was a man. It was gentle and smooth; one could relate on an emotional level while receiving good, hard penetration. There was a distance, but, unlike men, Darlene was not separate from us. We communicated. She was everything.

Yes. Darlene was fabulous. Perhaps we took advantage of her, extorted her, sensing, perhaps, that she might slip away, that she could not be for ever, so we had to see all the things that could happen. Sometimes we were obsessive as both Mel and I tried to lock Darlene into our cunts.

How did it go, you might wonder. Who slept where?

We all had our own bedrooms in a maisonette in Kensington that belonged to the Lord my father. We tended to end up in my bed as it was the biggest and the most comfortable. A cloud of duck-down, feathers and Egyptian cotton, it had suitable posts for those who needed to be restrained.

The candles would flicker around us, wafting scents of vanilla and lemon, and a low cloud of marijuana smoke tended to hang in the air.

Lucky us and lucky Darlene, for she had two tongues to serve her, two lips to massage her penis, both at the same time. Two mouths were devoted to worshipping her; four hands were ready to caress her breasts and balls and buttocks.

We worshipped Darlene and then she would fuck us both, though sometimes Mel – because she is a bitch – tied me down and made me watch, my pussy twitching, my pelvis gyrating in a fury of need. I would have to watch as Darlene's lean, white body climbed all over Mel and penetrated her. I would have to watch as Mel got fucked until the tears came into her eyes and Mel, even Mel, became emotional.

She would untie me, pull me towards her and make me sit on her lap with my back towards her face and my legs spread far apart so that my pussy was presented to Darlene: wide, open, and wet.

Darlene would kneel down between my legs and tease me for long, awful minutes with her tongue and I could not struggle in any throes of abandon because Mel held my arms and enjoyed herself, muffling my moans with her tongue.

Then Darlene would stand up and look down at me, displayed and presented by Mel, knowing in that moment that she was the only thing that mattered. And, the groin being at my eye-level, I would stare at her unwavering phallus and Darlene, had she-male, would make me beg for it.

There was a priapic man in there somewhere. He would kiss me and finger me and play with my wet pussy but, best of all and most of all, he would push his huge, hard point into me so that all I knew and felt was that dick and, with eyes open, what did one see? A beautiful woman at one's face; a hard man below.

She was a tease, Darlene. But he was fun. He loved his power. So did she. I liked sitting on top of them both, riding up and and down, satisfying myself on his penis, fondling her breasts, filling myself up with them both. Girl, boy, man, woman. Darlene was everything.

Then, one day, a man told her that he would manage her and we never heard from her again.

It was as if she had died. Mel actually went into grief, saw a doctor, couldn't stop crying. Sometimes I think she never got over it. Darlene scarred her and Mel was a very difficult person to lacerate. I, too, was difficult to wound, but for different reasons. Mel was genuinely detached; I was conscientiously guarded. I was difficult to wound because the portcullis was up and nobody could enter.

Creeping horror was telling me that, somehow, and without my permission, Jim had invaded my psyche. He was letting himself in, or I was allowing him in. He might not know this, but he was getting to me, and with that came fear of all the terrible wounds.

I changed the subject. Talking about Darlene was never constructive. It was a long time ago. She was a shade, an interesting shade, perhaps the most interesting one that had passed through our lives, but now she had slipped away into time and could never be revived.

'What happened to Bernie last night?' I asked Mel.

'I don't know. We listened to you being fucked by Jim. Rick got hot and started kissing me. Bernie just watched and went on and on about wanting to marry you. Rick told him to go home. He looked really upset, slammed the door off its hinges . . .'

'Oh, dear.'

Jim appeared in the kitchen looking dark and beautiful. He wandered around to me to make sure that I was sitting, as instructed, with my bare buttocks touching the seat of the bench, smiled, paused for an indecipherable second to appreciate Mel's breasts underneath her starlet peignoir, and then placed himself at the end of the table in the manner of a person who knows that he is the most important person in the room and everybody has been waiting for the moment when he will appear which, in my case, was true, but not in the case of Mel, who, I suspected, still needed to be impressed by Jim.

'Coffee, Stella,' he said.

I got up to make him his breakfast.

'So,' said Mel. 'Bernie and Rick seem very taken with little Stella.'

She was never one to pass on a game and now,

already bored of Rick, she was ready to engage this new player.

Jim saw her coming a mile off. He was not going to let this manageable minx have any ground. He gave her unreadable neutrality.

'Oh yeah?' he said, without much interest. 'How does Stella feel about that?'

'I do as I'm told,' I said, waving a Marlboro Light nonchalantly in the air while stirring some eggs in the frying pan.

'You'd better,' he commented.

I put plates of fry-up down in front of both of them and administered ketchup and coffee.

'I want you to be careful of Bernie,' Jim said. 'I think he could be dangerous.'

I seemed to remember that I was the one who had originally drawn his attention to Bernie's instability and he had claimed that everything was as it should be.

'Be careful, like what?' I said petulantly.

'Be careful, like don't lead him on unless you're willing to take the consequences. I'm serious, Stella. I can't always watch out for you. He's very volatile. He doesn't really understand what's going on and you don't know what he is capable of.'

'I think he's cute,' I argued. 'Harmless. Like a nice, little dog.'

He rolled his eyes.

'Just do as I say, Stella.'

I looked at Mel, but she just shrugged.

Jim's instruction made me look at Bernie in a new light. Here was a good game. Disobeying Jim. Where once I had seen Bernie as a cerebovascular accident in Mel's circle of 'characters', now I saw him as a firm cowboy with potential.

Disobeying Jim always held sensual frisson. To

annoy him was to incite him and to incite him was to encourage a sexual showdown where he would retaliate and I would be forced to submit. His fury was sexy and I played with it, loving the risk, entertaining myself with the inevitable outcome.

I was perverse and perverted and he, knowingly or unknowingly, encouraged me. Our foreplay had never been confined to the bedroom; our minds were engaged in intrigue long before our bodies combined. These were psychically disordered fertility rites whose luxurious habits were self-indulgent.

The end result would be the fantastic excitement of knowing that he was the master. He had the birch, the rod, the whip and the dick. It was all about Jim but, as a perverse result of this, Bernie had a playmate. Moving towards this new excitation with a cool insouciance, I nodded affectionately when this oddball swain whooped and threw his hat into the air and delivered long monologues about how the CIA wanted to recruit him to aid them in their covert operations in Chile.

Bernie placed me firmly on a pedestal. He was a courtly lover. In the past, I would have been bored by this: now I was moving in a realm of occult voluptuousness where there were rules but even the most experienced players did not really know what they were.

These subtle tricks were designed to force Jim to pay attention, keep guard, keep looking at me. They were validated and strengthened by the fact that Mel, now bored of Rick, wanted to tease Jim. I would have to fight to hold his interest.

The desert was suddenly fermenting with febrile temptations. The inchoate borders that separated its teasing entities were beginning to dissolve, unfettered by any of the traditional tenets that served to constrain mayhem in suburban convention.

I knew that the man who did not feel restrained by

the emotional blackmail that is enforced monogamy was the man with the freedom to choose. If he chose me, when he could have any slut walking on the earth, then that decision was an accolade cemented with a stronger bond than any attempt at orthodox supervision or unreleastic diktat.

Jim was not and never would be my possession. He would never do what I wanted. He probably would not have been able to, unless some freak wind blew in and altered his basic essence.

I had to be brave and let him loose. He would do as he wished, but so would I. I knew the elements that founded these diversions. Sometimes I wondered if I had invented them, I knew them so well. Of course, I did not know whence they came, why I was motivated by these cross-currents of sensuality, swept this way and that by them. Bored, perhaps. Fatherless, certainly. The Lord had never looked down on me. He had given me money, a car or two, things, but he was exiled by his wealth and moved in those marinas where grim tans hold offshore accounts.

Perhaps I was just a hominid waiting to feel something, wanting to know the animal inside her. Modernity had tangled all the wires; boredom inspired duality; the reasons in the end were unimportant. In my experience you could know the reasons but you couldn't do anything about them. It was easier to relish the minute and refuse to recant.

It did not take Jim long to discover the stables. They were no longer used, but they bore the legend of their former occupants. The smell of horse and hay pervaded the atmosphere, and much of the equipment had been left behind. Bridles hung from pegs and there were several saddles lying on stands in an antechamber. There was also a loft full of hay, as well as stalls and troughs and all the usual effects required by those who ride.

A series of hooks offered old snaffle bits, girth buckles, stirrups, and bridles. Grooming brushes lay about the place, as did various leading reins, halters and harnesses.

Riding horses, I soon gathered, was not on Jim's mind. I did not know exactly what was on his mind when he told me to meet him at 2 p.m. in the stables. I suspected he had thought up some imaginative scenario but I could not envisage the details and did not try to do so: it was always more fun when one did not know.

He made me wear my skintight jodhpurs, knee-length, polished riding boots, and a neat, tailored white shirt so tight it was impossible to do up in the front, particularly when wearing an underwired bra whose design, in this particular case, allowed the nipples to poke through two holes.

My hair was in bunches, as requested, and I wore no make-up, so that it looked, for all intents and purposes, as if I was about to go away to pony club camp.

The jodhpurs always made me feel sexy. I loved the way the fabric clung to me, granted me two fleshy protuberances and an instant look of lasciviousness. My nipples were already hard, poking through their lacy apertures, by the time I had walked across the old corral and opened the old, wooden door.

He had told me to wait there for him, so I sat on a bale of straw in the semi-darkness, appreciating the cool, for it was hot outside, the sun was high and the desert heat was beginning to bake everything.

Small droplets of sweat began to ooze on my chest and drool down my cleavage; the heat between my legs also began to intensify as I sat there waiting for him.

I did not know how long he would make me wait. It

could be ten minutes, it could be an hour. He would time it perfectly, appearing just as I was beginning to stop wanting him and start getting bored and angry; it was then that he liked to punish me, not when I loved him, but when I hated him. He always found that more interesting, punishing me back into love for him.

And I knew he probably had some form of pain in mind, for the instruments were all around me: the carriage whips, and little crops, and various straps made of leather. Even if there had not been, he would have improvised, used his hand if necessary, or shoe, or anything.

I lay on a hay bale with my feet up, dozing, thinking of him, slipping fast into a realm of my own as the minutes ticked slowly by.

I did not hear the creak of the rusting hinges or see the shaft of sunlight as it cracked through the open door.

The first thing I knew was the sharp slash on my upper thigh as the stinging blow came down on it. I looked up at him. He was holding a single tail whip, three feet long with a steel, reinforced handle and a leather lash at the end of it.

'Ow. Jesus Christ.'

'Get up. What do you think you're doing! Get up!'

I was still on the bale and he was standing over me, face set in angry determination. Frightening, and merciless. I knew that face. And I knew that I was in trouble.

I stood up so that I was facing him. He was wearing khaki trousers and a white shirt and he was brown from the sun; the smell of him rose up and under my nose making me want him at once in that weird, olfactory mystery that underlies the biochemistry of lust and love, and over which one has no control.

131

Certainly I did not. Merely to smell the subtle scents of him was to seep into my panties.

I wondered if my excitement would show through my jodhpurs. I was wearing a little, white satin thong. He had demanded it because they improved the line of the jodhpurs. He did not like the smoothness of the fabric over my buttocks to be altered by a visible line.

'Get down on the ground and lick my boots.'

I looked up at him, furious and defiant and with no intention of obeying such a stupid and humiliating command.

'Do it!'

He pushed me down on to the ground with one hand so that I lay sprawled in front of him.

'Do it.'

Begrudging, hating, I licked his shoes, leaving a little wet glob on the toe.

'Not good.'

He pushed me down again so that now I was sprawled face down on the dusty floor. A spider ran across the surface in front of me. Jim squatted down, rubbed his hands in the filth, and then rubbed the dirt on to my face and chest where it coagulated with the sweat and turned into little, dirty mud balls.

'That's better,' he said, ripping the front of my shirt so that it fell open at the waist and my nipples popped out at him, brown and hard. He licked them and then pinched them. I cried out but I did not dare voice the insults that were rising in me, ready to shoot at him like hard, verbal missiles. No. I did not dare emit these. And then I could not, for he brought out a bridle and tied it to my head, placing the bit in my mouth, gently fastening the buckles to make sure that I could not speak, but also that the tender part of my mouth would not be damaged by this punishing apparatus.

'Get on all fours.'

I did as I was told and the next thing I knew something heavy had been lowered on to my back. A saddle. He offered me a bowl of water.

'Drink this.'

I tried to lower my head to the bowl, but it was difficult: the saddle was heavy and my mouth was impeded by the bridle.

He removed the saddle, somewhat to my relief, for it was very heavy and I was growing hotter and hotter all the time.

'Go and stand over there.'

I stood in front of a hook designed to hold tack and Jim tied me to it. Then, standing behind me, he sliced through the cotton shirt with a knife so that it fell in shreds off my back. Slowly, his breath hot on the back of my neck, he pulled down my jodhpurs.

'I am going to whip you now, Stella.'

The sweat was now beading my brow and running into my eyes. I could just breathe, but I could make no noise with that metal bit in my mouth.

I saw him remove a carriage whip from a hook. It had a long, black leather handle and a snakelike tail of braided leather designed to prick the hide of a horse.

He stood some way away from me. I heard the crack well before I felt the pain. A short, hot surge seared through the top of my back, and then again and again, some seconds between each strip, so that I had all the time to feel it before the next one came, on and on, back, lower back, then top of the buttocks, then the full, fleshy orbs themselves, and then, most painful, the top of the thighs. I could feel each one of those lines, and then they all melded with each other into one hot, unbearable torment.

The tears sprang into my eyes. Not for the first time, I thought, why do I like this? Why do I want this? Why do I allow this? And then, one day I will get my own

133

back and implement furious revenge. I will pull down those khaki trousers and whip his butt until it bleeds. And I will go on and on, despite his screams for mercy. I will see him in pain and tearful in submission, beat him like the bad boy that he is.

But these thoughts were quickly ousted by the sensual charms of the after-effects, the calm as the endorphins kicked in like a narcotic rush and the lubricants eased themselves between my legs, and all I wanted was his dick.

My clothes and back were torn and shredded, but I cared about nothing. All was ease and lust.

He cut me down with the knife and carried me over to the bale. He sat down on it and made me kneel in front of him. Then he removed the bit at last, and looked down at my face, red, filthy, and tearful. A thoroughly obedient slave, now. He had won, as usual.

He undid the fly of his trousers and pulled out his hard prick and eased it into my mouth.

I sucked on him with all the lewd lasciviousness that I knew he loved, and he grew harder and harder in my cheeks until I thought this was the hardest he had ever been. My mouth could hardly contain him; my throat was full of him. I gagged, but I went on, the tears now flowing freely down my face, my jaw aching, my cunt aching in a different way.

I began to lose any sense of where or who we were: there was only the smell of his flesh, the musty groin, and the crown and shaft driving into my mouth and throat.

'Take off the jodhpurs and sit on me,' he said.

The breeches were still halfway down my legs. I removed the polished riding boots and then took off the trousers and gently eased the thong down my body.

I took off the remnants of the shirt and, wearing only the peek-a-boo bra, slowly sat astride him and, teasingly at first, brought my hot, wet hole slowly down on the tip of this cock. He pushed up towards me but I smiled and pulled away.

'Go on, little Stella, stop teasing, and fuck me,' he said.

I brought my warm lips slowly back down and allowed him to push all the way into me. Then I rode him. We were in the stables after all, so I rode him, rising to the trot, up and down on him, bouncing and shaking and taking my own pleasure, using him like a vibrator almost.

And, as I began to screech out my climax, he put his hand over my face so that my cries were muffled by his calm, and then, with the final shudders of release, so too he lost that final control and allowed himself to erupt into me.

I closed my eyes, and as I opened them again, I saw two things. I saw Jim's face, calm with release of orgasm, and I saw Bernie's face staring through the crack of the open door.

As I looked at him, his eyes widened like a terrified animal, and I heard the crunch of his boots on the ground as he ran away.

Oh God, Bernie, I thought to myself. How much did you see that time. Am I destined always to be watched by your staring eyes?

Chapter Eight

O ver the next couple of days Bernie would not leave me alone. Every time I turned around he was there and, such was his omnipresence, even when he was not there I thought I felt him following me, or thought I saw him out of the corner of my eye, like some flickering ghost.

He bought me trite little presents: one rose with a pink ribbon; a box of chocolates in a heart-shaped box; an awful Furby which he insisted was cute, like me. I don't know from where he had gleaned his knowledge of women, but his information was made of cliché and stereotype. I assumed he had been allowed to watch television in prison and had believed what he saw on commercials.

Sometimes, if I saw him arriving, I would duck down and hide. Once I even crawled under a bed to avoid him. Although I had initially enjoyed the flirtation – if only because I thought it would incite Jim – the plan backfired as Bernie waylaid me with his romantic suffrage, his mood rings and his Hallmark card credulity. His manner was cloying and his presence became suffocating.

Mel and Jim thought that this was very amusing. They teased Bernie by encouraging him and making him think that he had a chance. It was a cruel game and Bernie did not know the rules. He had no capacity to understand complexity; he simply believed what he was told and acted on how he felt. He did not understand conundrum or subtext, and so he pressed on, convinced that I was to be his.

Occasionally he managed to catch me on my own. He would press himself very close to me as if to kiss me, and whisper that he loved me, that I was the most beautiful woman in the world. He wanted to make love to me and he wanted to marry me.

I oscillated between being flattered and being irritated but, wanting to annoy Jim, I sometimes allowed Bernie the privilege of letting his hand rest on my thigh, or the light brush of a lip on lip. Sometimes I was polite and received his blandishments with a semblance of gratitude.

He was a man obsessed. I could see that, and I knew I was not handling the situation with any common sense or integrity. I was using him for my own ends, but I thought that I was not doing anything harmful and I went on with it. Teasing and withdrawing, withdrawing and teasing.

One morning Bernie arrived in his jeep to take us to Satan's Golf Course. A picnic was planned and there was some talk of Bernie teaching us how to shoot. I was the only one ready. Well, nearly ready. I couldn't decide between a marabou slipper and a particularly pointed Manolo and had one on each foot when Jim walked in and told me to take them both off at once.

'For God's sake, Stella, you're not Barbara Stanwyck . . .'

'Barbara Stanwyck was very good with a gun,' I pointed out. 'Haven't you seen *Double Indemnity*?'

'I don't care. Those shoes are not right, either for the desert or for shooting. You can wear those lace-up boots I bought you.'

'It's hot!'

'Just do as you're told, Stella, and stop being such a princess. In fact, you can crawl on all fours to the wardrobe. Go on, I want to see that arse wriggle.'

I was wearing a very tight, black, low-cut Azzedine Alaia micro mini-dress with no panties. It was barely there. When I dropped down on all fours it rode up my backside and exposed my nether regions, so that as I crawled slowly across the floor, Jim was availed of the full, fleshy view that he had been seeking.

'Slowly!' he barked.

My buttocks perked up at him, the material slowly riding further up my back as I eased myself across the room. I could feel his eyes scorching into me, hot as a branding iron, and I began to ooze.

'Stay there, you little slut,' he said. 'Just stay there.'

He left the room, left me crouched there on the cold floor, on my hands and knees, arse in the air, waiting there, smouldering and wanting him, labia presented like some bitch on heat in the jungle, glistening and wanting.

He made me crouch on the floor for ten minutes, but it seemed much, much more. My knees and arms began to ache, but I did not dare to move.

He walked back silently into the room, and it wasn't until I heard the whistle of the switch that I knew what was happening.

He stroked the thin wood across my backside and then brought it sharply down across my buttocks so that the sting seared through my flesh. Again and again, silently, six times, until the weals blistered and my stomach started to smoulder with want. As the pain suffused my being, my will became subsumed by deep obedience where the only sexuality was the surrender of individuality and submersion into a de-personalisation where one was totally free.

I glanced around at my behind. There were six livid stripes across it. These lines were welts or trophies, depending upon how you looked at them. I liked them; I liked Jim signing me with his hand, but they would show if I bent over, or raised my arms, because the dress was tiny. It was designed to show the panties and entertain all who were lucky enough to notice them. I had put it on to amuse myelf and tease Bernie, to allow him flashes of pussy and thigh and pudenda. Now, though, with my arse signed by Jim, Bernie would see this livid demarcation.

What would he think? What could he think? The complicated twists of role-play and the non-exploitative power games of gender politics were not the stuff of life in Hicksville. He would see the stripes on my arse as surely as he could see the lines on his own hand, and there would be nothing I could do about it.

Jim would not let me change. He said it served me right for being such a little tart. Now the world would see what I was and they would know that no matter how slutty or how tarty, I was not the boss: there would always be a stronger hand than I, and that hand would fuck me when and where it wanted to.

If he chose to, he said, he would spank me in front of Bernie. If he chose to, he would stripe me in front of Bernie. If he chose to, he would push me up against the bonnet of Bernie's car, spread my cheeks and he would bugger me then and there.

He would show Bernie that he, Jim, was the cause of

my pleasure and there were very few contenders to this position. This was not because he was jealous, I suspected bleakly that he was not, but because he was the one who pulled my strings and he enjoyed the fact that, as I liked to know this, so he got off on others knowing it. He liked the idea of a stranger looking at my lines and knowing that they were the mark of a property as surely as a mark on the hide of a ranch animal.

'Just be grateful –' he said '– that I'm not sending you out with a gag in your mouth. You've got a lot to learn, Stella. You haven't even begun to understand total submission. Submission is the pleasure, little one, not the pain. When you know how to truly surrender, that is when you will understand euphoria. You're a learner, don't forget that, you're a little learner. You think you would do anything for me, but you don't: you constantly fight and struggle against me; you're constantly looking for ways to rebel when you should be turning towards acquiescence.'

Did I really know who Jim was? Everything had seemed much easier in London, perhaps because I had more control, or perhaps because there, I knew less about him. Now that we had been pushed into a forced intimacy in this barren place, provoked to push each other's buttons, new, unfamiliar emotions were rearing up.

A breeze that was the intimation of terrible disaster, death even, trembled through my body like a wave of fear and nausea. I did not really know this man. I had once known Mel, but I had not seen her for a year: I did not know what she had become. I was totally alone and unable to defend myself. And, though once I had been stimulated by the challenge of experiment and of freakish foreplay, now I was scared. If Jim chose to lead Mel into outlandish psychosexual drama, would I want to follow or would it be too much? Unsure of his affection, I suddenly felt very estranged from Jim. Bernie seemed to be the friend and Jim the enemy.

I looked into the angular, adonic face and I hated it. Hated it. Loved it. Wanted it to be only mine, wanted to desert it. My head spun. The terrain and the games were confusing me and I was dizzy. I no longer knew who I was.

Jim, oblivious of the temerity instilled by my insecurities, laced me into the boots, and they did look fabulous with the mini-dress.

His eyes melted with desire as he rubbed his hand across my mouth, smudging my lipstick across my face, wiping it away so that he could kiss my mouth. And I stared back, little girl sideways, wondering if he would push up that mini-dress and fuck me. I was accessible, after all. No bra, no panties, bare legs, now smooth and brown and kissed by the desert sun.

He pushed me towards a wooden chair in the corner of our room and spread my legs. Kneeling in front of me, he gently prised the lips of my labia apart and slowly licked my clitoris. He kissed and tickled and licked until I suffered and then shivered and then quivered and screamed and, as I moaned in that triumph of primal exuberance, I saw Bernie's face staring through the French window. As soon as I saw it, he disappeared, a fleeting image that dissolved as if he had never been there.

How much had he seen?

Had he seen Jim thrash my arse?

Had he seen the boots being laced tightly on to my calves?

Had he seen Jim's face buried in my pubis, tonguing me, kindling me and forcing me to erupt, abandoned, into a seizure of delicious torment?

I hoped that he had seen it all and that it had turned him on.

Mel was still in bed. She had overslept, so Jim told me to go ahead with Bernie, and that he and Mel would catch up with us later when they had finished preparing the picnic.

'Why can't Mel go with Bernie?' I said. 'You tell me to watch out for him and then you make me go with him.'

'Mel isn't ready and you are. It would be safer to have two cars anyway in case that thing he drives breaks down in the middle of the desert. Go on, baby, it will be all right. We'll be there within twenty minutes.'

'Twenty minutes can be a long time,' I countered, hoping that he would appreciate to what I was referring.

Jim glared at me, his mouth set in a hyphen of anger.

'Stella, if you want to fuck Bernie fuck him: it's your choice and your responsibility.'

I flushed with anger and frustration. I did not want to fuck Bernie particularly, but neither did I want Jim to stay behind with Mel. I felt now that he was throwing me at the bloody weirdo so he could have some time with her alone. I composed a magnificent expression of dull disinterest but inside, acid was bubbling and it was slowly eating every single one of my organs.

I considered bursting into tears, knowing from past experience that the sight of a woman weeping gave him an instant erection. Once I had wept, not because he had tormented me, or humiliated me in delicious, tense game-play, or even because he had fucked me deep and hard. Sometimes, of course, a man can make you cry by the simple act of reaching into the womb. Then, on some level, the woman has been found out; she has been touched in a deep place that is usually protected and the shock takes her by surprise and

142

induces an incredible relief that surges like the outpouring of hundreds of old regrets. Sometimes this feels like true love. Sometimes it is omnipotent misery.

On this occasion, though, the tears were a hormonal outburst that arrived as unpredictably as a storm on a sunny day. He hurt me with a throwaway remark, a weapon against which I had, at that moment, no defence, and to my surprise, tears had welled out of my eyes and down my face.

His cock had swelled as if in some Pavlovian reaction. He widened and lengthened and the tip blossomed like a swollen bud. And, as the shaft stretched and strenghtened, so he lost himself to unfathomable propulsion. Accelerated by wordless instinct, he had fallen on me in crazy lust and thrown me into the plush carpet of some penthouse suite in Milan.

The soft, cotton bathrobe had dissolved into a pool around me and he had fucked me while the sobs were still strangling my throat. The tears had been a trigger, a turn-on to him as surely as some men are turned on by lacy garters, fishnet stockings or corsets.

Afterwards, I had asked him why and he said he did not know, but seeing me more vulnerable than he had ever seen me before made him want to protect me, and to want to protect me was to want to fuck me.

That was his explanation. There were no deeper insights. Jim never stopped to analyse. He marched forward with terrible confidence in his right to dominate and intrude because that was his sexual power and it was a power that had given pleasure since he first started wielding his dick.

I concluded that he had never had to question his prowess and that, since he was young, every woman had been surprised and pleased by what they had discovered between his legs, and had wanted more.

Jim behaved like a man with a big cock. His lucky

endowment was an inherent part of his personality. He was so sure of himself that he never boasted or bragged and, even more significantly, he was comfortable around those born with different sexualities. Drag queens, rent boys, effete art collectors, diesel dykes. They never perturbed him; his inner confidence was immutable. He knew that he carried an enviable trophy, but he did not need to applaud his own victory, his gift that had been appreciated for years. He had nothing to prove. He did not need to.

I was out of control. Inwardly, I was out of control and the tension of hiding it was killing me. The repression of truth was worse than wearing a hair shirt, and certainly worse torment than anything he could have chosen to inflict, with his devilish imagination and constant incitement to make me play with lese-majesty.

I felt like throwing myself on the floor at his feet and begging him to love me, but I did not. I wafted silently away from him, inwardly resolving to do anything and everything to undermine his harsh insentience.

Bernie's jeep was a frightful thing, camouflage green in colour, with a rusting body and no roof. Empty cartridge cases littered the floor and one of the seats was patched with Sellotape and a copy of Universal Soldier. One of the bent doors was peppered with bullet holes and the windscreen bore a peeling sticker with the words TRUST NO ONE.

'I used this here vehicle when I was fighting the contras,' Bernie informed me. 'Government gave it me. They wanna keep me on their side, see, in case everyone rises up against the Majestic 12 and there's a breakdown of social order. They'll need me then 'cos I got the arsenal and I'm on their side. I've had the training and we're ready for Them.'

'Who are the Majestic 12, Bernie?'

Bernie, though obviously genuinely scared of the Majestic 12, did not seem to be familiar with their exact identity. He was, it seemed, running from an invisible enemy, and I could not help thinking that this would make the job of fighting them very difficult.

'Er, they're majestic,' he said.

'So are the British royal family,' I said. 'But I doubt they are out to destroy the structure of society.'

'You don't know that,' he said crossly. 'It's a well-known fact that they are everywhere. The Queen of England could be one of them, you could be one of them, there could be one right now taking photographs of us out of a black helicopter. The illuminati are everywhere.'

At that moment the illuminati seemed to be living in my bra, judging by the way that Bernie was staring down it. I edged my breasts minutely closer to his face and looked at him with an expression that said, 'These are yours for the taking: all you have to do is take. Are you brave enough Bernie? Do you want it enough? Will you fight for me?'

Bernie paused, momentarily transfixed. Undermined by some arcane mental confusion, he seemed to be swimming blindly in a current that was flowing against him. I wondered how much experience he had had. Had there been simple dates in drive-in movies, pulled-down panties in the back of Buicks? Or had there been darker adventures slammed up against the cold walls of high-security penitentiaries? Was he high-school drop-out, or ex-con hardman?

He did not bear the outer shell of a man who had enjoyed the lessons learned from experienced women, but he was difficult to read. The innocence was combined with a subtle steeliness.

He looked young but there were lines around his

eyes and a sense of weariness in them. He was twenty-three, going on forty-three.

He leaned forward as if to grab something: me, the gear stick, I would never know, because the nano-second was dispelled by Mel who appeared on the passenger side as I was carefully checking my lipstick in the wing-mirror.

She leaned into the door, grinning at me. She was wearing cowboy boots, a pair of jeans, and a gingham shirt which was knotted at the waist and open enough to reveal a black, lace demi-cup bra over which her breasts were spilling. Her wild black hair tumbled, wanton and wild, around her face. She was a feral gypsy and trouble with a capital T.

'Behave yourself,' she said.

Then she grabbed my face with her hand.

I thought for one terrible moment she was going to slap me, but she did not: she pushed her lips down on to mine and forced her tongue into my mouth, caressing my breasts as she did so. And, of course, I threw myself into her, melting momentarily with her chest and neck and mouth, wanting her.

'Behave yourself,' she said again.

'Are you going to fuck Jim?' I whispered. 'I'd just like to know.'

She looked at me, surprise on her face, but she said nothing. I took these reactions to mean that she planned to do exactly as she pleased but did not plan to discuss her plans with me. She was ready to exclude me to serve her own ends and I would be left to flounder in the dismal desolation of isolation and sexual jealousy, simply because she was a self-indulgent egomaniac without the discipline or the sensitivity to address the widespread emotional possibilities that her actions could initiate. As I loved and hated Jim, so I loved and hated Mel. But, at that moment, I only hated her.

146

She smiled sweetly at Bernie and waved at him.

'Jim and I will meet you up there,' she said. 'We'll bring the picnic.'

I slumped back in my chair, fermenting with resentment.

'You look good, Mel,' I said, 'but you'd look better gagged with a dildo.'

Again, she looked surprised and now slightly confused.

'What's going on in that imagination of yours?' she said. 'I love you, baby, you know that.'

She stroked my cheek with her hand and cooed, 'Don't you, baby?'

'Why don't you bring Rick on the picnic?' I said desperately.

'I'll see if he's at home,' she said, and then, in a lower voice so that Bernie could not hear, 'I don't particularly want to spend the afternoon with Albertine.'

'Albertine?'

'His wife! She'll probably want to come. She's so straight: Martha Stewart crossed with Doris Day and a canapé.'

Bernie, thoroughly disorientated by the sight of overt ambisexuality, stuck his head underneath the steering wheel and concentrated on revving up the engine. This involved an operation whereby magical incantations had to be mumbled from his lips and several multi-coloured wires had to be knitted together.

This accomplished, a loud detonation was followed by a thick cloud of acrid smoke and the dissonance of metal clanging against metal.

Conversation was impossible but this did not stop Bernie making it. He shouted at me at the top of his voice, his manifesto belting over grinding, crunching and a strange whistling somewhere between a flute and two owls trying to peck each other to death.

147

'I'm going to teach ya to defend yourself,' he shouted, clanking the gear into four-wheel drive as we juddered painfully down a sand track, the dust billowing behind us.

The desert flowed out as salt plains to either side while the mountains stretched into multi-coloured ribbons of antediluvian beauty.

'You need to be able defend yourself,' he yelled. 'It's a basic American right.'

'I'm not American, Bernie,' I pointed out, but of course he could not hear over the twang and thrum of all the clashing mechanisms.

I wondered why all mad people were so similar with their clichéd neuroses and predictable paranoias.

Bernie was an obtuse *faux*-revolutionary damaged by B-movie rampage, but I was making myself fancy him, promoting him from bar brawler to sexy idiot-savant. He was becoming what I wanted him to be, not what he was. And, as I chose not to listen to his nonsensical cant, so I drew towards his physicality.

He had a good body. The arms were strong and muscular, the butt was tight. He had strength. And so, through powerful self-hypnosis, I found myself wanting to sit on that cock of his, feel its width and know it. Maybe I would even put myself out and teach him. He was a young dog, after all, and they can always be taught new tricks. Perhaps he could be my slave. I had never had a slave before, never really wanted one actually. They always seemed to be so drippy, with their 'yes Madam, no Madam' and their 'shall I lick your shiny, shiny boots, oh mistress of mine?'

Mel had had hundreds of slaves, always, to do the housework and typing and cleaning. She picked them out of clubs where they hung out, waiting to worship her. Perhaps, for once, I would take up the power and manipulate Bernie into supplication, order him about, use him as a fuck factotum. I could think of worse things.

We bumped and clattered through Indian Creek to Satan's golf-course, which looked much like any other part of the desert, except that Bernie had nailed up a series of targets on various trees. These were made out of colour photographs stuck on to hard wood.

Nancy Reagan's nose had been blasted off; Cindy Crawford's face was pock-marked; and Tom Cruise was without the benefit of his left eye.

Bernie opened a battered, metal trunk in the back of his car. The case, secured with a thick link chain and a padlock the size of a man's hand, revealed an armoury of weapons whose identities he revealed to me in excited tones, as if he had just availed himself of the latest Beanie Babies.

There were semi-automatic hand-guns, several double-action revolvers, and an Enfield Mark 1 rifle. He had a pump-action Remington, a Mossberg 500 and a Winchester Defender filled with bird shot. There was a Glock and a Ruger and an old Makarov ready loaded with hollowpoint.

'You have to be prepared,' he said, gently fingering a Berotta.

'Prepared for what?' I asked, wondering if those hands would be as sensitive if they were playing inside me.

'This is the year when the Bilderberg will finally reveal themselves,' he said. 'The numbers add up; everyone says so. It's the anniversary of the Club of Rome. They will kill ninety per cent of the earth's population. But you won't see them coming until they are right smack on top of you ma'am, no sir, they'll hide themselves with mirrors and holographs. David Copperfield is one of them, and Claudia Schiffer, well, everyone knows she's an alien. Came out of Hangar 15

when she was seven and then doesn't remember anything until she was found in a discotheque in Dussel-
dorf. So you won't see them 'cos they'll be illusions.'

'What good is a gun then,' I said, 'if the enemy is an
illusion?'

'The gun isn't for the enemy; the gun is to defend the
home against all the folks who take up their own arms
and join in the anarchy, as has been prophesied.'

He pointed to a small red Bible lying in a pile of
rope, tins of Mace and several sheath knives.

'This is one of my favourites,' he said, easing the
Enfield rifle out of its case and stroking it as if it was
his newborn son. 'Beautiful gun: you can stop a man at
several hundred yards with this.'

After caressing his artillery for five minutes or so,
Bernie finally picked out a Smith and Wesson Model 14
.38 Special with a six-inch barrel, rubber grip and a
body made of blue carbon steel.

This is not a gun a girl can fit into her handbag. It is
a man's gun and its use is limited to blowing heads off
at a distance of 25 yards.

Bernie loaded the revolver for me. I positioned
myself in front of Tom Cruise and fired. The bullet
soared to somewhere in the treetops and the kickback
pushed me over so that I staggered and nearly fell. It
took some time for the ringing in my ears to stop.

'I don't think this is very me,' I said.

'Come on, babe, it's easy.'

Bernie stood behind me and held my arms straight
out. He could not have got closer if he had tried. I've
seen less intimate positions in the *Kama Sutra*. He
enveloped me in his warm muscles and I could feel his
breath on the back of my neck as he whispered instructions. His groin was pushed up against my arse which
was bare, still warm and sore from Jim's cruel
attentions.

I could feel the bulge broaden and sprout as the hardness began to strain against his jeans. He eased it closer to me so that it was pressed against my soft, throbbing cheeks. I did not draw away, but allowed him this frottage, and enjoyed this swollen sign of longing.

'Just pull the trigger,' he almost moaned.

I fell back into him, closing one eye and looking beyond the front sight. Bernie clasped his hand around mine and around the gun and pushed my finger over the trigger. The bullet again blasted into the far distance. I was about to turn around and face him, kiss him hard, allow those fingers to dig into me, perhaps receive the cock, in my mouth, in me, I didn't know, but I was about ready to make out with this gunslinging horny cowboy when a voice of cool sarcasm slapped me back to the reality of the present.

'Well, they won't be employing you to stand on the grassy knoll.'

Jim's voice was jovial and he seemed unaffected by the sight of Bernie and I locked in a clinch of arms, legs and gun.

Bernie stepped neatly away from me.

'Takes practice,' he said. 'Takes practice. It's not a shooter for a proper lady.'

'Lady?' said Mel. 'I hardly think so.'

Bernie handed Jim the gun and, hardly taking four seconds to aim, he flung one arm, closed one eye, and shot out Tom Cruise's mouth with the calm efficiency of a hired hit man.

'That'll shut him up,' he said smugly.

Bernie's jaw dropped.

'You done this before! Yesiree,' he said.

Jim shrugged and put his shades back on.

'Grouse in Scotland,' he said. 'It's not that different.'

Mel, revved up with competitiveness, almost

snatched the revolver from Jim, flicked it open, checked the chamber, flicked it shut again and stood in front of the tree with her legs apart, squinting over the barrel.

She was Grace Jones in *You Only Live Twice*, Jamie Lee Curtis in *Blue Steele* and Rene Russo in *Lethal Weapon 2*: a fem-dom babe with a gun and an erotic death wish. Honey, she seemed to say, I can blow you or I can blow you away.

Every muscle in her thighs tightened so that you could see them straining underneath her jeans. Her buttocks clenched; her tits threw themselves out of her unbuttoned shirt. A bra strap appeared on a bared shoulder. She was tall and hard, taut and flexed. She held death in her hands and she looked as if she could serve it up as calmly as a short-order cook serves up a hamburger.

Bernie gawped at this mistress, wielding action girl hardware as if it was a three-speed hairdryer.

'Jesus,' he said. 'That gal knows what she's doing.'

Mel fired one sure, sharp shot without flinching. The bullet whistled through the air and ripped through Nancy Reagan's nose.

She lowered the gun, smiled, raised her arm again and shot Nancy again, three times, in the same place.

The air rang with the blasts and a flock of birds shot out of one of the trees, screeching.

Jim was still wearing his dark glasses. His eyes were hidden and his expression, as always, was immutable and unreadable, but I knew as well as I knew the name of my own mother that he was staring at her and that he was excited. On some level the master was submitting to the chick with the fistful of steel but he would not fall down without a fight. He would do everything in his power to disarm her.

Nothing was said. They simply left together, leaving

the picnic basket on the ground. There was nothing I could do except stare after them.

I turned round. Bernie was staring at my behind, noting, no doubt, that my tight mini-dress had ridden up to just below my cheeks and that there were the marks of the whipping.

He seemed in suspended animation, hypnotised by the pale flesh moving in front of him.

'Let's eat,' he said, and spread out the tartan rug. 'Then we can go for a ride, I'll show you where the aliens landed. Come on, it'll be fun. Perhaps I'll shoot something for dinner.'

Anything would have been more 'fun' (for want of a better word) than moping around thinking about Jim and Mel.

Jim then was not mine any more. He had never said that he would be, but he had been more mine than anyone else's. I had never really had to fight for him, as I had known that I was the focus of his attention, if not his life.

I picked at a piece of chicken, drank a beer, sulked behind my shades. Bernie ate quite a lot and smoked a joint which left his mouth slack and his eyes rimmed with red.

'Come on,' he said. 'Let's go for a ride.'

I was numb and would have done anything. I didn't care. I was subsumed by cold melancholy. Had I lost Jim? Why didn't they want me to join in? I had never felt like this before, never minded what my lovers did or with whom, but this departure was painful and dreadful and it made me want to kill.

I hardly noticed that Bernie guided me into the jeep and practically lifted me into it, hands pushing against thighs, palms on bare buttocks.

I hardly noticed the smell of my own sweat or saw it staining the fabric of my tiny dress. I hardly noticed the sun belting down on my nose and eyes or the dust thickening and stiffening my hair into wild, white strands that stood in dirty efflorescence, like the living dead. And I hardly noticed the way that Bernie was driving, jolting the gear into four-wheel drive and slamming down dust tracks, going ever and ever faster until the speedometer stopped flickering and stuck at the end of the dial. Too fast.

'This here vehicle is good in all terrains,' he shouted over the noise.

He turned up a steep track where the cacti were burned out and boulders littered the way. Up and up, further into the mountain.

He was in a stoned world of his own, concentrating on avoiding the obstacles in the path, on keeping the jeep from tipping down any one of the precipices that were now appearing to either side. And I now saw that we were high, very high.

The desert and mountains stretched towards the horizon on all sides and there seemed to be no one in this world except me and Bernie and a boot full of guns.

Bernie's cowboy boot was flat on the accelerator and his muscles flexed as he handled the steering wheel.

'That's where the spaceship landed,' he shrieked, pointing up to a cragged mountain peak. 'The army took the bodies away, but old Farmer, he saw 'em. Some say he's still got their windscreen wipers hidden away in his outhouse somewhere. As proof.'

'Oh for God's sake, Bernie,' I snarled. 'Why would an intergalactic vessel have windscreen wipers?'

'Why not? Rains, don't it?'

It was growing dark and we were still driving, now round and round the top of a mountain with no reason except adrenalin and compulsion and not caring about anything. Round and round until the tyres of the jeep made their own track. Then Bernie took a corner too fast. It was inevitable when I think back on it. He took every corner too fast, but this one was tight and he misjudged it. The jeep lurched over to one side, balancing on one side on two of its wheels and I fell out.

I crashed on to the hard ground and rolled a little way down the mountain, hard edges slamming into my flesh, dirt everywhere. And I lay, face down, filthy, dazed and disorientated.

I could not move, or perhaps didn't want to. I was exhausted, and at that point I really didn't care what happened. And I felt no real pain; just numbness and a kind of loss of will. Laziness almost. I felt Bernie pick me up, literally pick me up, and carry me like a baby, back to the car. He cradled me like a child until I came round.

'One of those wheels must be outa line,' he said. 'You hang on, baby, Bernie'll get you back home now. Are you okay, honey? Are you OK?'

I didn't know if I was OK and I didn't care. It was dark now. There was blood on my legs. Aches in places that I could not have named if I had been asked to. I was very, very alone.

Bernie couldn't handle it. He was like a child who had burned down a barn by mistake. He drove more slowly, the lights catching the road, patting me occasionally on the knee. I saw the lights of the ranch with no feeling, for the ranch now seemed to be a den full of strangers who would offer no comforting companionship or friendship. They would have to be handled, they could not be communicated with, Mel and Jim. Suddenly they were back in me, worse than a real bruise or laceration.

Bernie carried me into the house. He was a scared animal now and he did not plan to take responsibility or the consequences of delivering me, damaged and dirty and very, very late.

He staggered into the kitchen and lowered me on to a sofa. Mel and Jim were sitting at the table drinking glasses of red wine. They didn't look as if they had had sex, but who knew?

I noticed that my left arm was bruised and that there were bleeding scratches on the hand.

'What happened to you?' said Mel. 'You've been hours.'

'Bernie turned the jeep over on some precipice,' I said.

'God. Bernie, you could have killed her, you bloody idiot,' Mel said.

Jim stood and looked at me. 'Jesus, look at your face,' he said. 'What did I tell you?'

I was silent. Sulky.

He came up to me, looked at my arm and examined my face.

'What did I tell you?' he said again.

'To be careful,' I muttered.

'Yes. To be careful. And were you?'

'No.'

'Did you do as you were told?'

'No.'

'Did you stop to think that we were here waiting up for you, that we might be worried?'

'No.'

'You're a naughty girl, Stella. Mel and I are both cross with you.'

So now it was 'Mel and I'. They were as one, a union set against me. Why was Mel a part of him?

I noticed, for the first time, that Mel had showered and changed her clothes. She had tied her black hair back and loose curls fell on her face. She was wearing a pair of four-inch-high patent leather ankle boots with needle-thin heels and zips up the side. Her long, black ciré dress seemed to have been poured over her, like

156

oil, and it was split all the way up the front to the waist, so that with each movement, the shiny fabric fell back to reveal the lace on top of her stay-up stockings and the edges of a black, satin thong.

'It wasn't my fault,' I said.

'It wasn't her fault,' said Bernie.

'Shut up, Bernie. Go and sit down and shut up. You've done enough.'

Bernie sat in a chair in the corner.

'You need to be taught a lesson,' said Jim.

'No!'

I stamped my foot on the kitchen floor.

He lifted my chin with his finger and stared down at me with dark, merciless eyes.

I was not going to escape.

I suspected that he and Mel had been planning something all along, something that was going to give them pleasure. But me? Me? I did not know.

'I'll be good!' I yelled.

'Ah,' he said, 'but you never are.'

'I will.'

Jim twisted both my hands behind my back and pushed me towards the kitchen table.

'Lie face down on top of it,' he ordered.

I paused.

'Lie on it, Stella! Face down, now!'

I knew there was nothing I could do. I knew I wanted it. The day had been about this in many ways, finding out if he cared. Now I was finding it out. I had succeeded in remaining at the centre of his sexual attention, but I was going to pay for it.

I crawled on to the top of the kitchen table so that my face was hanging over one end and my body was stretched down the centre of it.

Jim reached down and tied my wrists to the table leg on either side of my shoulder, weaving the soft, nylon cord through my fingers and around my wrists and tying them securely so that I could not slip out of them. He knew me. He knew my wrists. We had long ago given up on handcuffs, for my wrists are narrow and my fingers long. I had alway been able to get out.

He then attached ropes to the other two legs and tied down my ankles.

'Get your flogger, Mel,' he said.

I heard Mel's footsteps. The tips of her stiletto heels clacked a staccato across the stone floor and then clacked back again.

I knew this whip. A mistress in San Francisco had made it for her. It was made of Elkskin and it was known for its bite.

The handle was bound with green and purple dyed leather and the tendrils of the whip sprouted from the tip like a hydra. She had used it on the famous Canadian porno starlet, Faith Plating, in Leon's film, *Slave Farm*.

Mel knew how to wield that whip professionally. She had been trained by one of the most famous dominatrixes on the West Coast, a Madame named Candida. The Madame had taught Mel everything, from simple lashing to complicated ambidextrous hand techniques. There was nothing she could not do with it.

I heard her footsteps and sensed her presence but I could not guess her plan.

Jim turned off the light so now there were only candles and the wind outside and the four of us. Bernie still, silent, gazing out from some shadow in the corner, Jim, Mel. And I, Stella, helpless and squirming but totally triumphant.

Jim sat down on a chair at the end of the table so that my face was bent down towards his groin. He lifted his hard dick out of his jeans and he pressed it towards my mouth.

'Suck, you little bitch.'

I brought my mouth down on the tip and then further down the shaft. He pushed his pelvis up towards me. Now my mouth was full of his flesh.

Mel slowly peeled my dress up so that my back and buttocks were bare.

She kissed me on the back of the neck, stroked me on the hair-line, causing me to shiver with pleasure and apprehension. Then, stroking her fingers down my back, enlivening all the nerves on my spine, she inserted them into my sphincter, gently opening it.

'You're going to like this, baby,' she whispered.

She slapped the tips of the flogger down on my back, gently at first, so that I began to tingle and then grow warm, and then harder, up and down my back to my buttocks, the tops of my thighs, slow but sure, so that I felt every sensation.

She did not stop. An expert, she carried on bringing the simple warmth to pain and the pain to more pain so that I began to ride the wave with her. It was not too much, just enough to know that I was being cared for in the worst possible way, cared for and caressed with the endless bite.

As Mel whipped me into a crazy endorphin high, so my head bobbed up and down on Jim's moistening corona, hard and red. He pushed my head up and down, guiding my movements with his strong hands, harder and harder, up and down, until, without warning, he withdrew and expelled his come into my hair.

Mel, still working on me, still warming me up, spread my warm, throbbing cheeks and slid one finger in, then two, then three.

'I know you like this,' she said.

She was right. The glow on my back and butt was pain and pleasure meshing and marrying as one. I did not know who I was or where I was and I did not care.

There was only warmth and thrill and uncanny elevation. Certainly there was no hate now – or love, as it is
easily explained – just indefinable emotions that served
to take me away from my self.

Vaguely I sensed or remembered that Bernie was
lurking somewhere out there, watching my legs struggling in their laced boots, seeing my naked body flat
and squirming, tied down and helpless on that table.

Mel gently pried the leather handle of the whip into
me, as if she was a man – stern pelvis, hard, fake
phallus – deeper and deeper, and now Jim was hard
again, so there was the smell of his come and he was
again in my mouth, and all was moist and hard and
abandoned and rampant.

He began to moan, and I was surprised, for he rarely
uttered any of the usual growlings of pleasure, or
appreciation: he was mostly silent in his enjoyment.

Mel drew the dildo softly out of my open anus and I
felt as if I had lost something for ever. It was like a tiny
flickering of real grief: I had not wanted her to leave
me.

Jim got up and walked down to the other end of the
table. Mel took his place, sitting on the chair underneath my face, then caressed my mouth with her fingers
and kissed me. Then she opened her dress and showed
me her bare breasts ornamented with hard nipples and
pushed them into my mouth.

Positioning herself so that I could see her lower half,
she allowed the folds of the dress to fall open, and
spread her legs. She had taken off the thong, so I could
see her immaculate pubic hair and her tumescent scarlet labia, but I could not see her face.

One long, painted fingernail eased open her lips and
pushed into her wet opening. So now I had her cunt in
front of me; I could smell it; I could see two inches
away her fingers rubbing on her erect clitoris, gently,

160

slowly, her pelvis beginning to gyrate as if in some synchronised dance with Onan.

But aroused though I was by Mel's enjoyment, so too was I by the familiar place: being in Jim's power. I had been in his power before. It was where I liked to be. He knew, I knew it: the fascination fed on itself.

He looked down at the flesh of my arse, reddened by Mel, flushing as if with mortification which, in some way, it was; mortified flesh that would liberate my soul. But to do what? Who knew; who cared? All I knew was a mystical alliance that gained strength with every connection.

He stroked my tender flesh with a careful, kind hand.

'Not a bad job, Mel,' he said.

Mel's hands were rubbing herself now. Emerging towards a climax, she was beginning not to care.

'Just take her,' she said. 'Go on. Just take her. I've made her ready for you. She's open. She wants it. She wants you.'

He eased his stiff dick into my anus, slowly at first, then he pushed all the way up, suddenly and with the full force of all his strength. It was almost too much. He was too big. I screamed.

'Christ, stop, baby, please stop.'

'Open up, little one,' he said impassively. 'Open up, or I'll have Mel whip you with my belt.'

The pain of his dick surged through me again, but as he pushed further and further in, he simultaneously pushed his fingers into the opening between my legs, past the tender, hurting, huge labia, up and in, rubbing me towards a climax as he took me.

And now, when I was as open as I had ever been for him, open in the front and in the back, in my heart and in my womb and in my soul, receiving all of him, willingly and with all the intense drama of bodily pleasure, my eyes looked down to see Mel's fingers

161

deep in her cunt, pushing herself to the same thrill, moaning as she did so.

'Are you coming, Melanie?' said Jim. 'Are you coming?'

Mel jolted back, pussy out, wet, red lips in the air, gasping and moaning, eyes rolling, blinking, going to some place far, far, far away.

Jim came into me from behind, fucking my arse again, pinching my buttocks with tight fingers, telling me that I should do as I was told. He was with me: he was mine again. And as I yelled that I was coming, that he must let me come, he must get me there or I would die, so Mel was bringing herself to the same place, knowing that she was going to join me on that strange plateau and he, knowing everything, saw us shriek out the weird joy together, saw us shudder and our bodies vibrate together and, as they did so, so he expelled into me, and we all reached the same place of true decadent joy; we all knew what that was like all at the same time.

All his juice burst forth. He fell on me, and I lay still beneath him, satisfied and at peace.

'Mel liked that, didn't she, little one?' he whispered.

'Yes,' I muttered, coming round slowly.

'And so did you.'

'Yes.'

The following morning, I remembered that Bernie had seen it all. And then I realised that slowly, inexorably, Jim and Mel were joining forces against me.

162

Chapter Nine

*I*t was strange that three people who were so close could become so distant, but then human relations are full of these anomalies and, in some ways, to nurture successful intimacies is to lay the foundations for harsh denial. Only the special soul, it seems, can embrace *ménage* without clawing back its individuality with long, aggressive fingernails that slice and cut and slash so that all the other players, the ex-friends, the former lovers or spouses or conspirators, are left lacerated and limp, wet rags on a sodden washing-line, sucked of all energy.

The dance is never as simple as it looks. The steps may be learned, the music may be comforting and familiar, but there are always unpredictable intangibles thrown in by Mother Nature, the most sadistic mistress of all. And so, someone is out of step or tone-deaf or wants to play the instrument themselves, and the smooth quadrille is disrupted by clumsy egos. Futile manipulations and doltish presumptions: these destroy the dance.

As I have said, three is a dangerous number. It

promises sexual synchronicity but often delivers confusion. Its rewards are plentiful but so too are its perils. And three is a particularly dangerous number when those involved are bright and wilful and proud to stage-manage psychic notions over which they might have implicit understanding but over which they have no real control.

It is arrogant to hope that one can ever know another person well and it is misguided to try and know oneself; to know oneself is to become familiar and to be familiar is to lose interest. It's far more entertaining to remain a stranger to the world and a stranger to oneself, just as it is more amusing to continue to explore a country than it is to set down and live in it. New horizons are exciting; familiar landmarks are not. They are boundaries, and boundaries are the same as prison walls.

Mel and Jim colluded. They drew together and, as they did so, I became the target of their inventive diktats. It was two against one and it began as a subtle, unspoken dynamic of which, initially, they were unaware.

Mel and Jim did not observe and analyse as I did. They were extrovert travellers, more concerned with action than introspection, more motivated by physicality than philosophy.

They walked while I lounged; they rode while I read. I could stare for hours at my own inner space, carried away in imaginary ramblings that served to transport; they could not wait for anything. Easily bored, they had to go somewhere, do things, feel the present.

But they could not stop. To stop was to get off the ride and to get off the ride was to be stagnant and die. They were both running and they both set up a vortex of energy that fed on itself and each other, whipping each other up into a pagan orgy.

164

I had taught myself how to withdraw and could protect myself as surely as an octopus protects itself with an amphora at the bottom of the ocean. I could hide behind myself and push my tentacles out to feel the danger, and then pull them back in again if I felt like it. I could be physically present but emotionally absent and I was the only one equipped with a mastery of this particular skill.

Jim could make himself unavailable, but his tactics were obvious and usually involved physically disappearing. In London he had controlled the interaction with telephone calls and notes, choosing exactly when he was to be present in my life and knowing when he was going to leave.

There would be a call telling me to meet him here or there and I would find myself in a scenario that he directed. There would be instructions on how to dress and some clue as to what to expect, but little more than these. I fell in with these antics and appreciated his inventiveness. There was always something different: another role, another costume, another fantasy enacted in some far-flung place.

I had been fist-fucked by a poet in Barnstaple; I had watched a man in Kent perform fellatio on himself; and I had been sodomised underneath a table in a teashop in Penrith.

I had attended meetings held by rubber fetishists in Otterley St Michael and I had been dressed up in Victorian bloomers and severely birched by a governess.

The cotton underwear, long and white and lacy, was made to the original design, and the original design was made to easily free the buttocks.

He had made me wear a little, lace camisole on top of this, then a long, wool skirt, and Mary Jane shoes. We went to Nottingham for the day. I did not see anyone else there though I believe there were 'classes' with men and women all disciplined by Miss Turbeville, a lipsticked martinet and a complete bitch.

We had lunch at a long table and I was reprimanded for my manners. Then I was reprimanded again when I failed to finish the washing-up to a standard that she required. She called me into a classroom, where there was a blackboard and authentic desks and where Jim was standing by the window at the back of the room. He was some distance away and I realised afterwards that we must have looked as if we were in a play.

She, the Turbeville woman, looked the part, in a high, frilled collar and long, heavy, cotton dress and hair scraped bleakly back from a high forehead.

She made me lean with my hands against the wall so that my back was flat and my rear was up and out. She undid the skirt so that it fell to the floor and slowly pulled open the gap in the back of the white cotton bloomers, crawing the lace and damask aside as if they were curtains.

'If you move, you will get more,' she said.

My cheeks were poking through the lace frame. I had never been switched with a birch before and did not know what to expect. It was a fierce thing, made of gathered reeds, and it stung as she thrashed me with experienced strength, reddening my flesh until the tears poured from my eyes and I started to sob.

She did not stop there, but carried on to a new level of pain, slashing those thin twigs against my poor body until I collapsed on all fours in front of her.

Jim stroked me, his fingers cold against the heat, and picked me up.

I could not sit down for a week, but every time he looked at me, looked at that crimson smear that she had left, he wanted to fuck me, and did fuck me.

I had watched Jim sandwiched between two spectacular Scandinavian women, both armed with hard-throb three-speed vibrators, and both naked except for G-strings and black spandex masks with wide gashes cut to allow their mouths to perform the necessary requirements. I do not recall their names; we never saw them again. But their purpose was to teach me how to fellate. They were, Jim informed me, the best he had ever had with regard to this particular art, and art they had made it, with both their tongues licking his balls and glans, touching him ever so lightly, and then pushing their hands, soft but firm, on the base of his dick.

They knew just how to touch and when, how to make him rise, let him drop, and rise again, how to play him with their mouths so that he retained a long hard-on, on the brink of climax.

He came, it seemed, just when they wanted him to, and I liked seeing their beautiful, long, lean, tanned bodies entwining with his. I liked the way he pushed their legs back over their heads so that they were trussed by his hands and showing their bald arseholes and smooth, shaven pussies, all lewd.

I had carefully creamed their back passages with warm, slippery lubrication, fingering their internal muscles as I did so, ensuring that they were open and ready for any object to slide into their lascivious posteriors. The translucent gel oozed abundantly from the bald, brown orifices now seeking brazen attention from the dark curves of their smooth cheeks, and I inserted identical red vibrators, poking through the inadequate guard of their sphincters and deep inside them, while Jim fucked them both hard from the front, one after the other, so that they shrieked and moaned and clasped each other, almost blind in their masks, but trembling in happy bliss.

I had had my nipples pinched with the very latest

adjustable duck-bill clamps and my anus examined with a procterscope. I had given an enema to a leather king in Earls Court, and I had watched a den full of *demi-monde* experiment with the latest innovations in electricity. They had set up a small stage and enacted a burlesque drag-queen show, performed to Wurlitzer music and demonstrating the most effective uses for cock-ring electrodes and pulse-generated plugs.

In Essex an essayer had performed coitus between my breasts, and in Sloane Square one of the richest landowners in England had emptied a bottle of champagne into my vagina and sucked it out while I lay spread-eagled on his antique billiard table, observed by portraits of his periwigged ancestors.

He had had a big mouth and a long, wet tongue. Kissing me hard all over my sticky labia, he had gobbled at me greedily, sucking out the liquor as if it was to be his last drink, enjoying himself without much thought about me.

Jim had presented me as an unpaid prostitute and that is how he treated me, this Marquess or whatever. The thrill for me? The thrill for me was not the sight of that man sucking Ruinart out of me, the bulge straining at his trousers, but the fact that Jim retained eye contact with me throughout the whole scene. His eyes did not waver from mine, and just staring at me with this unblinking intensity was to enslave me to his will.

He was a greedy man, the Marquess. He had a coat of arms and a family motto and claimed he could trace his ancestry back to Frederick the Fierce.

I had sucked him back, gobbling on that excited member for Jim's delectation, sucking and licking and massaging his balls until he let himself go, howled like a dog, declared passion, declared love, and wanted possession.

Jim would lend me but he would not give me, and

of course his simpler friends were confused. They did not know whence I came or who I was or where I was going. I did not care what they knew and what they did not: they were bit parts in the main drama that was my devotion to Jim.

I had once driven to a deserted cottage in Hove to find the sitting-room bare of furniture except for a rape-rack, hewn in polished oak, upholstered in leather and carved with quatrefoils.

A man who I had never seen before and would never see again watched as I shed my tailored, shiny, leather coat and revealed myself in the tightly woven black corset that I had been told to wear. There was only the corset, pushing my breasts up. I wore no panties and no stockings. My feet, in six-inch-high platform pumps, pushed my body into the appropriate fuck-me posture, and I was spread over that rape-rack like honey over toast.

He, the stranger, had tied me down with chains and padlocks and then wound a lever so that the equipment turned into a raised bed where my legs were spread, my pelvis jutted out, and my orifice was exposed as if for an examination. And there he left me, this implausible official, fanny up and akimbo.

It had grown dark. Some candles flickered and there was the vague smell of the sea. A fire burned in the grate. I had not known when Jim would come, of course: all I could think of on that rack was being raped. By the time he arrived, an hour or so later, I was ready for him. I would have wanked myself if my hands had not been tied down, and I would have been punished if I had been caught doing so. Jim did not like me to masturbate unless he was present and he had given me permission. Then I did. But only when he said yes, you can, and he could see, watch my fingers, and inspect the secret pleasure zones of my elusive autonomy.

He had stood looking at me, enjoying me as a spectacle of want, body and breasts, and guiltless fanny, all splayed and waiting for him.

He had slipped his belt out of his trousers, very slowly. I love that sound of the leather easing itself out of the fabric, the thrill of not knowing whether one is going to get strapped or fucked or both. He had strapped me that time, slapping me with the edge of the leather on the thighs, little slapping leather licks, not much and not for long. I fancy he wanted to fuck me as much as I wanted to be fucked. He had not undressed; he had simply pushed his big, hard penis into me. Taken me on the rape-rack.

I remember being frustrated as he pushed me to excruciating orgasms, opened up all the channels to surrender and affection, made me want to love and kiss him, while all the time my arms were tied down. I could not hug his neck; I could not whisper gently into him. I could only shout and thrash and be 'raped'. I could only feel the tip of his dick inflame my G-spot and my pelvis melt down towards him. I could only be wet and out of control. And that time, he withdrew his dick as I was about to come, and there I was, strapped down, shrieking at him to fuck me, crying with desire.

He had laughed, shot himself all over my stomach, and left me like that for some minutes before pushing his powerful fingers into me, deep and fast, guiding me fiercely to relief.

Afterwards I wondered why it was called a rape-rack, since it had not been about assault so much as waiting and wanting. Jim told me the Chinese had invented them and called them 'romantic chairs'. The clasps had automatically snapped around the wrists of unsuspecting women and the chair had then collapsed into a bed.

He wanted me to be as trained and as expert as a professional. He wanted me to learn all the tricks, and then perform them. He believed that it was good for the soul to provide favours unconditionally, a kind of sex charity-work, like dropping a penny in the hat, only dropping the panties into the lap.

He was very creative, very strict, and believed that the expression of his predilections was his right. It was also his thrill and his *raison d'être*.

He was fixated by sexual plot and focused on enaction. He turned everybody into actors and manipulated them to perform his private screenplays. We were all in his pornomovies; we were all his porno stars.

Real life and sensual plan melded into one until they became as one. Sometimes he did not know the difference. Everything could be used to further the game and provide ideas for the next show.

He was always watching, directing, and he was always hard. We would play over the scenarios verbally afterwards, and they would always arouse him, some more than others, maybe, but, in general, he enjoyed anything over which he had had some creative control.

Unlike many fetishists, he did not play over the same rites, did not restrict himself to the same PVC-pervert constrictions that restrained the SM scene. He enjoyed Nazis and nurses as much as anyone else, but he was more excited by improvisation and avant-garde ideas. He preferred to see costumes that he had never seen before and involve his cock in new games.

I sensed that he wanted to feel unfamiliar emotions, though this was difficult to know. He was so detached, so implacable, so rarely anything except the unassailable auteur. The shards of love that he did throw my

171

way, so unexpectedly and so innocently, went deep and far. They were intense because of their rarity, and genuine in their sincerity. When he expressed devotion he was truthful. He would not have been bothered with those kind of lies. But they only went so far and, for me, it was never, ever far enough.

Mel, like Jim, was distant, and it seemed to me that I had never known her centre. I did not even know if she had one, so elusive and so mercurial was her essence.

As the days went on, the hours were full of heat and dust and a landscape that had not changed since the first arthropods crawled upon it. One could be dizzied by the space, the oldness of it, and wonder at her immutable detachment, the endless cool of her, the robotic responses and oblique perspectives.

I sometimes thought that Bernie was not a maundering dingbat but a sage who knew the truth about extraterrestrial landings. Mel was an alien; not an alien in the science-fiction sense, but she was different, triffid different, robot different, not of this world.

When I thought of how much I really knew, I recalled the sinister but salient fact that, though I knew her sexually, I could outline few real details. Her birthdate, the towns in which she had lived but not the birthplace.

There had never been any parents. She mentioned once that she had been adopted and had changed her name but refused to reveal the original. She had a fluid identity with no core.

When I thought of Mel, she was almost spooky; when I described her to myself, I hated her. But then she would arrive, all swollen, maternal tits and unembarrassed buttocks and deranged black hair, big and sexy and with a smile that could make an orchid burst into flower.

172

How could she be so emotionally cool and yet so sexy? To see her was to want her, to meld with her. She was always hot.

They looked natural together, mutually feeding on a physical narcissism that forged a sexual alliance of vanities.

They were both tall and dark and strong while I was smaller, slighter and gamine. They were destined to rule with their physical strength, and this I enjoyed, revelling in deviant guidance and stimulating myself with inspirational thoughts of powerlessness.

But was I powerless, or just playing? I knew in some ways that I was equipped with perspicacity and thus stronger. I did not submit instinctively; I submitted as a considered antidote to boredom. I, not Mel, had always been the top of the class. I, not Mel, always saw things coming. I, not Mel, made up the games, although she, more exhibitionst, saw them as reasons to perform.

Perhaps Jim was right. I did not understand about pure submission; I did not know how to go all the way or want to; my heart and stomach were always rebelling against him. I relished his directives but only because I had asked for them and allowed them.

Now, slowly, almost imperceptibly, he moved away from me. Looking back, I wonder if it was a considered ruse to retain his hold over me, a way of retaining control.

They hiked. I did not like to hike. I did not have the shoes, for a start. They went off shooting, a skill in which I was not interested. They drove to the market. Together.

They were closing ranks and, as they did, so I became a part of their plots. At first I didn't mind because it was fun.

* * *

Once he sat in a chair and I sat in his lap while Mel spread my legs, kneeled down in front of me, and tickled my clit with her tongue until I screamed to be fucked. And she did. She strapped on that leather dildo of hers and she fucked me while Jim held me in his arms. She jolted into me, pushing her phallus into me, first slow, then harder and harder, and faster, knowing what she was doing, knowing how to pace her performance, and knowing that I liked it when I thought I had had enough, and was yelling at her to stop, knowing that that was when I liked to be taken further, fucked when I thought I had had enough, because, of course, that was when I gave her the control.

He stroked my breasts and then pinched them, pinched my nipples, kissed my neck, and breathed filthy words into my ear as Mel sat on top of me fucking me with her leather dick.

They were both fully clothed and they both engulfed me. And when she was finished, she withdrew like a man, strode to the kitchen, put her cowboy boots up on the table, smoked a cigarette, left me for ever, as men like to do, airing her masculinity. Fucking me with her fake phallus made her feel like James Dean. She became the protector. And that was when I was mesmerised by her.

One day Jim made me wear a lacy pinny and high pumps and nothing else. Then he tied my hair into a pony-tail and tethered me to the kitchen table with an ankle cuff and a chain. I could reach the bathroom and the sitting room, but I could not go out of the house.

I was there all afternoon and all evening while they went out, to a rodeo I think. I didn't want to go with the heat and the crowd, and I had sulked when they tried to make me, so Jim pulled up my dress, slapped my thigh with his hard palm and said, 'Well, you can stay here, then,' and made sure that I did.

174

I didn't mind being chained. The leash was long enough, though I dreaded lest a stranger call and would see me in this weird humiliation. Left to myself, though, without the stress of having to explain, I caught myself up in deviant Doris Day scenarios, enjoying being a housewife, 50s style, and enjoying subverting the camp symbolism of the little woman. I was literally chained to the stove.

I would have liked all those big bras and cheesecake girdles and pointy heels. I would have liked to pretend to be perky and satisfied with what society had handed me in the form of the biggest freezers and cars while, in fact, being bad and wet and wanting to screw Elvis.

So when they came back I had made an apple pie, of course. Apple pie. I had been in, 'home cookin'' all day. And I served it up, all meek and good, and they had both watched as I bent to get the dishes out of the bottom of the oven and my bare buttocks were pushed up by those pumps with cute little flowers on the front.

'Good girl,' Jim had said, and put me to bed, tucked me up, kissed me and told me that he loved me. And then, the next morning, I sat in his lap at the top of the breakfast table and he fed me like a baby, whispering sweetly to me and cutting the toast up and engulfing me in muscle and protection and total security. Allowing me to be small. Looking after and loving me as no one ever had.

I was swept away by him and I was aware again that the scope of his understanding made him special.

I was sitting on Jim's lap at the kitchen table being fed by him when Bernie arrived and I loved it because Bernie could not come near me as I was wrapped up, small, in Jim.

Jim did not bat an eyelid, but performed as a father, and then brushed my hair with his big, flat-back brush that had gone across my knickerless behind in the past.

175

Bernie didn't know what to make of it, of course.

These deviant attentions did not dispel my primary fear. In some ways, they fuelled it because, as Jim catered to me, so I loved him again and so I didn't want him to spend much time with Mel. I wanted to ask if he had fucked her but I didn't. I didn't dare and I didn't want to deal with the consequences of knowing.

Then, one afternoon, she started to taunt me with cruel remarks and snide asides that, maybe in another mood, I would have batted back at her or laughed off. But it was hot, and I was tired and annoyed anyway because she had been dropping rude remarks all day: undermining and catty, not sexy. She said something about the fact that I would 'probably end up having children and be a milk cow'.

I slapped her very hard in the face.

She was momentarily astounded and then slapped me back. Then I lost control and went wild. We were both wearing bikinis, so it must have been a scene from some catfight club in Los Angeles. 'Mud Wrestling is Us'. Only I fancied that this was bloodier and bitcher and, of course, it was real.

I threw myself at her, punching every surface that I could find. She fell on the ground and I put my fingers around her neck and squeezed them. I probably would have squeezed the life out of her if she had not pushed me off.

We were rolling around and around in the dust, scratching and screaming, very ugly, very undignified, when the next thing we knew was the cold splash of a bucket of water and Jim was hauling her off me.

He separated us, God knows how: pure superiority of strength, I suppose.

'What the fuck do you think you are doing, you little bitches?'

I was easier to calm down; I was more accustomed to admonishment, after all.

'Go and sit in that chair, Stella, and shut up.'

Mel was big and red, heaving and furious, but he physically restrained her and she, realising that she was not going to win, surrendered.

He dragged her across the floor and padlocked her wrists with a firm, silver chain and leather restraint. Then he attached one end of a rope to a silver hook in the wristband and threw the other end across a beam and then attached it to the leg of a table, so that she hung there, body filthy from the floor, still shrieking terrible insults, writhing in white anger.

He strung her up over the beam and made me watch while I sat in that chair in front of her.

She was yelling and struggling but he brought out his twin-lash whip, three feet of braided leather with two lashes that I knew from experience would sting the flesh like heat from hell.

He was so strong and his right arm did not flinch. He whipped her good, bringing back the tails again and again, hitting his mark every time, her wide, full, quivering buttocks, her back, the top of her thighs, each time leaving a red line.

He put all his force into it, drawing his arm far back, hurling like only a man can, pausing for a second between each strike to regain his position. He whipped her until she begged him to stop. And then, while she still hung there, placid now, tears staining her dusty cheeks, black hair in wormy tails all over her sulky face, I argued and said that it was her fault, that she had started it.

I tried to get him on my side, but he placed a ball gag in my mouth, tying it tightly so I could not yell. Then he pushed me across his knee, angry daddy now and, unforgiving, pulled down my bikini bottom and

177

brought a solid wooden paddle down harder on my arse than he had ever before, so that she could see that I was getting as much as her and that we were both to blame.

When he let her down, she was quiet. The fight had left her. He undid the black bra bikini-top so that her full breasts flowed out towards him and he twisted each nipple with his fingers so that she groaned, gasps of need gagging the back of her throat.

He laid her, face up, on the floor, drew her legs up to her shoulders, and tied her at the ankles, behind her head. Then he tied me in the same way, leaving us side by side, silent and tied, so that we were sisters in bondage, smarting from the blows, forcibly silenced, both of our cunts wet and exposed and helpless, two of us helpless to do anything except wait for what he chose to dole out to us.

Now we were joined together in our hatred of him. He had trounced us and thrashed us. We were hot and angry and smarting and very, very excited, but still we hated him, because that is what the pain can do: make you angry and then make you beg for the person who inflicted it. It is strange that way, pain, how it makes you want the tormentor, how it makes you do anything for them.

He was the cruel master and we were back at school, together in brave, defiant conspiracy against the punishments of an outside force.

Fighting and fucking. There's nothing like it.

He left us like that, to think about our sins, he said. We were left, trussed up on the floor, to calm down, and by the time he returned we were both quiet.

He removed the gags from our mouths and demanded that we apologise and we did. Then he fucked us both, still tied, one after the other, as if we were some anonymous holes there for his use, and he used them as if we were his private harem, me first, then Mel, then me again, drilling us hard until, against our will, we came and there was the final placidity that only a big man can enforce with the pure strength of his dick.

We screamed as we climaxed and afterwards we did not complain about the hot pain all over our bodies. It was what I enjoyed, after all.

Mel was not destined to be his slave: we all knew that. She had enjoyed being ravished by him for some arcane reasons that lay at the bottom of her strange psyche. Perhaps she knew she had been out of control and it had frightened her. To be given the cold discipline of imposed boundaries had helped her return to herself. Perhaps she just fancied something different. Perhaps she did not think about it, merely enjoyed a distinguished love-maker with wood rarely seen outside the profession in which she had worked for so long.

Afterwards he made us apologise to each other again and watched, satisfied, as we pushed our tongues into each other's mouths and kissed and made up.

'Go down on Melanie, Stella,' he said. 'Show her you mean it.'

She spread her legs for me and I crouched on the floor on all fours, licking her pussy, making her feel good, while he kneeled behind me, his fingers up my anus, investigating and pleasing themselves, making my arse wriggle with their playing.

'Go on, little Stella, I want to see Melanie come, I want to see you please her.'

I licked and it was easy. She was tender and aroused and in orgasmic lust anyway because she had just received him. She was ready to have another orgasm, as women are. One is never ever enough. Remember

179

that, boys, if you ever decide to get too big for your boots.

I flicked the tip of my tongue into her wet orifice and over her nasty puss, nasty, self-indulgent, wanting, spoiled puss. And I made her come again. And again. Her moaning and moaning. Lost.

'What do you say, Melanie?'

She came back and focused on us, eyes looking at us as if she had never seen us before, coming back into the room, having been away for some time. And we had sent her there, Jim and I. I hoped she would not forget that.

'Thank you, darling little Stella. Thank you, you make me feel so good.'

'Yes,' said Jim, kissing me on the back of the neck and caressing my hard nipples.

The episode did not finish there. The following day, Jim piled me into the jeep and drove me to Indian Creek Springs, a town twenty miles to the south of Complicity.

'Where are we going?'

'You'll see.'

He was wearing shades and a white shirt and his dark hair flopped over his forehead. He looked angular and determined and beautiful.

I wished I did not find him beautiful, but the rigidity of his cheekbones and jaw and the set of authority around his mouth – his basic glamour – were more than I could bear.

He had so much strange charisma, exuded so much heady mystery, that sometimes I just gazed at him secretly, enjoying the visual experience.

Would I always think he was beautiful? Or was he merely a tourist attraction whose landmarks would fade in time? Eventually one would walk past them without noticing their unique characteristics, just walk right past without noticing.

Would the day that I failed to be enthralled be the day that I would cut off from this slavery and walk free from the fetters of loving him?

Would I ever want to stop pleasing him, stop caring, see him across a crowded room, as I had seen so many of the other ex-boyfriends, and think, oh, there's so-and-so, and wonder what I ever saw in him, how I had managed to even sleep with him?

So fluid and so transient are these sexual impulses; they ebb and flow, carry you here and there, never staying still for one minute, but are all-consuming while they are happening.

I could not imagine at that moment being anything except hopeless and pitifully subsumed by a desire to meld with him, so that he could never, ever drop me because I would always be part of him.

Indian Creek Springs paid its respects to civilisation in that it had a supermarket, a barber, a shop selling cowboy boots, a saddlery and a bar. It was also in the proud possession of Chief Jeremy's Tattoo Parlour, run, as it turned out, by Chief Jeremy himself, whose cultural influences were drawn from a range of disparate sources of unwavering eccentricity and widespread geographical location.

He had, it seemed, at some point visited New Orleans. To this end, he wore the battered top-hat of a voodoo shaman and carried a stick with a skull on top of it.

Indian beads and feathers hung around his neck. There was a turquoise T-shirt bearing a picture of Jim Morrison and an old, patched jacket with brass buttons down the front. His face was brown and wrinkled and his mouth had suffered none of the dental privileges traditional to the average American citizen.

The teeth ranged in hue between yellow and green and there were very few of them, presenting a pitiful sight, as his mouth regularly gaped open in order to release frightening guffaws of laughter that were unrelated to any obvious joke.

'So,' he bellowed, stamping his stick on the ground, 'this is the little lady.'

I looked at the shrunken head on top of the wand. The eyeless sockets stared back; the tiny mouth stretched into an unpleasant, rictus grin.

'Yes,' said Jim.

'Well, it won't be a big job. Over in twenny minutes or so, I'd say. Over quicker than the coyote takes to find a mate in the spring. Let's hope she doesn't howl like one.'

He led us to an antechamber where there were pictures of his designs and a range of metal implements, twisted and paint-spattered.

The chief lit some candles and placed a cassette in a dusty player. The sound of Native American drums filled the room.

The flames of the candles flickered against the designs, filling them with grotesque breath. The chief seemed to be an accomplished artist, but his works inclined towards the Gothic: there were demons and two-headed babies and crustacea.

'Lie on the bed, Stella,' Jim said.

I lay face down on an old, fur cover that smelled of dead horses and oil cans. Jim pulled up my summer dress to show the chief my buttocks exposed by a little satin thong.

'There,' he said, pointing to a place to the top, near my hip. 'There, I think.'

The chief bent down to have a closer look, as if he was in the need of a pair of glasses, which, as it turned out, he was, since he then extricated a pair of gold-rimmed bifocals from a leather case embossed with his initials.

'Ah yes,' he said. 'That will be mighty fine. Won't hurt there so much because of the flesh.'

'Jim,' I whined. 'What is he doing to me?'

'Don't whine, Stella.'

The Indian wiped antiseptic on to my cheek and started up a whirling needle that made a terrifying, high-pitched buzz and drowned out the thumping of the shamanic drums banging from the cassette player.

He crouched over me and pumped the needle into the skin on my bottom, working, at least, with some skill, that meant he was quick and sure and did not pause to stare or make artistic decisions. Wiping away the blood, occasionally, he ploughed on and on, and soon I was inured to the points stabbing into me. There was just a dull pain.

'Easy job,' he said.

I got up and twisted around to look at my buttock. I could only just make it out as I was looking at it upside down. There, in reddish black letters, in capitals about a centimetre high, was the word RESPECT.

'Very nice,' said Jim. 'Let's hope she now shows some.'

The chief stood over my throbbing cheeks and examined his work. Brushing my stained skin with a delicate finger, he said thoughtfully, 'You two should come to our party. We're having a big pow-wow – all the tribes are coming – then you'll see some real tattoos!'

'Thank you,' said Jim. 'We will.'

Jim took me to the bar and I sat on the stool, the ache making me aware of this new sign on my tender flesh. I resented the fact that there had been no decision, but I was accustomed to that. I rarely made decisions when I was around him. He ordered and I obeyed. He chose and I acquiesced. So, by following these rules, I had set the scene for this and I could not vent any rational rage and anyway, soon I began to think that these letters bound him to me for ever.

I hoped that this meant he was serious, for surely this modification was a form of commitment of some kind. This eternal graphic was for him. Now I was his. He had made me his, his own possession, as surely as if he had put his name on my arse. I bore his signature. Those words would never go away; I had respect burned into me, so I felt as if I could not get away from their effect.

It seemed as if the indelible word worked a spell on me. I began to feel respectful. I began to think about what this meant and I realised that though I obeyed Jim, I did not respect him, as I did not respect any man, on principle, because they had never given me any reason to.

Did this really mean that I was to be like this for ever? A tattoo is not just for Christmas, right, it is for ever? What would other men think? Would they enjoy it? Would they resent the message left by another man? Would they fail to understand?

How would it be when – and if – Jim left my life and I was left old and wrinkled, a bent old person with RESPECT written on my arse. It was surely as clear as a banner that said: I'm bent, I'm twisted, I'm kinky; don't come near unless you are the same. Would I change; would this thing allow me to change? Or would it hold me to its meaning for all of time?

The tattoo pleased Jim and I liked to please Jim. In the car park, he lifted up my skirt to check the swelling and to see if there was any bleeding. He stroked me with his fingers, reading the letters, and whispered to me that he wanted to fuck me and, when we drove back into the desert, he took my hand and led me out of my high seat then laid me over the bonnet. And he did fuck me.

Chapter Ten

There are some very strange people living in the desert. Lizard-skinned tribes, burned by the sun and deranged by the long, black nights, scratch out a living and celebrate extremes.

The modern primitives gathered at the chief's mobile home for a solstice whose original meaning had long been hidden by the new-age a-go-go of pansexual sybarites. The scene saw shifting cabals of tattooed pagans and shoals of undulating drifters, white-trash types with modified extremities and lesbian witches with dangerous rising signs. Here they all were, the disparate human insignia that represent life on the edge of America.

Different pioneers these. Once their forefathers had trounced the boundaries of land; now the desert delinquents defied convention by assuming their own uniforms.

The disenfranchised, the forgotten, the uneducated, the fat, the deviant, the violent: all eked out an existence in the vast tracts of dusty anonymity. Noses cut, faces scarred, eyelids pierced, hair dyed, earlobes of metal.

Some were wondrous, but many were lumpen. Readers' wives with scars. Their skins were the discoloured shrouds of a bad diet, years spent on grape-flavoured soda and chilli fries and all the other unnatural savouries of mass-market cuisine.

The chief had not changed for this occasion and, in some environments, tube stations for instance, or certain municipal parks, he would have been seen as another victim of urban dystopia, for he had the vagrant look with the fraying and smudges and shoes in need of replacement.

His eyeballs were red and he smelled of serious drinking. He wove about, followed by several giggling tattooed girls, some with neon fronds sprouting from their scalps, some bald. One beauty, lean and mean, had a solid gold hand with articulated joints.

'She's the editor of *Bod Mod* magazine,' I was told by a gamine with green hair and pierced lips. 'Learned everything she knows from Fakir Musafar, King of the Modern Primitives. She's spiritually exploring herself and reclaiming her identity.'

'How did she afford the gold?'

'Her father made a fortune on Wall Street in the mid-eighties. He's in prison now, of course, but she got the dough.'

'Is she, er, involved with anyone?'

'Aw no, they're all free spirits. I'm told she's married to her motorbike. Y'know, travels round with a sleeping bag.'

The chief's tribe was not made of the Native Americans as we know them from traditional representation. No Pocahontas here. But Native Americans there were, some befeathered and fringed, all smoking long, wooden pipes, drinking whiskey and nodding over hands of poker read by the light of the candles.

The first sight, the first creature who was a preview

to the wider picture of this party, was a naked man with a shaved body and a bald head, upon which a high headdress composed of shivering, green feathers had been attached.

And, though you could see that his eyebrows were painted and his lips made huge with clownish paint, his features were encased by a mask made out of metal links and perspex cubes.

His fingers were tipped with three-inch-long talons painted silver. His body was shaved. He was lean and he was naked and this allowed even the most casual spectator to observe that he did not have a penis. He was all man, hands, knees, adam's apple, bony joints, but no dick. There was a smooth space of nothingness between his legs.

He whooped and danced, the masked bird-man. He had bells on his ankles and behind him were three bald cronies, also feathered and shaved, and one tattooed from top to toe with scenes from the Garden of Eden. A green and red snake wound around his arm and stretched to his torso, its forked tongue flickering over his pierced nipples.

Two members of this pack banged on upturned oil cans with pieces of flint, and wailed like babies, while one played the violin, setting up a dissonant symphony of uncanny discord to the twisted posturings of the dancing bird-man.

'Peyote, I suppose,' said Jim shrugging, as if the scene was some mundane event from everyday life: a snooker match, perhaps, or the delivery of a pizza.

Mel and I had been dressed by Jim but we were smalltown librarians amongst this menagerie. Mel was in a leather catsuit and shiny, black peep-toe platform shoes like the lap girls wear down on the Strip. They eased her height to about six foot three, and she swayed over the crowd like a black mamba.

Her long leather coat, tailored at the waist, fell down to just above her ankles. Her ears were tricked out with long, diamante earrings. Her hair was the usual arrangement of untidy tendrils, almost rasta-tailed from the dust and some nostalgia pomade that she had applied when in the mood.

I wore a tiny, black, pleated skirt that barely covered the cheeks of my arse, and a tight, black cardigan, half-open to expose a white, lace push-up bra that thrust my breasts into a cleavage to cause car crashes. It was a bra that forced the wearer to take responsibility for an unfettered prominence that could only cause trouble. The right kind of trouble, I hoped. And then, to add to the snuff-movie Lolita, long, black knee socks and a pair of lace-up walking shoes with five-inch stiletto heels.

My eye make-up was carefully smudged, my lips as glossed as it was possible to be. My fringe flopped into my eyes and my hair was in a pony-tail with a black ribbon tied by Jim.

He said he didn't know if I had just escaped from jail or St Trinians. He liked me that way.

'And what does Mel look like?' I had asked carefully.

'Mel?' he said. 'Mel looks like the Queen Bitch that she is.'

He meant this as a compliment.

'Sit on the sofa in front of the fire, Stella, and we will find drinks.'

Jim and Mel disappeared into the crowd and I was left to slide into the corner of a big sofa that had been placed outside in front of the fire. And I stared silently at the shifting penumbra of post-modern freaks who contorted themselves into a mutual millenarian ecstasy of transported selves.

A man with two guns in embossed leather holsters

sat beside me and said his name was Dan. He was a Cancer and he had once maimed a man in Mexico City.

'Why?' I said.

'He took my parking space, hon'.'

His wife Bobby-Jo Anne had the highest wig I have ever seen. A billowing cloud of hard, white nylon blew around the top of her head like the poisonous gases that form a ring around a volcano. They said they were swingers.

'Dan's had an implant,' Bobby-Jo Anne said proudly. 'He's so big.'

Dan, it turned out, had flown to Miami in order to undergo a cosmetic reconstruction which had enhanced his girth and increased his length.

He unzipped his jeans and showed me the amended member. It bore little resemblance to any I had seen before, for the head seemed to have disappeared into a roll of flesh, much as a sausage disappears into the pastry of a sausage-roll. But it was very big, and very fat.

I wondered how it would be to sit on top of it when it was hard, although it was difficult to imagine what happened to this massy mass when the blood pumped into it, or what metamorphosis it could perform or shape it could take, having engorged itself with all the lucky reactions.

I watched Dan with invisible binoculars, for he was a new beast and his physiology should be noted for the future; implants were the thing, after all. As he said, 'Honey, it's no different to chicks gettin' their boobs done.'

'Very nice,' I said, prodding it gently. 'Was it expensive?'

'Honey, I had to mortgage the house and sell the horses. Nearly had to sell Bobby-Jo Anne here, but I don't think as anyone would have her.'

Bobby-Jo Anne thought this was highly amusing, and she giggled girlishly, beringed fingers pressed to lips.

'What are you doing, Stella?' said Jim, arriving and handing me a plastic glass full of red wine.

'Looking at that man's cock,' I said.

Jim sat down beside me so that he was between Dan and I. Dan put his expensive penis back into his trousers as carefully as a man replacing an Asprey jewel into its velveteen case.

Jim hauled me across his lap, lifted up my skirt and showed the swingers my new tattoo. He had refused to allow me to wear any panties that evening, so lucky Dan and Bobby-Jo Anne must have been presented with the full, peachy view of my bare arse and shaven lips.

'She got that yesterday,' he said. 'It's healing nicely, don't you think?'

'Sure is,' said Dan, leaning forward to inspect my buttocks more closely. 'Cute butt that gal has got there.'

'You can have a piece any time you like, sir,' said Jim.

'Yesirree,' agreed Dan

Mel picked up a tall man with a beard who turned out to be a woman. They started to slow-dance together. The man-woman's mouth rested in Mel's cleavage where he-she, as many before, found comfort and rest, and I pondered on the oddity of the penile arrangements in this domain. Those who were supposed to have them did not, while those who wanted them had bought them.

The bearded beauty looked as if she had availed herself of something, though it was difficult at this point to conclude exactly what.

Dan's hand crept between my legs. I was wet. He assumed it was for him and his implant but it was more than that: it was the nerves and the new sights and Mel getting off and Jim being so close that I could smell him.

'We could use ol' Ellie's caravan,' Dan said.

'OK,' said Jim.

Dan led the way. Jim held me by the hand.

Ellie's caravan was a mobile home decorated with the trappings of a lifestyle that described a woman whose children had not left home. There were Star Wars curtains and Barbie duvets, a playpen full of Fisher Price and a ceiling full of juddering mobiles whose aeroplanes and elephants knocked the visitor in the side of the head on entrance.

There was also a smell of patchouli and dope.

I caught a glimpse of myself in a Mickey Mouse mirror. I looked young because of the pony-tail and sulky because I always did. My face, in repose, was a permanent pout. No wonder men always wanted to slap me.

Dan removed his stetson, went down on his knees, lifted up the little pleated skirt, and tongued my wet pussy. Jim asked Bobby-Jo Anne to strip, which she did, revealing herself in a tasseled silver bikini brief. Her breasts were big, the nipples brown and hard, the muscles young and holding them firm.

I looked down at Dan. He was working hard but he did not sensate the area of my interest. I wanted to see how that expensive appendage worked.

'Show me your beautiful dick, Dan,' I said, kneeling down in front of him and reaching for his fly.

'Oh, hon',' he muttered. 'Honey, honey.'

It was not a disappointment. The shaft sprang out, swollen with excitement, and although not of a traditional design – in that there was no differentiation between the head and the shaft – the girth was huge.

I wondered, briefly, if I would be able to take it.

Of course I would.

But I had never seen anything like it. Would Jim be offended by this greater dimension? Intimidated at all?

Of course he wouldn't.

'Please may I sit on Dan's dick?' I said to Jim, for I always asked permission in group scenarios.

'You may,' he said.

Bobby-Jo Anne was sucking his dick. He was happy. I was glad it was her and not Mel. This thought flickered past with no time for further analysis, for now Dan was lying on top of Barbie with his offering of tension and elevation and, looking at it, weird though it was, I felt all the muscles of my inner pelvis relax and widen, as if the nerves themselves had eyes and were getting ready for this new experience.

'Baby, it's only an old car with a new engine,' he said, as if, in the past, women had needed encouragement. 'You're not scared, hon'?'

''Course not,' I said.

'Sit on Dan at once, Stella,' said Jim, whose erection was funnelled down Bobby-Jo Anne's throat. She kneeled in front of him, naked except for the bikini and cowboy boots, but his eyes were watching me, as they always watched me when I was making out with somebody else. Even when he disappeared into orgasm, he would come back quickly, look around, check up on me, see where I was.

I was never alone when I was in a crowd with Jim. He understood all the subtleties of this sex, all the little dynamics and dangers, and he was always at his most sexy and protective, and so it was like making love to him by proxy. I was only ever really with him, no matter with whom I was engaging.

I straddled Dan, pushed the condom down on him and lowered myself slowly, heels digging into the nylon cover, shaved pussy sensating every surface, and

192

tingling before I got all the way down and filled myself up.

'You're home, hon',' he said. 'And you sure do feel good on ol' Dan's pecker.'

I closed my eyes and moved up and down, massaging his shaft with my excited groove. Dan closed his eyes and allowed himself to push all the way into me.

Jim came in Bobby-Jo Anne's face, which I thought slightly impolite. Then he spread her on the floor and gave her the full force of his hard-on so I knew she was having a good time.

I fucked the medical miracle, sliding up and down, feeling every bit of it. It had power. It would have had more if it had not been attached to Dan who, in the end, was not Jim, but closing the eyes helped, for then I found myself in some other place with a range of new, clitoral sensations.

'Now I'm gonna fuck you,' I said.

And again I caught myself in the Disneyland mirror, my face flushed, my mouth sulky and determined, my lips swollen with sex.

God, I was selfish. I didn't care about this man at all. All I cared was whether his surgically reinforced dick was going to get me off. I was just a mindless body, psyche moulded into a masochist-minx by Jim, body a ganglia of narcissist nerve-endings, but in control; on top and in control. It was a different power, this butch-femme aspect. I did not play with it often. I like to relinquish rather than organise, and Lord knows I did not want to teach. Still, the assertiveness was a change and I wondered briefly if I would go from switch to total bitch, leaving behind the child that wanted to be ruled and emerging into cruel authority.

Jim didn't know what he was playing with, allowing these Technicolor philanderings. Who knew what I might find in these experiments? I could become someone new and that person would no longer be interested in conforming to his rulings.

I rode Dan, relishing the frenzy of his supplication and bathing in my own prowess, the power of my pelvis and the intimations of the woman's natural strength, a strength in which I was only perfunctorily interested. Still, it was always entertaining to enjoy a new show.

So I did: I got myself off, thanks as much to my own selfish skills as to his erect prowess. He, experienced in such things, as swingers are, knew the art of sexual orchestration. He achieved a simultaneous orgasm with impeccable timing. And again, because swingers are like that, his wife echoed her release at the same time with a screeching noise that reminded me obscurely of a country-and-western song.

'Did you enjoy that,' said Jim.

'Yes.'

'Yes what?'

'Yes, thank you.'

Mel was still dancing with the beard. She looked as if she was in love but I knew that she probably was not. Jim stared at them, unblinking.

'Perhaps I should break them up,' he said.

'Why?' I said.

'For something to do.'

Suddenly I was bored of his endless plurality. Why did everything have to be manipulated? Why couldn't he let things be and allow things to evolve naturally, see what happened in the end? Why did he always have to have a say in the conclusion? He was an egomaniac and a solipsist and I was tired of being invisible.

'Do what you like,' I said.

I turned my back and got ready to go off to find the

girl with the golden hand. He could do what he liked. I wanted to love him but he wouldn't let me. Every little flickering of affection and generosity was served back at me; he did not want anything real and I was bored of it.

I had an ineluctable attraction to resolve and this did not involve penile operations and lacquered wigs. And it did not involve Jim.

He stared at me, surprised and, for the first time, he did not know quite what to do. Switch bitch was something he had not seen before. I had always been so malleable. Now there was a minute in the midst of this carnival where he knew the chaos of the unknown. It took him by surprise and he could not handle it. He even looked vulnerable. If he had kissed me, I would have melted back into him, but he did not. He was angry, I suppose, and confused, and I was untethered. The dynamics had shifted and he was no longer in charge. This was a flickering mercurial thing, but in that moment, an element of true reality. He was at a loss for words.

He was about to gather himself up and pull back his command like a man in a river grabbing at an offered branch, but by that time I had disappeared into the night. And, for the first time since I had met him, I did not care what happened or what he did. He could even fall in love with Mel if he wanted. He could marry her and have five children and talk about the prices in Mothercare, for all I cared. He could push strollers and talk wet and be a big girl's blouse. God. He could even join the race of straights who thought they knew it all because they had managed to plant their seeds, blissfully, smugly ignorant of the basic fact that if there is one thing anyone can do, it is replicate the monsters that lurk in genetic pools. It is not a miracle: it is a boring fact of human life. It is the one thing that makes everyone the same.

Anger made me insult him in my mind and expect the worst. I saw him submerged in the ultimate horror of submission which was to conform to the universal codes. But what did I want from him? This was a cruelly unanswerable question because the truth lay in a chaos of ill-defined emotions and not in any of the canny analysis of rationale.

My head wanted him all to myself, but my cunt knew that would erode erotica as insecticide burns weeds.

The detached observer might comment that he was a man in a no-win situation, but at that point, I did not know anything much, though, if it had been discussed, I would have argued that I had never won anything.

Ah, the power and the people and the love. I was still fighting, I was young and I was fighting. I hardly even knew what for, driven as I was by the simple but complex forces that are uncontrolled hedonism. I was thirty. Why shouldn't I do as I pleased? You're old at thirty, then sometimes it feels as if you will never get older.

And so I strode out into the inferno of oddities, a stranger alone in a strange land, a slave-slut with a tattoo on her arse and a head full of anger and confusion and decadent requests.

I was in luck.

She was sitting down, looking at the fire, a joint in the fingertips that weren't gold.

She looked like a young boy. She had dark hair cut short and her face was flushed from the glow of the fire.

'Hullo,' I said.

'Hullo,' she said, handing me the joint. 'I'm Max.'

I waved the joint away. 'No thank you: makes me paranoid.'

She shrugged adolescently. She was a mixture of girlish innocence and boyish belligerence. Her eyes were dark brown and sad and decorated with long, black, lucky lashes. A scar ran down one side of her face, its origins difficult to determine, as with most facial scars, for what can their meaning be except for some gangland fight or freak accident or terrifying, childhood thing?

She had a good mouth, full lips set in an expression of determined subversiveness.

She wore a T-shirt saying WEIRD AND WONDERFUL with a plaid shirt worn over it, defying the observer to understand how her mechanical digits were attached to the end of her arm.

Her leather belt had a beaded holster with a knife in it, a working knife as if she spent time gutting fish or cutting rope. Her drainpipe jeans were quite clean but her cowboy boots were scuffed and old.

I arranged myself on the ground with some care, as the skirt was very short. I made sure my buttocks eased comfortably down on to the rug on which she was sitting.

'You're not wearing panties,' she commented.

'No.'

'You should wear panties, girl. You'll catch cold.'

'Please may I touch your hand.'

She blinked, surprised. 'If you wish.'

It was cold and hard, of course, since it was made of gold. Each joint was articulated and the nails were long and made of pointed metallic flecks, gold also, though darker. It seemed possessed of nearly as many movements as a normal hand, but less delicately accomplished, and less graceful. It was sinister, beautiful and efficient.

She had been a member of an anarcho-pyromaniac performance group working out of a Dumbo warehouse in Manhattan. They were judged to be a success in that they had managed to blow quite a lot of things up without getting arrested – and their GI Joe Inflammatory 1996 had earned them nationwide attention – but one day she had got the mix wrong and a canister had exploded in her hand.

She had decided to turn her deformity into a jewel. So now she was a walking confrontation or liberated disabled person, depending upon how you looked at it. I thought the mechanical digits enhanced her and I could not imagine her without them.

She was sexy because she was centred. She was sexy because she slept with women and had never even considered a man and this was a strength unto itself. She was sexy because she had lived in San Francisco, she had suffered the spiritual rigours of advanced body modification (cutting, burning, scarrification) and she knew it all.

She saw pleasure as a chemical sea whose currents were controllable if one knew how. As a fisherman knows which currents will bring in the whitebait, he also knows that those familiar currents are part of nature's insurmountable power, an unpredictable and stronger force over which no one can rule; so she knew this about the body. Its currents could be used. But she also knew they dredged emotions from the deep bed of the psyche and these must be seen and cared for if they were not to destroy. She respected unpredictability. She was a wise woman.

We rode her motorbike away, away from Jim and Mel, away from the twisting oddities and feathered shamans, into the desert night, and in the midst of nothing, we lay on her sleeping bag.

She lit a candle and I took her clothes off because I

wanted to. She was lean and had beautiful skin and a pierced labia from which chains hung in various ropes.

I would have fought off anyone who came near her. Something about her made me jealous and possessive. I wanted to protect her. And, of course, you would never have guessed this to look at us, two young women, limbs tangled in limbs, smooth flesh, pelvis on pelvis, lips on lips, breast on breast. Our bodies entwined like an Indian drawing or some kind of erotic decoration, and there was a brief, interesting moment when, lips locked and legs plaited together, with my shaved pussy brushing on her chains, that we wrestled for control.

Somebody had to be on top, somebody had to be the strongest and the fittest, and so there was a struggle of rolling buttocks and clenched biceps, determined faces. It was very subtle, and nothing was said, but one minute I was underneath her and the next she was underneath me, then, as subtly and as silently as the struggle had begun, it stopped and we lay side by side, not caring who was where (this a first for me), equal, really.

None of these things were said, as they rarely are when one is making love, but the intangibles floated over the thought processes and were gradually played through, little dramas of actions and emotions and thought all meshing together, until finally, some time later, looking back, one assimilates and is amazed by the unfathomable complexity.

Her hand was lethal and she used it as an implement of arousal and tease, an erotic threat, running the nails down my back, gently at first as a tickle that spread all over the spine, and then harder, delicately slicing the skin and then licking away my blood.

And yes, there they were, the endorphins, for she eased me into the pain of the cutting and then let me stay there, allowed the pleasure to come up to the pain and work against it, and then lifted her hand, her natural hand, deep inside me, manipulated me into a shivering wetness and, though she was doing these things, I could only see her as the girl, a girl, an innocent in need of protection: this was, I think, because I saw the deep wounds in those soft eyes, for, in the end, scars were scars and they signified old pain, and the public did not revere little lesbians with scarred cheeks and deformities.

There was unseen anguish and this, I think, was responsible for the effects she had on me. I was her vixen mother.

This was a new. It took me by surprise. I did not say anything, but I wondered where it had come from and where it was going to go.

As I watched her and she came, I reflected that this was the first time for a long time that I had been without some kind of costume. I was accustomed to being dressed in tartlet guises, slithering in and out of skins for all the various dramatics that excited Jim.

Now, here I was, all the imperfections laid out for the observation of this strange girl-woman. I could not tell what she thought of me at all. She was very silent: even when she came, it was to herself, and though she liked to play and tease, she rarely laughed. Everything seemed very serious to her but she knew where to put her fingers and she knew how to kiss.

We lay in post-climax calm. Nothing was said, but there was familiar intimacy. She had met my body. We did not know each other, but there was an eternal familiarity that made one believe in the concept of old souls meeting again.

We rode back. It was around 4 a.m. but the energy of the gathering was not flagging. It was more frenzied if anything, unnaturally so.

Mel had attracted an audience and was slowly and

deliberately taking her clothes off to a soundtrack by Sonny Lester, king of the tease track. She was starring in this show for the woman with the beard and for Jim, both of whom were staring with sensuous enjoyment on their faces as the leathers peeled off to reveal breasts and belly and buttocks. Mel as leather-woman Salome: an intriguing tableau.

And she sure was lewd. Presenting herself for the tribe's delight, she slowly caressed herself, fingering her own nipples, and making them hard, pushing her hands down into the front of her black thong. Now she was only thong and boots and big, wild hair, in some erotic dreamtime of her own, everything shaking, dervishlike, whipping the hypnotised gawpers into wanting only her, teasing them because they would never have her, though they would see it all; those two firm, round buttocks pressed into their faces, all lewd winking orifices and puckered provocation. She spread her cheeks and pushed her bunghole out, dropped down on to all fours like a cat, spread her cheeks again, pushed her bunghole out, swept up on to her feet again, belly-danced fast and furiously, leaped down into the splits, scissored her legs above her head, her excited cavity flowing into the satin of the thong and making a patch, dancing to be fucked, but cavorting only in the torment of tease.

She knew what she was doing, showing nearly all and pulling back, and because she was big and tall, long-legged, fleshily built, Amazon woman, she could present and pull back, present and pull back, and always retain her power.

I could see Jim, mesmerised by this act (learned from many years spent in *demi-monde* Soho clubs), wanting to struggle, then lay claim, then control.

He ignored me. He simply pretended that I was not there. This was his anger; genuine anger, not playtime anger. My heart lurched, but it was not stimulated to erotic rebuttal as it usually was, now abhorring the vacuum that he had set up and wanting to fill it with my need.

'I'd like to go home,' I said to him. 'I'm tired.'

'I want to stay,' he answered. 'Get your little girl-friend to take you.'

This was as good as a slap, which I probably would have received if I stayed near him for many more minutes. Then everything might change again. Who knew? Perhaps I should have stayed and fought with him and for him, regained my ground on the terrain of his emotional life, steered him away from Mel by offering him my fanny and my mind and playing the old tunes that we knew so well.

I was vaguely aware that I had this power and I could have done it. All it needed was a little energy, a little nerve. I was equipped, after all, with all the knowledge of his predilections.

I could have simply dropped down on all fours and crawled across the ground in front of him. I could have kneeled down at his feet and kissed his feet and played in a place of total submission. I could have begged for his cock, begged to suck it, have him come in my face, let him come in my face, that task of the submissive. I could have looked up at him from semen-dripped cheeks and kissed him with my dirty lips and been as lewd as any x-rated slut. I knew these things would have lured him back, despite the delights supplied by Mel's judicious pleasing.

In the past we had never reached this stage, as he had never lost control and I had never wanted him to. I liked him to command and I liked to know where I was and this was simple.

He pulled down my panties, pushed me up against

the wall and fucked me. He turned me round, pushed me down, took my arse.

He lifted my skirt and fingered me when and where he pleased. He tied me and bound me and deliciously licked me. He whipped me and raped me but never hated me. I had always, basically, done as he wished, though playing imaginatively so that everything remained interesting.

I was his when he wanted and this had made things simple. My body submitted and my heart was his, but my mind? My mind had not and this, in the end, was probably what fuelled his hostility. He wanted my mind.

It was difficult to fathom why he had reacted to this little liaison. I could not imagine that he felt threatened. He never felt threatened by anything. I am sure he did not know himself. He certainly would not have asked himself: men so rarely do. They do not tend to question their inner workings or untangle their complexities. I had made him jealous in the past, on purpose, as part of foreplay. We both knew where we were. I would provoke. He would punish and fuck. It was a good old routine, a line dance to which we both knew the steps, and a show of immense pleasure.

Genuine anger, though, was now settling about the place, the genuine anger that arises from familiarity and frustration and hostility. It was as if all the cards had been played and nobody knew how to end the game.

He could have slapped me and I would have wanted to kiss him and then we would have made out. Fighting and fucking: there's nothing like it. But the energy had drained out. I was very, very tired. I wanted to be alone, and in bed, and away from this horse-playing heterodoxy.

'I'll take you home, honey.'

Bernie appeared from nowhere, his face suddenly very close to mine. His breath was full of beer and his eyes were mad and staring, but at least he was there.

'Bernie,' I said. 'I didn't know you were here.'

'Came about an hour ago,' he said.

'I'll go with Bernie,' I told Jim.

'Do as you please,' he said coldly.

'I will.' I wanted to add 'you motherfucker' but I did not want him to gain the benefit of my anger, for this would have shown an interest in his petty moodswings.

Max gave me her card. It had a Celtic graphic, an e-mail number and the information that she was the editor-in-chief of *Bod Mod* magazine.

'Will I see you again?' I asked.

'I don't know,' she said. 'Who can tell?'

She was right and sensible. We were from two different worlds that had momentarily collided. Now I was returning to mine and she would ride her bike to hers. I lurched towards an instant life-changing romantic decision: to get on the back of that bike and disappear into the unknown horizon with Max. Mad Max. There would be a seismic upheaval and I would leave the known places to find new adventure. Travel sandy plains and through pump stations, be Marilyn in *The Misfits* or girl on a bike, a gypsy woman. I would just trust the love, turn my back, and go. But this is the stuff of movies and all the *faux* promises of screenplay romance.

No one really lives happily in the end. Nothing is perfect. There are only ever fleeting moments. Maybe if she had encouraged me, I would have acted out the movie, spurned by Jim's rejection, but as it was, I kissed her long and hard and felt my heart pierce with all the pinpricks of regret.

Bernie drove me home, jamming the jeep through dusty tracks and slamming it aggressively around corners so that we swung this way and that in our seats. The desert was dead black. Only the headlights lit the way and it wasn't until we had been jolting along at fifty miles an hour for twenty minutes or so that I realised we were not going in the direction of the ranch.

I did not know where we were going, but the landmarks, such as they were, were unfamiliar. We seemed to be winding further and further up a mountain and through a dark forest, the trees sprouting up as thin, black silhouettes against the dark-blue sky.

'Is this a short cut?' I shouted.

'Wa'?'

'Is this a short cut to the ranch?'

'Nah.'

He wiped his mouth with the back of his hand and stared at me, eyes wide, lips stretched into a laughing rictus of triumphant glee.

'I want to go home, Bernie. Now!'

'Well, you can't,' he said. 'We're goin' up the mountain to Jake's cabin and we're gonna have ourselves a little campin' expedition.'

'I don't want to, Bernie. I'm tired, I want to go home. Please.'

But he just started laughing maniacally and slamming his hands up and down on the wheel and kicking his legs and then accelerating so that even the jeep in four-wheel drive was skidding on loose stones.

'For Christ's sake, Bernie!' I shouted, furious now rather than frightened. I was not frightened of him. He was a child, after all, eminently controllable. He would do as he was told in the end: he was just having an annoying and selfish episode, propelled by the wild imaginings of over-excitement and liquor.

'Bernie!' I shouted again.

But he took no notice and slammed the jeep up the hill, further and further into the woods and up the mountain. Miles, it seemed, of rocking up and down on those hard seats.

'Bernie, please. I'll come with you another time. Not tonight. I want to sleep in my own bed tonight.'

'Oh no, lady! You're staying with me tonight. We'll have a lil' slumber party.'

Now I was nervous. Jim had warned me. Bernie could do anything. I hardly knew him and now he was abducting me. He had been in prison. He had a history of violence. And I realised, as exhaustion was replaced by the adrenalin rush of panic, that he might well be capable of anything. Anything at all.

The headlights flickered on to a sign saying WARN-ING! RATTLE-SNAKES and then a sign saying DANGER! KEEP OUT!, and Bernie pulled the hand-brake up in front of a wooden cabin.

There was an oil-lamp flickering in the window and the door was ajar.

'Bernie, I'm not going in there. You can bloody forget it. Take me home.'

He got out of the car and went into the house.

'Come on,' he said. 'It sure is cosy here. You'll love it.'

'I will not love it. I want to go home, you fucking bastard.'

He ignored me and went into the house. I could hear his boots thumping up and down on a wooden floor, clattering about. I could smell a fire.

Oh, God.

It was cold and it was getting colder.

I was stiff with cold and cold with fury. My jaw started to ache, as did my back. My teeth started to chatter and tears welled in my eyes.

Oh, Christ.

Bernie reappeared. I stared at him pathetically, too tired to resist.

206

'Come on,' he said, then lifted me out of the passenger seat and carried me into the smoky cabin and laid me down on the soft fur of some bed.

He was going to rape me, and I was too tired to stop him. He was going to fuck me and do God knows what to me up there in this deserted mountain where no one knew where we were. But I was so tired, and for God's sake, it was Bernie. Surely he couldn't be a criminal sex-killer. Surely not.

Chapter Eleven

I awoke with a jolt to see a window with a view, to clustered hordes of pines through which dawn was filtering. My head ached, my back ached, my bladder ached and, I quickly realised, my wrists ached because they were tied together with nylon rope. My clothes had been removed and placed in a neat pile on the end of the bed. I was wearing a pair of baby-doll pyjamas, pink, frilly and cotton, and I was accompanied by a teddy bear.

'Bernie's gonna look after you.'

I twisted around on the bed to see that he was sitting in an armchair, fully clothed, staring at me. There was a rifle across his lap and a sheath knife in his belt. He stared at me with a look that could have been described as affection if the context had been different; as it was, in these circumstances, the softness became the inappropriate leer of the delusional.

'Well, you can begin by untying me and letting me go to the bathroom,' I snapped. 'Right now.'

He smiled slowly and stroked the tip of the barrel of the gun with his finger.

'You're gonna stay here with Bernie for a bit,' he said. 'I'm gonna save you . . .'

'Well, I'll piss on the bed, then.'

'You piss on the bed and you'll lie in it . . .'

'Please, Bernie. It's beginning to really hurt.'

'The toilet's outside.'

'Oh for God's sake. Where are we? Just let me go. I won't run away, I swear.'

He came over to the bed and pressed a hand down on my stomach so that I nearly wet myself there and then.

'Bernie!'

'OK, you can go to the bathroom. But I'm taking you.'

'OK. Anything.'

'Put on these little slippers I bought you.'

He put a pair of white, towelling mules on my feet and dressed me in a short, pink, satin dressing gown.

'Untie my hands, Bernie. I can't do it like this, can I?'

He untied my hands, took one of them, led me out of the cabin and across a patch of land to a group of small outbuildings where an evil-smelling loo stood. He swung open the door and watched intently as I squatted. By then I was too desperate to relieve myself to care where I was or what he was doing.

Then he led me back into the cabin and re-tied my hands in front of me.

'Bernie's gonna make you a nice breakfast and then we're gonna have a lovely romantic day together, just you and me.'

My heart sank. I could be in real trouble here. Bernie had kidnapped me and who knew what he was capable of? He was living in his own fantasy, gleaned from witnessing the events at the ranch.

He had seen me drunk and naked. He had seen me tied down, tied up, whipped, fucked and buggered. He probably thought I was anybody's, which, in some ways, I was, but he did not understand that the choice should be mine. He did not understand anything.

'I love you,' he said.

'If you love me, then let me go and take me home,' I said. 'I don't like it here and I don't want to be here. I want to go home.'

'This is your home now,' he said. 'We're gonna be very happy. I'm gonna look after you. And now I'm gonna make you a special breakfast.'

At least he didn't plan to starve me to death, but of his other plans I did not dare imagine. Anything could happen, and I did not like to be faced by the thought of anything.

The cabin was a large, open-plan room surrounded by windows on every side. There was one double bed on which I was lying, and a big sofa, sunken and lumpen with age. In one corner, there was a kitchen with a wooden table, a fireplace and two armchairs in front of it. It was very basic.

I had no idea where we were. My only hope of escape would be to steal the car key from Bernie, and how was I going to do that, unless I somehow got hold of the rifle, or incapacitated him in some way? And how was I going to do that? Even if I managed to free myself, I was never going to be able to physically disable him, unless I took him by surprise. I was well and truly his prisoner.

I thought of Jim and wondered how long it would take before he came to look for me. I wondered if Rick knew about this cabin, if anybody knew about this cabin. Certainly there were no local police to help. Jim and Mel would have to take the matter into their own hands and find me themselves. I wondered dismally if Jim would care enough to come and find me, or if he was enmeshed in some passionate affair with Mel and

would just leave me to it. He might think that I had
gone with Bernie on purpose. I had flirted enough with
him after all. Jim might think that I had gone volun-
tarily, left him even. After all our last contact had not
been friendly.

Bernie fiddled about in the kitchen and the smell of
frying bacon filled the air.

'Bernie,' I said quietly. 'You're not going to hurt me,
are you?'

He turned around, genuinely surprised.

'Of course not,' he said. 'Why would I want to do
that? I love you. You're beautiful.'

But who knew what love meant to Bernie? I doubted
that he had had much experience of this particular
affliction, and any experience that he had had doubtless
served to derange his mind and imprint conclusions
that did not lie within any traditional tenets.

Bernie's understanding of love, I suspected, was a
mixture of naïve delusion and wrong-headed deduction
based on a range of unhealthy experiences.

Jim and I and Mel were to blame. We had allowed
Bernie to observe our maverick scenes and provided
him with a live peep-show for the purposes of our own,
unthinking amusement.

Blinded either by vain conceit or lack of understanding, we had been mistaken in this arbitrary choice. Our
excitements had somehow fermented in his mind,
twisted up with his simple perspectives, and created a
series of ideas of which this scene was now the result.

He thought that I should be saved from Jim's cruelty
because he could not understand the tapestry of complicated subtexts that interwove these dynamics. How
could he have done? They would have confused many
people more experienced and sophisticated than he.

So now there was this predicament: an enforced
elopement where I was the princess bound in the hands

of Bernie, forced to react to his deluded will, all power taken from me, forced to face rough uncertainty.

I was nervous and anxious, and angry, but I was not mortally terrified. This was Bernie, after all. A child. I could not believe that he intended to inflict genuine injury on me on purpose, though in my bleaker moments, I realised that he could hurt me out of sheer stupidity, clumsiness and incomprehension of reality.

He was stronger than I, but I fancied that I was cleverer. I fancied that I still had some control, but I was to come to realise that there is no control when the second person is as determined and as deluded as Bernie.

The sun rose and warmth seeped into the cabin, trapped inside by the wooden walls. Bernie opened some windows and the front door, which opened out on to a vista of tall pines and, in the distance, a river.

'There's bears out there in the woods,' he said. 'Friend of mine, Dirk – used to be in the CIA – he got killed by a bear. This was his cabin before he gave it to me. He lived up here on his own, for years. No one knew where he was; tax men, nobody. He was on the run, I think; seen terrible things in South America, I reckon; knew the government's secrets, germ warfare 'n' all. Bit of a drinker, too, I have to admit. Liked his liquor, did Dirk. And those hallu hallu hallucinogenerics. Anyways, they found his body all twisted up like a pretzel, and bloody, with gore an' all.'

I sat up on the bed. My wrists were still tied. I looked around, trying to be grateful that at least he had not blindfolded or gagged me.

He clattered around in the kitchen with a frying pan and bacon and eggs, put a plate on the table, then led me over to it and untied my hands.

'Now,' he said. 'You're not gonna run away, are ya?'

'Where am I going to run to, Bernie?' I snapped.
'How long are you going to keep me here, Bernie?'

'Eat your breakfast.'

I wasn't very hungry but I knew that I had to keep
up my strength if I was going to work out a way of
getting on top of this situation.

'Good, huh?'

He shovelled lumps of bacon and egg into his mouth.

'Yes.'

'Yes, thank you.'

'Yes, thank you.'

'Good girl. Now. Bernie's gonna give you a lovely
bath and show you all the beautiful things he has
bought you to wear.'

'There isn't a bathroom!'

'I know that, honey, but there's hot water and there's
a bath.'

He left the room and walked back into it, dragging
an old-fashoned tin bath, the kind the Victorians used,
in front of the fire. He filled it carefully with hot water
from the kitchen sink.

'Now, honey, take off those little pyjamas so Bernie
can bathe you.'

Now he was staring at me, blue eyes unblinking and
fixated, the stare of immutable concentration. I don't
think anyone had wanted to see my body as much as
this man, and for a fleeting moment, a few seconds, no
more, I was pleased. He was staring and I basked in
the stare, forgetting the circumstances. I liked the
attention.

This thought was routed by the basic irritation that I
was not here of my own accord, and I sulkily removed
the little cotton top so I was naked except for frilly
knickers. My nipples were brown and hard from anxiety rather than excitement, or perhaps both. I was
confused and did not know.

I peeled down the frilly knickers and now he had it all. I stood in front of him, nude, pussy bald as the day Jim had forced it to be painfully waxed, smooth, long legs, curved hips, firm breasts, round cheeks that swayed when I walked and served to give me a wanton wiggle.

All of me was here for him to see. I felt an old innocence that I had not known for some time, some pre-virginal memory where I had once been untouched and untainted, when my body had been fresh and smooth and young and there had been naïve pleasures.

I could not understand why I should feel like this, Bernie was beginning to affect me, and my flesh was not conforming to any messages supplied by my brain, messages where reason might rule. My body was reacting to some unseen sense of security and admiration and irrational trust.

His breath withdrew and then became heavy.

'You're a very, very beautiful lady,' he said with genuine awe.

I know that, Bernie, I thought to myself, but what I don't know is why I am conforming to your outlandish lores and why your presence, your idiotic naïvity, your irritating denial of reality, why these things are luring me to enter a state of sensual innocence that existed many years ago, before the first awakening.

I shivered and a small beat of panic pumped into my stomach. I was vulnerable. Very vulnerable. And I still did not know what I was dealing with.

I stepped into the tin bath so that I was knee-deep in the hot water, and then slowly lowered myself into it, watching his face as I did so. I was still uncertain. The rifle lay harmlessly on one of the kitchen chairs, but he still had the power to push me down into the water and drown me if some maniacal urge overcame him and he turned out to be the murderer of his reputation.

'Not too hot?' he asked.

'No. It's OK.'

'Sit down, then.'

I lowered all the way in, easing my body slowly under the water.

He picked up a large tin jug and poured hot water over my shoulders. I had to admit that this felt good, and comforting, despite myself.

Then he soaped a big, soft sponge and he washed under my arms, on my back and over my breasts, his breath hot on my face, his hands gentle but firm, as if he knew what he was doing. His arms were powerful, biceps swollen from labour or working out. He was strong, I could tell that. I hoped that he was not going to us this strength against me.

Finally he made me stand up and face him and he washed between my legs, attending to my most intimate place and arousing it. There was nothing I could do but allow him this privilege. I could have tried to slap him away, or scream but I did not want to ignite any violence that might lurk within him.

I still did not know him, or what he intended to do, what he wanted to do with me in the end. I did not know if he could suddenly erupt in mad fury and vent old rages and frustrations. I had to handle him carefully and so I offered him my fanny as a gift of appeasement. Meanwhile, I watched him with animal cunning, observing his every action, his very demeanour, to glean information that could be used to my advantage.

He massaged my clitoris gently with the sponge and, without any warning, I found myself in a strange place of intimate trust. He was gentle. He was turning me on. Against my very will, he was turning me on. My head was still resisting but my body was behaving independently of sense and reason. My groin tingled, and then ached. My cunt moistened inside. I could feel it. It liked

215

that soft sponge and those big hands and the way that he adored me, caressing me with humility and love.

Suddenly, terribly, unreasonably, insatiably, I wanted to get fucked. I wasn't sure if I wanted Bernie to fuck me, but I wanted to be penetrated by a well-proportioned tool and I wanted it as soon as possible. I was accustomed to getting what I wanted. I closed my eyes and groaned. What was happening here?

He continued to rub me, gently and carefully, as if he knew where every single one of my nerve-endings were. Bernie! Bernie, who could not even have pronounced the word erogenous, was homing in on those zones with surety and uncanny expertise.

'That's good, huh, baby?'

Now I was little girl in the bath being cared for by kind daddy. Climbing into a realm of sensuality, my reason climbed further and further away. I was no longer myself.

'Yes,' I was forced to admit. 'I want to come.'

'You'll come when Bernie says you can, and if I catch you playing with yourself, there'll be trouble, you understand?'

I groaned. My cunt was on fire; I was past caring about repercussions. I didn't know if I could stand it and, instead of thinking of escape, I began to wonder how I could get away, finger myself in private, get myself off without him finding out.

'Yes, I understand.'

He wrapped a voluminous cotton bathtowel around me and dried my body, again making sure that his hands passed between my legs, rubbing me up into a frenzy of wet need.

But he made no effort to kiss me or to engage in any form of foreplay. I half expected him to force me down on to his hard dick and fellate him, but he did not. He was just hands and touch. It was like being with a master masseur who knew all the muscle groups and did not have sex with his clients.

I became dazed with conflicting sensations. It was as if the circuits had jammed because they could no longer analyse the impulses and relay any coherent message. My clitoris was swollen and begging for attention; my head was ringing with alarm.

'I want you to wear these pretty little dresses that Bernie has bought you,' he said. 'I don't like those things he makes you wear, those –' he shuddered and rolled his eyes '– those prostitute's clothes.'

He laid out three cotton dresses, some cotton bras and panties, all very plain and innocent, but not so in these circumstances.

The dresses were all roughly the same style: very short, loose smocks with puffed sleeves and scoop necks and buttons down the front. The hem floated high on my thigh, so that when I bent over, it floated over the bottom of my buttocks.

'Stand there in front of me.'

I did as I was told, still naked, but warm from the bath. He sat down on the edge of the sofa and drank in my breasts, my waist, my thighs. Then he held out a pair of the cotton panties which were blue, to match one of the dresses, and indicated that I should step into them. I obeyed and he eased them carefully up my thighs and over my arse. I was still dribbling and prayed that he would not notice the little wet patch that would inevitably seep on to those panties, screaming out my want as clearly as if I had fingered open my lips and showed him the inside of my pussy.

'Turn around. I wanna see your butt.'

I turned around.

'Beautiful. Come here.'

The matching bra clasped in front. He stroked my breasts very lightly, perfunctorily even, and then dropped the blue and white gingham dress over my head. It was very short.

'Go over and sit at the kitchen table,' he said.

I sat down on a chair and he walked towards me with a hairbrush. At first I thought he was going to pull down my knickers and use it on my bottom, but his intention was more innocent than that. He wanted to brush my hair, as he had once seen Jim brush my hair and, perhaps, assumed that was what one did. He pulled the bristles back and forwards over my scalp and scraped my hair into a pony-tail which he wound into an elastic band.

'There,' he said. 'Look at yourself in the mirror.'

The mirror was old and cracked, and blemished with stains of green, but I could vaguely see that I looked five years younger. He had made me look like some voodoo Baby Doll.

He went over into my handbag and got out my compact and lipstick.

'See these?' he said, holding them up.

'Yes.'

He went over to the open front door and flung the make-up out with that powerful flick of arm, wrist and shoulder that men use when they are skimming stones or underarm bowling. The compact and lipstick flew into the air and landed somewhere in the far distance with a faint clatter.

'No make-up!'

'Oh, Bernie. For goodness' sake. There's nothing wrong with make-up.'

'Don't argue with me –'

'But –'

He walked up to me, looked down at my face, shook my shoulders and looked for a second as if he was about to cuff me.

'Don't argue with me! You do as Bernie tells you;

218

you be a good, little girl and we will have a nice time, but if you're bad, if you disobey ol' Bernie, then . . .'

He shook his head sadly.

'Now, there are some other rules that I want you to keep.'

I continued to sit at the kitchen table, remembering that he had untied me now and if the situation erupted into serious danger, I had at least a chance of escape, or even of defending myself.

'One. I do not want you to play with yourself, do you understand?'

'Yes.'

'Two. You will do all the cookin' and the housework.'

'OK.'

'Three. You will ask permission to go to the bathroom and you will not go out at any other time unless I give you permission and I am supervising. Do you hear me?'

'Yes.'

'Do you understand?'

'Yes.'

'Good. Now you're gonna lie on that lounger outside and I'm gonna tie you up while I go and look for some wood to chop.'

He led me to the day-bed which stood on the porch of the cabin and manacled one wrist to it with a pair of handcuffs, which, despite the slenderness of my hands, were impossible to escape from. I grimaced, thinking of Jim, who had never managed to find a manacle that would efficiently entrap me. But here, Bernie had availed himself of cuffs that truly bound. Where did he get them from? I could not imagine him frequenting a fetish shop, should there even be such a thing in these wild parts. But found them he had, and they provided more evidence that he was a quantity whose resources could not be predicted.

I looked up at him sulkily and he stroked the side of my cheek with one finger and smiled.

'Behave yourself.'

I was silent. When he had gone, I inserted the finger of my free hand into the leg of the cotton panties. Excitement was dribbling down my cervix and seeping into my pudenda. My pussy was hot and it was very, very wet.

'God,' I thought. 'This for Bernie? What's going on?'

Arousal, it seemed, was the result of Bernie beguiling me with a mixture of adoration and mastery. And all this with the frisson of fear that travelled in waves and passed through my body as a shiver and a racing heart.

I resented his actions, the presumption of them, but now he was gone, I could not help thinking about his dick: how big it was, how smooth, how the glans and corona and shaft looked when erect.

I imagined the tip of the head nestling into my burning outer lips, gently at first, and then slowly pushing into me so that I could feel every inch of it.

I rubbed myself slowly, and then more quickly, sending myself those compliments that turn into surges of pure pleasure until your throat opens, your head cricks back and you scream from the transcendental completion.

My fingers crept inside my panties. My legs were spread apart and I was rubbing faster and faster, dependent on my body to yield itself, succumbing totally to the vigour of my own hand. There was no self-control; my own vibrations led my own gyrations. I did not need love, I did not need scenes: all I needed was this. And I did it so well. So very, very well.

He was in my mind, naked, his prick quivering, ready to plunge into me and bring me to mad apoplexy. Then I opened my eyes and he really was there, standing two inches away, watching me with an expression that mixed surprise with fascination.

My fingers did not stop playing on their fleshy target. I could not stop. I hardly knew he was there, for my hands were guiding me to the top and the only thing that mattered was that final release. I was lost in this. I had to come and I did not care about anything else.

'Oh, yes! Yes! Yes!'

My voice echoed around the pine trees and a bird flapped out of the leaves, surprised by the sudden sound.

I was about to have my final reward, I was so nearly there, when he slapped my hand away from my groin and then slapped my thigh so hard that the red stain of the mark of his hand remained in the stinging flesh, each finger clearly defined.

I jolted into the present, desperate with savage frustration, everything in my body aching to finish myself off, prevented now from doing so, so all there was was terrible emptiness and need.

'What did I tell you?'

'Oh, Bernie. I'm sorry. But I was so turned on . . .'

'I'm gonna make sure you don't do that again, honey. From now on, both hands will be tied behind your back.'

He tied both hands behind my back, flipped me over on to my stomach, pulled my arse into the air, pushed the dress down over my hips and pulled the cotton panties down so I was positioned on the day-bed in a semi-doggy postion with my buttocks exposed to the mountain air, shameless and vulnerable.

I knew he could see that my lower regions were swollen and wet from where I had played with them, and I knew he could see my puckered back hole. He could see everything and he was not about to let me move from this position of abject passivity.

'Stay there and do not move,' he said. 'I want to see you in exactly this position when I return.'

I groaned. I was uncomfortable and I was frustrated and presenting my every orifice as open targets served to arouse me more. As they were naked, so my attention focused on them, and as my attention focused on them, so I wanted them attended to and filled up.

After ten minutes or so all I could think about was sex. There was no hunger, no fear, no thirst. Even the position in which my arms were forced caused little anguish. The only torment was the presented spectacle of my womanhood shrieking out to be gratified. And, of course, because my buttocks were naked and projected as a target, so all the scenes that Jim and I had entertained flickered through my mind; all the times that he had pulled apart my cheeks and inserted his rigid cock anywhere he pleased, slowly through my sphincter and into organic sanctums that would always remain mysterious, and hard and violent into my pussy, rapist, hardman, master, father, lover.

I resonated with the erotic memories of flesh flicked by the stinging tip of the whip, lined and burned until the heat spread ineluctably to my pulsating lips, and everything was on fire. The slap of the slipper on the thigh, the crack of the crop on flesh, the tears, the catharsis and release of old trauma. Where was he now, then? Where was he now, when I was alone and helpless and needed him?

I must have sat there, crouched, tied with my naked buttocks in the air, for half an hour or so. When Bernie returned, I was still wet because I still wanted it. In fact, when Bernie returned, I was beginning to feel desperate that he might not fuck me. I was actually beginning to want Bernie. He was triggering some arcane responses in my body, and this adversity was arousing me.

I would have done anything to receive his dick. As I heard his footsteps on the wooden boards, I prayed that he was going to give me instant satisfaction, that he was one of those men who could not hold themselves once they wanted it, that he would simply fuck me there and then. There need be no preliminaries after all: there were two available holes gaping and winking at him. He had put them on display and now he should relieve my torment.

But this was not going to be.

Bernie was a master of the fine art of withholding. He slowly came up to me and very gently stroked my bottom with light fingers, running them lightly over my anus and even more lightly under my pubis to feel my moistness. Then he withdrew. I nearly screamed out loud. What was going on? Did he not want me? Did he not fancy me? Why had he hauled me up to this deserted place if he did not plan to make love to me, to make love, or something akin to that, surely? What were this man's plans? What was in his mind? I had never met anybody like this before. He seemed beyond the range of the usual manipulation.

I did not know how I could make Bernie do what I wanted. He seemed to adore me, but he did not seem to want to fuck me. I shuddered with a spasm of violence. For about three seconds I wanted to kill him. This was replaced by a feeling of rejection and insecurity. This was mad. This could not be understood. He had taken me against my will and now he was making me as insane as he was.

'Get a grip,' I told myself. 'You're becoming carried away.'

'I have collected the wood,' he said. 'Now I am going to chop it. I want you to clean the house and then make something to eat.'

I was sulky and silent now and refused to look at him. And, of course, when he asked me why, I could not tell him the truth: I am angry because you will not fuck me. I could not let him know that. I didn't want him to have that much control. But in my mind, my hands were closing round his throat and I was slowly squeezing the life out of him.

He locked the front door of the cabin so that I was imprisoned inside while he worked on a block some distance away.

There were various aged brushes and dusters, and rusting cans of polish and bleaches that must have been in that cabin since Nixon was in power.

Crouched amidst the filth and dust and sticky cobwebs, watching the long-legged fauna scurry here and there. I half expected to find the remains of old Dirk, the CIA man.

It was a difficult job. Clouds of dust rose and settled back in their original position, rendering the task rather pointless. I seemed to have wiped through one smear when another appeared. There were patches of sticky, coagulated grease that had settled in the corners like some Josef Beuys sculpture and could not have been moved if I had tried all day.

And all the time I was thinking: if this pleases him, then he will fuck me.

The same thoughts kept coming as I dressed the chicken and peeled the potatoes.

He seemed pleased, wandering around the cottage inspecting the work. He sat down at the kitchen table. I served him silently and then sat down beside him. My hands were free but he had locked the front door with the key hanging from his belt. I could not have escaped unless I knocked him out.

'I think I saw bear prints out there,' he said. 'Big ol'

thing. I'll have to make sure I have the gun with me when I go out. Could be very, very dangerous.'

Outside the window, evening was falling, the silhouettes of the trees growing spiked and black against a royal-blue sky.

He lit an oil lamp so that shadows danced around the walls of the cabin and then crouched in front of the fire and blew it into life.

'Clear everything away from the table,' he said.

I washed up and he watched me as I did so.

'Come here.'

He indicated that he wanted me to sit in his lap. At first, I hesitated. The rifle was down by his feet. I still was wary. But I was also hot.

I climbed on his lap, the little dress disappearing into my waist so that my thighs were naked and my knickers were exposed. He kissed the side of my neck.

'There you are,' he said. 'Better, huh, here with me?'

'Yes.'

'I'm very, very pleased and I am going to give you what you want.'

He slipped his finger into my panties and started to rub my clitoris. Excited already, I moaned and instantly succumbed to the pleasures.

'I'm gonna give you what you've been waiting for.'

He lifted the dress off over my head in one movement. Then he unclasped the bra so that my breasts were offered to him, naked and firm. He took each nipple and licked it slowly so that spasms shot up and down my body from clit to tit, tit to clit. I wanted this man.

'Lie on the table.'

I lay down on my back over the kitchen table, the fire flickering behind me and keeping me warm, the night growing darker and darker outside. There was a smell of smoke and fire and oil.

My body stretched over the length of the wooden surface, like a sacrifice on a pyre, ready for him to do as he wished, and when he wished.

He walked around me, studying every curve and every part of me, his expression slipping between far away, and a present where he had given himself this gift. Now it was finally his, my body, the thing for which he had longed since he met me; now it was totally under his power to watch or touch or kiss or fuck.

He was enjoying these seconds as a person might enjoy the beauty of a thing they have longed for in a shop, and have finally brought home after weeks of torment and longing.

He leaned forward.

'Do not move unless I tell you to. Do not speak unless I tell you to. Do not come until I give you permission. And do not close your eyes. I want you here with me.'

Then he kissed me very hard on the mouth, his tongue forcing his way down my throat, his right hand pressing down on my face, his left on my neck. On and on, insinuating his tongue, live and hot.

He pushed his fingers into me and he knew I wanted it. My pussy had been whining for it all day. Sexual overdrive and sensual self-interest had twisted my nerves and shouted into my brain, get this man on your side; get him on your side so he will fuck you.

I saw the bulge in his trousers and at last I knew for sure that this was not all a head-game. His pelvis had finally caught up with his instincts and, yes, he did fancy me.

'Do you want me to fuck you?'
'Yes.'
'You want me to fuck you?'
'Yes.'

226

He walked to the end of the table and pulled off my panties, inserted a finger to ensure I was wet. I wanted to scream, but I did not, I stayed silent, watching his eyes intently, as he watched mine. He was not going to let me escape into any private haven away from him: he had not brought me here for that.

He climbed on top of the kitchen table so that he was sitting astride me and, after undoing his flies, pushed his hard cock into my mouth, watching my eyes as his swollen organ was engulfed by my greedy lips and throat.

I gobbled, concentrating, wanting to please him, still terrified that he was going to withdraw again and leave me in the state of puzzled frustration with which I had been inflicted all day. And so I focused on enslaving him, because I knew that if I did not, he would not give me what I wanted. I stroked the shaft, and manipulated the base, flicking my tongue over the glans, up and down the shaft, bringing him to glistening excitement so that I knew he was climbing up towards a climax.

He could come in my face. He could fuck me. He could do anything he wished.

He pulled my body by the feet down to the end of the table so that my open labia were in line with the edge and my pussy was in front of his dick. He grabbed my legs and pulled them apart, and he entered me, using my legs as a brace to insert himself further and further in, his dick in perfect alignment with my pelvis. He could not have gone deeper if he had tried. On and on, he thrust and drilled me and gave me what I wanted.

I wanted to scream. I wanted to come. I could not bear it any longer.

And, as he knew that we both must finish, his eyes still staring at me, my eyes staring back, begging him to let me go, he said, 'OK.'

I screamed out as my body was at last allowed to go where it needed to go, my pelvis throttled forward into spasm after spasm, and the tears of this weird love that I could never understand prickled my eyelids, and, as one fell down my face, he continued to look at me.

Finally, finally, I was quiet again. He was still firm inside me. He pumped me hard, let me feel his release, let me feel the pulsing as the juices spumed from the end of it. His eyes remained staring at mine, but he did not lose control; he merely smiled and came and buttoned up his trousers. Calm.

He was a very strange man. Not the strangest I had ever known, but strange. Unreadable. I had fucked him but I still did not know if he was simple or complicated, stupid or bright, experienced or naïve.

Chapter Twelve

*L*ife in the cabin was both simple and complicated. Simple, because the amenities were minimal – there was no electricity – complicated, because the smallest tasks required effort. I remained Bernie's prisoner. He tied me up when he went hunting or if he drove to town to get provisions, and watched me closely if we were together and I was unfettered.

We spent two days locked in this surreal relationship. He bathed me, dressed me, fed me and fucked me, but did not share a bed with me. I would fall asleep as the oil lamp flickered and he would sit on the sofa cleaning his gun and drinking beer.

I was, of course, completely dependent on him for everything, from my food to basic freedoms. I was aware that if anything happened to Bernie, I could die up there in that cabin. He would not reveal exactly how far we were away from the nearest town but I knew it must have been more than twenty-five miles down rough mountain tracks.

Bernie did not speak of any plans – how long we were to stay in the cabin, for instance – or what was to happen in the future. I do not think he had any ideas. He spent his time in the present, and the present required all his mental energy to concentrate on me. He could not do more than this.

His conclusions about my character and what I needed were warped. Bernie was inevitably wrong if he thought about things, but, when it came to his instincts, he was uncannily correct.

He would play with me, sense me, and arouse me, and then he would fuck me. But he always, always made me wait. Always, always ensured that I had to complete various tasks, show the right attitude, do as he told me, before I was allowed to sit on that hard cock of his and ride him to my own pleasure.

He loved to look at me naked and I would spend much of the day wandering around the cabin without any clothes on while he would look at me, drinking me in as if I was the last woman on earth.

And, of course, he liked to control me. He would sometimes tie me to the kitchen chair and make me spread my legs so that he could see my swollen lips and the scarlet flesh of my pussy as it opened further and further, growing wetter and wetter in front of his gaze. And the more he made me display myself, the wetter I became. He would leave me in that chair, legs spread, naked, tied, becoming more and more aroused, and he would only look at me. He would not touch me. And I could do nothing. My hands were tied behind my back while my cunt became hotter and hotter and, eventually, I would start begging him to touch me. But he would still tease me. Leaving me tied, he would force his head between my spread legs and gently lick my aching button, licking and licking until I writhed and screamed and, though I would climax, and the juices would pulse into lips as he submerged his mouth into that most sexual of kisses, I would still want his cock. There was always something missing until I had that, filling me up, forcing me out of the cabin and leaving everything behind.

Bernie was more complicated than he appeared, and more imaginative. It was easy to dismiss him as a simpleton, an inept recidivist brainwashed by whatever wacko theory was doing the bars. He was uninformed and uneducated, but life had taught him odd things: how to survive in the forest, how to read tracks, how to distil alcohol in a bath, how to recognise one birdcall from another, and how to make love.

He could catch fish from the river that wound through the hills, trap rabbits and shoot birds. These we ate, though I refused to do anything with them until he had plucked or skinned or at least done something to them to make them less dead looking. The glassy, red-rimmed eye of a corpse was not my idea of either fun or dinner. But Bernie, of course, was accustomed to this form of survival. He had spent weeks up in this cabin alone, practising his gunmanship, tracking and snaring and pretending he was some soldier of fortune preparing himself for the final and inevitable apocalypse.

He had been in prison because he had held up a local bank with a knife. He had been drunk, he said. There had been a lot of drinking then, a lot of drinking and madness. He was a trailer-park kid: there had been five of them by different men; no one knew who was who because their mother had lost track ages ago. Two of them were still serving time in a federal penitentiary.

I felt I could handle him, but I was intimidated by the bouts of paranoia that threw his judgement into a realm I could not reach. He would suddenly insist that he heard the steps of men from the CIA outside the cabin and that their binoculars were trained on us. He would not let me out of his sight and, even then, he would level accusations that I was planning to run away, that I was seeing other men, that I didn't love him.

One morning we did see some genuine human beings. I was awoken by the crunch of their boots on the ground outside the cabin. Then a hideous face stared in at the window. It was wearing a green camouflage cap and a flak jacket and at first I thought that, at last, some special weapons and tactics operation had arrived to extricate me from Bernie's clutches.

Bernie leaped out of the sofa like a cat, grabbed his gun in one quicksilver, reflex action, and huddled against the corner of the window like a cowboy in a final shoot-out in a deserted building.

The stranger tapped on the window and shouted 'howdy'.

Bernie opened the door and let himself out.

The men were hunters out on expedition stalking deer. They had lost their way.

When Bernie re-entered the cabin, he pretended to be calm, but I noticed that there were beads of sweat on his forehead and his hands were shaking.

He behaved as if I were his wife. He believed the fantasy he had created in the cabin, forgetting that he had, for all intents and purposes, kidnapped me and that it was only by a freak of sexuality that I was not kicking and struggling and threatening police action.

As far as Bernie was concerned, we were a happy couple living in traditional, domestic bliss with clearly defined male and female roles. It was impossible to know when he would break through this delusion and reality would hit him. I suspected that it would not, and I began to form some contingency plans in my mind, but these were difficult as they all involved physically hurting Bernie so that I could take the keys and escape.

I did not want to hurt Bernie: he was deranged and

deluded but he was not vicious. Nevertheless, I knew that I would have to take matters into my own hands if I was not going to spend months in this isolated place. Bernie did not realise it, but I had a life to return to. He thought that my life was in the cabin with him, but he could not have been more wrong.

He had created a secret prison with incomprehensible pleasures. Nevertheless, it was still a prison and I would have to escape from it.

I had given up on Jim and I had grown angry. Why had he not come to look for me? Where was he? Did he even know that I had gone? Did he care so little that I could vanish into thin air and it was as if nothing had happened, as if I had never existed? If Bernie had been a serial killer, I would have been tortured and murdered by now. I would have suffered a ghastly, painful death. My mangled body might or might not have been found, but I certainly would not have been saved by Jim.

On the third morning, Bernie bathed and dressed me as usual. This was a ritual. Bernie allowed me no privacy. He was always watching and controlling. I was allowed no secrets from him; every private action was his to dictate and observe, whether it be the ablutions of the bathroom, or the basic necessities of bodily expulsion. At first I had found this more constricting than any chain or padlock. His presence was prison, suffocating and impossible to avoid. Then, I suppose, some codependent survival trigger set up its circuitry, and I found myself enjoying the constant guards, enjoying the security of knowing that he was always there, that I was not alone, that I was safe, strange though it sounds. For, in general, the men in my life could not be trusted. They were fabulous lovers, or imaginative freaks, chosen, in general, for their exciting proclivities and the size of their organs, but not for their reliability, a quality that had always bored me.

There had been men like Taylor: beautiful, six foot tall, with a horse tool that validated everything that was said about black men. He had liked me to stand face to the wall, with my hands outstretched, supporting myself, then sticking my cheeks and thighs out. He would place his hands around my waist, lift me towards his groin and lower my wet cunt slowly down on to that magnificent, ebony organ.

'Honey,' he would say, 'once you've flown first class, there's no other way to travel.'

And he was right.

Then there was little Bennie, the opposite in every way, for he was tiny. I would lie on the floor, legs splayed out, and he would climb in and out and around my body, agile and nimble because of his size, fingers, tongue, dick everywhere. He preferred me to be blindfold and, such was his skill, it was like surrendering to some little love-making machine dedicated to joining up the pleasure circuits. I would feel his hard, darting tongue dipping in and out of my pussy, jangling the clitoris, then his whole hand would slowly wedge between my legs and swim up my wet canal like a salmon. It was all sensation with Bennie. Sometimes he would flog me with a hand-made cat-o'-nine tails, a miniature version that he had had made to measure. He might have been small, but he was strong, and he could draw blood if he felt like it.

Bennie had taught me a lot about the endorphin rush. He had been the first to pace the pain until it turned into pleasure and, somehow, everything seemed clearer, the perception, I suppose, that all the religious maniacs were looking for when cultivating their tradition of flagellation. They shouldn't have bothered with the sin; they should have gone straight to the sex.

Bennie rarely allowed me to look at him. He would make me wear blindfolds or a soft, leather mask that he had had constructed especially for me. I think he thought he was ugly, but I didn't care what he looked like: he knew what to do with a girl.

After a series of interesting skirmishes, he went to join a circus. I think he married a trapeze artist.

Dan had wanted to watch while an alsation licked me in a nightclub in Amsterdam. Fred liked a little rubber nurse's outfit, white pumps and enemas. Christopher only wanted to rape me. He loved to follow me to a designated alley, or wood, or deserted wasteland, I wearing clothes that he had bought me, tarty little micro mini-dresses that extenuated my breasts and buttocks and thighs and rode up as I tottered about in the high heels. Or sometimes he would make me go straight, like a prim person walking home from some workplace; a good secretary, or junior executive, all tight, sensible skirt and clean shirt.

He would jump me, push me on to the ground, and there would be a moment when I was not sure if it was him or some real assailant, for he would take me from the back. I would hear his voice muttering that I was a dirty, little slut and I was going to get it, and he would physically tear my clothes off with his hands, pin me down on the ground, rip away the stockings, and cut off my panties with a knife. Then he would thrust his hardness into me, pumping for his own pleasure, using me purely as some anonymous vessel that he had managed to persuade to conform to his basic lusts. And, of course, I loved it. I loved it, even if the nervousness of this adventure initially kept me dry, for, by the time Christopher had thrust into me once or twice, and I felt his strength weighing down on me, his dick digging deep inside, I would inevitably moisten and join him in the abandoned pleasure of the socially unacceptable.

James wanted porn-film scenarios: double penetration and juices spuming into the face and mouth and ears, distended bungholes and dripping lips and all-over tans. He liked me to stand on all fours and suck the juice slowly out of his dick while a friend of his penetrated me from the back. And as the friend pushed, so my mouth would synchronise with his rhythm as it slid up and down his swollen shaft. He liked me to kneel astride him with my buttocks and fanny in his face and my mouth down on his dick so, as I licked, so he rimmed the brown puckering of my anus and tongued the proffered lips of my pussy. It became a competition to see who could concentrate for the longest without entering their own private realm of gratification.

Paul liked it straight. He liked to fuck me missionary then read his poetry. I soon got rid of him. I have not been placed on this planet to listen to the ramblings of a hothouse pansy cultivated by the heat of his own ego. Being forced to listen to poetry is the literary equivalent of allowing somebody to come in your face and frankly, the latter is more honest. At least you know where you are when a grateful cock erupts in front of you. There's some flattery and gratification in that.

Straights made me yawn and they never made me want to fuck. But this meant that one always had to look out for oneself: one was never sure what was going to happen next and one had to take responsibilities for one's own health and safety.

Now both my health and my safety, my basic life, was in the hands of Bernie, I had entered a place where there was pure submission without pain. It was an unusual feeling, and very soon my imagination managed to lead my body to be aroused by it. There was something very liberating about leaving one's identity and becoming a doll dedicated to aiding the whims of an expert puppeteer.

We ate breakfast and he announced that he was going to drive into town for provisions.

'I want to come,' I said.

'You'll be safer here,' he replied.

He took me to the bathroom, then tied my feet and ankles and left me lying on the bed.

'Bernie,' I said. 'Don't leave me like this. It could be dangerous. What if something happens?'

'Nothing will happen,' he said. 'I will be back in less than an hour. Don't worry.'

And so he left me. My ankles and my wrists were bound together with leather restraints and chain. The material was soft but the bindings were firm. I could not possibly have escaped.

'Why don't you just lock the door,' I argued. 'Then I can't get out.'

'No,' he said obstinately. 'It's better like this. Then I won't have to worry about you.'

'Thanks a bunch.'

He came over to me and pressed his fingers between my legs, working through the side of the cotton panties, and inserted two deep into me. He pushed with the true knowledge of a man who now knew everything about me; he had learned where all those little buttons were, how to ignite the impulses, the exact pressure that was needed to drive me into frenzy and supplication. He manipulated me, harder and harder.

'No, Bernie. No.'

But he continued and then, when he saw that I had become very excited and that now I wanted him – for my lips were coated in their sexy glaze and my pelvis was beginning to involuntarily gyrate in a begging dance – he withdrew.

'You think of old Bernie while he's away,' he said. 'Then, when I come back, I'll make you feel real good.'

'Why not now?' I said angrily. 'You're such a pussy tease.'

He smiled, put on his stetson, patted his gun, and said smugly: 'Yup. That's me.'

He went, leaving me helpless and trussed on that bed with a wet pussy and no way of relieving myself.

It was 10 a.m. I dozed off and woke with a jolt at 11.30 a.m. Bernie was not back, but I was not worried: he would be back soon.

I was slightly uncomfortable, my arms had gone to sleep and soon I would want to go to the bathroom. I wished there was a radio, or something to defy the silence. The only sound was the wind blowing through the trees and the rattle of loose window panes and something that sounded like footsteps walking across the roof.

I tried not to allow myself to imagine what these were. Nevertheless, my mind entertained everything, from bears to savage huntsmen. I was, after all, alone and defenceless. If any danger should present itself, I would have no course of action.

By one o' clock I was worried. Where was he? Scenarios played into increasing anxiety. Was he dead on the road? Had he been arrested? Had some mad scheme taken over his simple mind and he had decided to make a dash for the border? His absence was bad. My wrists and ankles were well tied. Bernie was an expert at this. I would never be able to free myself and I was seriously incapacitated with regard to performing any of the basic skills.

The first priority, though, was to negotiate a trip to the bathroom.

I eased myself off the bed and tried the handle on

the front door. It opened. I hopped out on to the veranda and struggled with tiny geisha steps to a tree where I relieved myself. The outdoor loo was too far; it would have taken hours to shuffle to it.

Then I sat down on a chair, looking out into the deserted mountain. It was beautiful, lush and green and silent, with the sun filtering through the branches and dappling the ground with shimmying golden spots. But I was alone and the intimations of real dangers began to claw at my stomach.

Bernie had still not turned up by three o'clock and now my mind was turning to survival. There was very little to eat in the cabin. That was why he had gone to town: to pick up provisions. Some old fruit, hard bread, a few eggs: all difficult to prepare with one's hands tied in front of one. There was water and a little coffee, but no milk.

I sighed. This situation was becoming more depressing by the minute. I tried to be grateful for the fact that at least he had forgotten to lock the front door, and for the fact that my hands were tied in front of me rather than behind my back, which would have rendered me completely helpless.

The previous owner had left some books, old, tattered things about Native American customs, hunting and fishing. I tried to engage myself in one or two of them, but they were hardly the stuff to calm the mind. I tried to retain some optimism, to believe that Bernie was being hopeless and he had just lost track of time. Certainly, it was possible that his dim understanding would not fully comprehend the very real peril of leaving me tied up for any amount of time. Furthermore, he was not a sadist. He would not do this merely to torment me in the hope that it would turn me on; he would not make that kind of mistake.

Darkness fell, and I gazed as the sun became a

flaming, orange ball bouncing behind the tall pines then dipped down and disappeared to leave a shroud of navy-blues and silver-greys, then total black. I managed to light the oil lamp and pick at some of the fruit. A mottled apple was about it. There were some tins of chilli beans which I couldn't face.

'You're not starving yet,' I told myself.

I did not sleep well. The black night brought real fear. I had never known the cold isolation of desertion such as this. My skin was beginning to crawl and I was beginning to imagine all the night-time ghouls of childhood. Things crawled under the bed and lurked behind curtains; blind monks with crippled legs crept across the floor; every draft was the breath of something inhuman lurking in the shadows armed with the unseen force of pure evil.

Dawn came at four as a grey-white sky and with it, some relief, as the fatal black was finally dispelled by the rising sun.

I was exhausted and upset but I knew that I had to work out some plan of survival. I had to free myself, but how? I was bound with chains. I might as well have been on a chain gang in Louisiana.

I spent a fruitless couple of hours opening drawers and searching the cabin for tools. There was nothing except a hammer which I took in case I should need some form of defence.

Tired though I was, my mind motored, playing with a myriad of possibilities. I could not believe that somebody would not eventually come and look for me. I had been missing for a week. Surely Jim and Mel would be concerned by now? Jim, in particular, had not trusted Bernie. Surely he would sense that there was something peculiar about the fact that we had disappeared together? I was unpredictable, but I was not unreliable. If arrangements were made, I kept to them.

I did not go absent without explanation. He must know me well enough to know this?

Where was he?

And where was Bernie?

Bernie, I thought angrily, should be done for endangering a person's life. If I died on this mountain, it would be his fault. It would be manslaughter. I hoped he would spend a very long time in a maximum security penitentiary. I could not believe he had done this to me. Where was he?

By the afternoon of the second day I was dirty, I was desperate, my wrists and ankles were aching and I convulsed into tears of desperation and anger.

I was beginning to feel weak. I managed to open a tin and make some beans in a saucepan. They tasted like cotton wool and I had no appetite, but I knew that they would sustain me. I drank water from the tap.

Should I pray? No. I did not believe in God. I had no faith except for some waves of basic Zen detachment that told me if I was destined to starve slowly to death, alone and abandoned, then there was nothing anybody could do about it.

I thought of the Lord my father in Monte Carlo. He would have to pay for the funeral, which would annoy him. Jim and Mel would have to organise to transport my body back to London, which would serve them right. I hoped that they would never recover from the guilt and misery.

The second evening, I had slipped into unthinking desolation. Perhaps I should try to struggle down the mountain? The steps would be minute and it would be painful but there was a possibility that I would be picked up by a hunter or a rancher. There was also a possibility that I would meet a bear from which I would not be able to run. And then, if I spent a day struggling down the stony track, I might have to spend the night outside, alone, in the mountain, and this I could not face.

I was stuck.

And I was watching the life slowly slip from me.

On the third morning, I discovered two things that I had not found previously. One was a passport showing Bernie's picture but claiming that his name was Wayne Wright III; the other was half a bottle of whiskey.

Faced with evidence of Bernie's criminality and depleted by living with fear, I slowly began to drink the whiskey. The liquor served to instil optimism. Somebody would come for me soon.

I looked in the grimy old mirror. My greasy hair lay flat on my head. I was filthy. There were bags under my eyes and my cheeks were hollow.

I poured another drink into a chipped coffee cup.

'Cheers,' I shouted grimly, raising the cup to myself and trying not to think of all the drinking and better times of the past, when drinks meant fun and fun meant sex.

I lay down on the bed, passing in and out of consciousness as the malt worked on my depleted body. I thought of Jim and all the love and sex. I seemed to feel his hands caressing my body, slowly stroking my buttocks, my breasts, my thighs. His tongue, passionate, in my mouth. His fingers opening me up, rubbing me, making me cry out for him.

I remembered with voluptuous relish the smell of his black, leather glove and the hot afternoon that he pushed me over the bonnet of his car, flipped up the cotton skirt, pulled down the pink, silk camiknickers and, with no ceremony or fear of being caught by any passerby, gave me a hard, careless fuck, the perfunctory kind that I always liked, with no speech or preamble or preparation. Just straightforward penetration.

242

He knew I liked this, as I knew he loved receiving oral sex while he was driving. I had become skilled in the art of teasing him in this way, leaning over from the passenger seat, gently pulling him out of his trousers, licking him slowly so that he was torn between his dick and his driving and it was agony for him. I would lick him so slowly, my tongue gently stimulating the nerves on his crown, watching it redden and watching the little droplet of excitement ooze from the eye on the head and then, finally, I would suck and suck, until, often, he had to stop (illegally) and allow me to finish him off.

I thought of his strong body enveloping mine, carrying me away from this to the haven of safety. I thought of his gentle hands stroking my hair off my face and of all the times that he had eased open my legs and pushed himself into me, controlling me with his unwavering virility. And then he turned into a monster master, a bloody zombie with a chainsaw, running after me, and I wearing high shoes, heels stuck in some swamp, unable to escape from the living dead.

'Stella!' he was shouting. 'Stella!'

His voice sounded so real. And then it was real. His hands were on my shoulders, shaking them. It was Jim's voice. His real voice.

'Wake up. Jesus Christ, wake up!'

I slowly came round, and through some strange mist, I observed him as if he was hundreds of miles away. He was there, but he was not there. I was confused. I just wanted to sleep.

'Stella!'

I vaguely felt myself being lifted off the bed by two strong arms. I vaguely smelled his smell of clean laundry and sex and Givenchy. And then there was nothing until I woke up in our bed at the ranch.

There was a smell of fresh cotton. The sun was

shining through the French windows and there was some ripe fruit in a bowl by the bed. Ripe fruit and fresh orange juice, and he was there, sitting beside me, watching me, soft love in his eyes, love not anger, and for this I was relieved, for I could not have borne any confrontation now. I could hardly understand all the things that had happened.

'Sweetheart.' He kissed me gently on the mouth. 'I was so worried. We've been looking for you for days, you know! There have been search parties all over the ranch. The police came out from Phoenix. But no one knew about that cabin until Bernie was picked up in a bar in Complicity. He was drunk and he told them everything.'

'I thought you weren't going to come.'

He sat down on the bed and lifted my chin in his hands and looked at me, his black eyes registering hurt and affection.

'Of course I would have come. Now, eat some of that fruit and Mel will make you some lunch.'

BLACK LACE NEW BOOKS

Published in December

STRIPPED TO THE BONE
Jasmine Stone
£5.99

Annie is a fun-loving free-thinking American woman who sets herself the mission of changing everything in her life. The only snag is she doesn't know when to stop changing things. Every man she meets is determined to find out what makes her tick, but her wild personality means no one can get a hold on her. Her sexual magnetism is electrifying, and her capacity for unusual and experimental sex-play has her lovers in a spin of erotic confusion.

ISBN 0 352 33463 0

THE BEST OF BLACK LACE
Ed. Kerri Sharp
£5.99

This diverse collection of sizzling erotica is an 'editor's choice' of extracts from Black Lace books with a contemporary theme. The accent is on female characters who know what they want in bed – and in the workplace – and who have a sense of adventure above and beyond the heroines of romantic fiction. These girls kick ass!

ISBN 0 352 33452 5

Published in January

SHAMELESS
Stella Black
£5.99

Stella Black, a 30-year-old woman with too much imagination for her own good, travels to Arizona with Jim, her dark SM master. Out in the desert, things get weird, and both the landscape and its inhabitants are more rough and ready than Stella has bargained for. A rip-snorting adventure of sleaze and danger.

ISBN 0 352 33485 1

DOCTOR'S ORDERS
Deanna Ashford
£5.99

Helen Dawson is a doctor who has taken a short-term assignment at an exclusive clinic. This private hospital caters for every need of its rich and famous clients, and the matron, Sandra Pope, ensures this covers their most curious sexual fancies. When Helen forms a risky affair with a famous actor, she is drawn deeper into the hedonistic lifestyle of the clinic. But will she risk her own privileges when she uncovers the dubious activities of Sandra and her team?

ISBN 0 352 33453 3

To be published in February

CRUEL ENCHANTMENT
Janine Ashbless
£5.99

Cruel Enchantment is an amazing collection of original, strange and breathtakingly beautiful erotic fairy tales. Fans of Anne Rice's *Beauty* series and Angela Carter aficionados will be enthralled. This collection transcends the boundaries of fantasy fiction and erotica to bring you dazzling tales of lust and magic.

ISBN 0 352 33483 5

TONGUE IN CHEEK
Tabitha Flyte
£5.99

Sally's conservative bosses won't let her do anything she wants at work and her long-term boyfriend has given her the push. Then she meets the beautiful young Marcus outside a local college. Only problem is he's a little too young. She's thirty-something and he's a teenager. But then her lecherous boss discovers her sexual peccadilloes and is determined to get some action of his own. It isn't long before everyone involved is enjoying naughty shenanigans.

ISBN 0 352 33484 3

If you would like a complete list of plot summaries of Black Lace titles, or would like to receive information on other publications available, please send a stamped addressed envelope to:

Black Lace, Thames Wharf Studios,
Rainville Road, London W6 9HA

BLACK LACE BOOKLIST

All books are priced £4.99 unless another price is given.

Black Lace books with a contemporary setting

PALAZZO	Jan Smith ISBN 0 352 33156 9	☐
THE GALLERY	Fredrica Alleyn ISBN 0 352 33148 8	☐
AVENGING ANGELS	Roxanne Carr ISBN 0 352 33147 X	☐
GINGER ROOT	Robyn Russell ISBN 0 352 33152 6	☐
DANGEROUS CONSEQUENCES	Pamela Rochford ISBN 0 352 33185 2	☐
THE NAME OF AN ANGEL £6.99	Laura Thornton ISBN 0 352 33205 0	☐
BONDED	Fleur Reynolds ISBN 0 352 33192 5	☐
CONTEST OF WILLS £5.99	Louisa Francis ISBN 0 352 33223 9	☐
THE SUCCUBUS £5.99	Zoe le Verdier ISBN 0 352 33230 1	☐
FEMININE WILES £7.99	Karina Moore ISBN 0 352 33235 2	☐
AN ACT OF LOVE £5.99	Ella Broussard ISBN 0 352 33240 9	☐
DRAMATIC AFFAIRS £5.99	Fredrica Alleyn ISBN 0 352 33289 1	☐
DARK OBSESSION £7.99	Fredrica Alleyn ISBN 0 352 33281 6	☐
COOKING UP A STORM £7.99	Emma Holly ISBN 0 352 33258 1	☐
SHADOWPLAY £5.99	Portia Da Costa ISBN 0 352 33313 8	☐
THE TOP OF HER GAME £5.99	Emma Holly ISBN 0 352 33337 5	☐
HAUNTED £5.99	Laura Thornton ISBN 0 352 33341 3	☐

VILLAGE OF SECRETS £5.99	Mercedes Kelly ISBN 0 352 33344 8	☐
INSOMNIA £5.99	Zoe le Verdier ISBN 0 352 33345 6	☐
PACKING HEAT £5.99	Karina Moore ISBN 0 352 33356 1	☐
TAKING LIBERTIES £5.99	Susie Raymond ISBN 0 352 33357 X	☐
LIKE MOTHER, LIKE DAUGHTER £5.99	Georgina Brown ISBN 0 352 34422 3	☐
CONFESSIONAL £5.99	Judith Roycroft ISBN 0 352 34421 5	☐
ASKING FOR TROUBLE £5.99	Kristina Lloyd ISBN 0 352 33362 6	☐
OUT OF BOUNDS £5.99	Mandy Dickinson ISBN 0 352 33431 2	☐
A DANGEROUS GAME £5.99	Lucinda Carrington ISBN 0 352 33432 0	☐
THE TIES THAT BIND £5.99	Tesni Morgan ISBN 0 352 33438 X	☐
IN THE DARK £5.99	Zoe le Verdier ISBN 0 352 33439 8	☐
BOUND BY CONTRACT £5.99	Helena Ravenscroft ISBN 0 352 33447 9	☐
VELVET GLOVE £5.99	Emma Holly ISBN 0 352 33448 7	☐

Black Lace books with an historical setting

THE SENSES BEJEWELLED	Cleo Cordell ISBN 0 352 32904 1	☐
HANDMAIDEN OF PALMYRA	Fleur Reynolds ISBN 0 352 32919 X	☐
THE INTIMATE EYE	Georgia Angelis ISBN 0 352 33004 X	☐
FORBIDDEN CRUSADE	Juliet Hastings ISBN 0 352 33079 1	☐
DESIRE UNDER CAPRICORN	Louisa Francis ISBN 0 352 33136 4	☐
A VOLCANIC AFFAIR	Xanthia Rhodes ISBN 0 352 33184 4	☐
FRENCH MANNERS	Olivia Christie ISBN 0 352 33214 X	☐
ARTISTIC LICENCE	Vivienne LaFay ISBN 0 352 33210 7	☐